Gift of Stone

Elemental Bloodlines
Book II

C.L. Carhart

GIFT OF STONE

Book 2 of *Elemental Bloodlines* series

Copyright © C.L. Carhart 2023

First Edition: February 2023

This is a work of fiction. Names, places, characters, and events are fictitious or are used fictitiously. Any similarity to real persons, living or dead, is coincidental.

ISBN: 978-1-954807-18-1 (paperback)

ISBN: 978-1-954807-19-8 (eBook)

https://www.clcarhart.com

Edited by Elizabeth Johnson

Cover Design © J. L. Wilson Designs | https://jlwilsondesigns.com

*For Becca
who prefers sagas like this
over my sweeter romantic tales.*

Other Books by C.L. Carhart

Elemental Bloodlines [series in process]

Gift of Fire, Book I
Gift of Stone, Book II
Gift of Darkness, Book III
Gift of Ice, Book IV
Gift of Water, Book V
Gift of Earth, Book VI
Gift of Air, Prequel Novella
Gift of Light, Bonus Novella

His Name Was Augustin [complete series]

Arcane Gateway, Book I
Mystic Passage, Book II
Astral Fantasia, Book III
Cryptic Pathway, Book IV
Lurid Curse, Book V
Numinous Fortune, Book VI
Veiled Magic, Bonus Novella
Winter Flame, Bonus Novella

Brief Pronunciation Guide

Anne – AH-nay
Befreiung – beh-FREYE-oong (eye is pronounced like eye-
    ball)
Erlangen – AIR-lahng-en
Leitaeri – Leye-TARE-ee (eye is pronounced like eyeball)
Leitalra – Leye-TAHL-rah (eye is pronounced like eyeball)
Teutonica – Too-TAHN-ih-kuh
Truhtein – TROO-tine (tine is pronounced like a fork tine)
Wuotan – VOH-tahn
Zehra – Zeh-RAH

You can find a full pronunciation guide and translations at
the end of this book.

Author's Note

All stories in the Teutonic Fantasy Realm take place in a world much like our own. Major historical events—like the World Wars—occurred similarly to those in our present world. Major locales—like München, Nürnberg, and Erlangen—can also be found in modern Germany.

However, all Teutonic history, customs, and magic, are utter figments of the author's imagination. As far as she knows, no actual elemental witches roam modern Germany in secret, nor is it possible for outsiders to seize their magnificent gifts. And no, the demon lord Wuotan is not a real being.

We hope.

Some of the businesses in this story—like Befreiung and Pritzl—are fictional. Others? You would have to visit Erlangen yourself to find out.

Turkish words are *italicized*.
Words in the fictional Teutonic dialect are *italicized*.

Table of Contents

Chapter One	Flames of Loss	1
Chapter Two	Choices	9
Chapter Three	Peculiar Craving	18
Chapter Four	A Spiritual Expedition	25
Chapter Five	An Unforeseen Pivot	37
Chapter Six	Henning Glossner	45
Chapter Seven	Investigations	55
Chapter Eight	Culture Clash	64
Chapter Nine	An Indulgent Heart	74
Chapter Ten	A *Leitalra's* Sway	86
Chapter Eleven	Sharing Burdens	97
Chapter Twelve	Community	106
Chapter Thirteen	Baring My Soul	117
Chapter Fourteen	An Empowering Fate	127
Chapter Fifteen	Blood Revelations	136
Chapter Sixteen	Rash Action	148
Chapter Seventeen	Abject Cruelty	156
Chapter Eighteen	Soulless Villain	163
Chapter Nineteen	The Bonded Pair	172
Chapter Twenty	Commitment	182
Chapter Twenty-one	A Peek at Eternity	193
Chapter Twenty-two	Ancient Justice	205
Chapter Twenty-three	Destiny Affirmed	215
Chapter Twenty-four	Mingling of Cultures	227
Epilogue	Six Years Later....	234
Social Links		237
Translations		238
Pronunciation Guide		239
About the Author		240

Chapter One:
Flames of Loss

Scorching agony consumed me from the inside out. The stench of rotting blood, mingled with fires hotter than I had ever experienced, choked my lungs. I could not think. Anguish clouded my reason, twisted my emotions into abject hopelessness. I tried to scream, tried to thrash against a torment barred from my eyes. This had to be hell. Complete darkness. The eternity I deserved as a former sex slave with a tainted body. I had always known this would come for me one day.

Heaven held no place for a maiden raped a thousand times over.

It will be the greatest suffering we've ever known. But only temporary.

Someone had told me that before this all began. Who? A spark of memory reawakened in my brain, somewhere apart from the trauma. A spirit that refused to capitulate to the fires, to the cruel drowning of blood. My soul, the essence of my inmost self. I had agreed to do this. So had he.

So had *he*.

Philipp.

My *Truhtein*. My magnificent, loyal, and gracious Teuton master.

When it's over, you will be just as strong as I am. Maybe even stronger.

I hope I'm dark energy like you.

These infernal flames charred my spirit, not my body. This was not death, nor was it hell. Sorcery beyond anything I ever imagined before I met Philipp. A terrible magic, one that could transform my standard human blood into something more. Something supernatural. Something Philipp insisted came forth from angelic forces, from the light that pointed all creatures toward the divine.

Something no ordinary human could obtain without deviating to the dark.

The Teutonic blood-transfer.

My spirit continued to convulse with pain, my screams tapering off as I tried to reassert my will. Death would be an easy escape. I sensed it lurking in the shadows, just beyond my reach, calling seductively for my surrender. If I released my tenuous grip on life, on the prospect of a future together with my *Truhtein* as his true equal, heaven may yet welcome me.

No. My master and I had too much to accomplish on earth. Freeing my mother from a conclave of human traffickers topped the list. We needed to work as a team to bring those criminals to justice. We could not do that if I surrendered to death, no matter how desperately I longed for it.

I needed to embrace the torment, fight the urge to flee into death's relief. To do that, I needed a distraction. Something to cling to while my spirit burned.

Philipp . . . .

For the first time since this awfulness began, I managed to project a name, rather than mere cries of agony, into the river of flaming blood. Philipp was here, too. He had agreed to give his blood for me, to offer his elemental magic in hopes of awakening mine. Both of our spirits would drown in this crimson river until the ritual was complete. Until we regained consciousness as Teutons in full. Partners.

Unless one of us chose to succumb to eternity's allure.

It occurred to me out of nowhere that maybe my *Truhtein* would fall victim to death's call. Maybe he was not strong enough to resist. In my mind's eye, he was invincible, his dark energy snapping in blackish-purple glory whenever he invoked his magic. But he was an old man. His spirit embodied resilience, but his mortal body? I had done my best to ignore its subtle signs of decay for months now.

Philipp!

I cried out his name again, shoving aside the torment of the flames. I could dissociate from this, too, just like I had done in my childhood whenever wicked males raped me on camera. This was no different. Temporary. I needed to focus, to find my beloved master. Grant him a portion of my undying tenacity.

Another memory flashed across my brain, a conversation I had with Philipp several days before my eighteenth birthday. *Lenz will put drops in our eyes to blind us both before he starts the ritual,* Philipp had told me, his blue-gray eyes grim and serious. *Teuton priests believe it's best for those who undergo the blood-transfer to do so in darkness, for sometimes frightening images appear in the bloody river. But there's a way to regain your eyesight if you want to, during the process. You must simply envision the blinding liquid as a shield draped over your eyes, and ignite your willpower to peel it free.*

Are you going to do that, when we're in the bloody river? I had asked him, nervous about the idea of facing torture while unable to see. Sometimes my handlers had blindfolded me while they committed their crimes against me—a demon that often haunted my nightmares.

Philipp pursed his thin lips, his gaze shifting from my face to the window behind me. *I might. If only for the privilege of seeing your spirit.*

Then I'm going to do that, too, I had pledged fervently, resolved to be just as strong as my *Truhtein*. That was what I needed to do right now, as fires ate away at my spirit. Peel the shield away from my eyes and find my master.

It took more effort than I expected to tear the curtain away. I was well versed in Teutonic magic already, thanks to a hefty stack of books and Philipp's guidance. But knowing something and doing something proved far different traits. Twice, I caught a glimpse of vivid red at the edges of my vision, and then the veil dropped back in place. I flexed my fingers and uttered a growl, trying again.

My fight to regain my eyesight took a tiny edge off of the torture, though the flaming blood continued to singe my spirit into dust. It surprised me that I was still alive. How much more of me could this place find to burn? *Enough to grant me the Teutonic magic I've wanted for years,* I told myself. An instant later, the shield fell away from my eyes. Fire immediately reached out to sear them.

Red everywhere. Anguish everywhere. I screamed again, my reason failing me. My arms appeared translucent as I thrashed against the thick liquid that drowned me. Translucent, yet glimmering with blood red fires. Madness.

No. I have to find Philipp.

I managed to transform my wails into Philipp's name, striking out into the river at the same time. I kicked my legs and worked my arms in the breast stroke, a talent my *Truhtein* had taught me. Water no longer scared me, because I could swim. This river of blood was just another type of water. And apparently my lungs could breathe even in this place, even without discernible air.

Was this what it was like to be a Teuton?

Philipp! I cried out, pushing myself further, fighting a current that sought to plunge me to the river's depths. Truhtein, *I'm here! Where are you?*

Somewhere in the distance, I heard his voice. The same one that soothed me when images of my past shackled me in iron, convincing me of my worthlessness. That no male could ever want me now that I had breasts. Now that puberty had altered my body. A broken maiden, a weak failure.

Throughout the past five years, Philipp had gently taught me otherwise. In his eyes, I was strong, a victor, triumphant. Every day, I fought to see myself the way he did. Right now, he needed the powerful Zehra. The one who would claw her way through tides of smoldering blood to reach him.

So I continued to swim, pushing waves of blood behind me as I pressed on. A corner of my brain began to wonder exactly how much longer this blood-transfer would last. How much longer must the two of us burn and drown? Had our priest—

Philipp's trusted friend, Lenz—placed two Teutonic arteries into my body and given my master two of mine? Would we wake to the morning sun and join our elements in mystical unity?

My eyes widened against the fiery blood as a strange new sense bombarded me from inside my spirit. I could *feel* my master's dark energy, quivering as though its vitality had already chosen to succumb. To seize death's sweet relief. Truhtein, *please!* I cried out in terror, desperation driving me toward him. *Please don't give in. I'm here with you. I'm here!*

I could see him now, his spirit barely visible against the flaming blood. Just a faint trace of energy sparked along his limbs and torso, his teeth bared in agony, his eyes squeezed shut. He did not lash out at the currents, like I had done. His arms hung motionless, his life fading before my eyes. *Philipp!* I cried, reaching my right hand out to his left.

The eyes of his spirit opened and focused on me, dark energy draining from the rest of his essence to magnify their glow. *Zeh . . . ra . . . my shining . . . star.*

His mental voice sounded so feeble. If it were possible to cry in this place, my face would have been drenched in tears. I closed my fingers around his, silently begging him to stay, though the spark comprising his spirit dissipated in my grasp. Truhtein, *don't leave me,* I pleaded, staring into his violet-black eyes.

Philipp's thin lips stretched into the most brilliant smile I had ever seen in my life, and he expended all of his energy in his last words to me. *Zehra, you are* so *strong!* His pride washed over me, binding me in unconditional acceptance and love. His final gift to me.

Then his spirit crumbled away, his sentiments dissolving into hollowness. I shut my eyes, clenched my fists, and screamed out my desolation to the fire, to the blood, to the void, to the demon that had stolen my *Truhtein* from me. The blood-transfer was Wuotan's ritual, and I would make him pay for this. Somehow. I would make him pay, and then I could seek the heaven Philipp had found—

I sat up straight in bed, the shadows of my master's private chamber falling over me. A thick comforter tangled around my legs, my torso slaked in sweat, my heart hammering so hard it might leap free from my ribcage. Panting, I touched a hand to my forehead as reality dragged me into despair. I wrapped my bare arms around myself and quivered, vivid visions spearing me in the darkness.

I had suffered that exact dream every night since Philipp and I had done the blood-transfer on Monday, April 5th. My eighteenth birthday. The day I charged into official adulthood with Teuton blood and a new last name. The day my spirit returned to my torn body to find itself manifested as stone. One of three earthen Teutonic elements. Not the dark energy I had hoped to claim.

The day Philipp Liebig died giving his blood for me, leaving me completely alone in an empty mansion, our plans to continue hunting traffickers shattered to pieces. Our plans to marry as Teutons forever lost. Our plans to bind our hearts in magic and dream together every night never realized.

Now I would have to watch him die every night instead. Face my nightmares without his presence to calm me, never discover how peaceful it would be to sleep in union with my master. Never learn what it would be like to mate as Teutons, binding spirit and element in sensual bliss. Philipp had held me at a distance for so long, requiring that our relationship remain platonic until I reached adulthood. He was not like the criminals who had stolen my innocence years ago. He wanted a grown woman, a Teuton woman, a Zehra whose blood status matched his.

He had promised that we would marry on Monday night, the same Teuton priest who had performed the blood-transfer officiating our ritual wedding by the pool outside, beneath branches of oak and elm. But my spirit had returned to my body that morning to find my master's unbreathing, his steady heart forever stilled.

A Teuton witch abandoned, her pining heart ground to dust.

After I had finished weeping over his body on Monday morning, I shut myself into his private suite, locking the door to the hallway in a mad attempt to seal reality away. Every morning since, I awoke alone in his bed, ripped from the bloody river into utter desolation. Philipp's familiar scent had already begun to vanish from the sheets. I would have to wash them at some point soon, catch up on the chores. I glanced at the blue numbers glowing from the digital clock on the bed-side table. Five forty-six, April 9th, 2004.

Friday morning. Day four without my dedicated partner.

"Get up, Zehra," I told myself, struggling against the urge to burrow under the blankets and moan for Philipp's return. "Get out of bed."

Despite the insidious weight of depression, I knew full well that eventually I would have to face the world alone. Step outside and find out whether the Teuton community could accept me as one of their own—a Turkish maiden who yearned to uncover the wonders of elemental magic, no matter the cost. As I made my way to the bathroom and switched on the light, my stomach grumbled, ordering that I assuage my basic bodily needs. I had eaten hardly anything since Monday morning, just a few snacks I found in Philipp's personal suite. Pretzels, Landjäger sausage, and excess hard liquor. The alcohol dulled my heartache, if only for a moment.

I would have to shop for groceries all by myself. I had not seen the inside of a grocery store since my mother brought me along with her as a little girl.

My eyebrows arched downward in pain as I stared at my reflection in the bathroom mirror, my deep brown eyes lightening into stone's flat gray. My vision sharpened, showing me every frizz in my tangled hair, every blackhead nestled in the beige skin of my nose. My flesh hardened as I granted my magic free rein, my lips curving into a frown. If only my heart could turn to stone, too. It had troubled me since late Monday night, rebuking my sorrow for my dead master.

Two dark red scabs trailed upward from the left side of my chest. My tank top revealed their course as they split to cross my shoulders and travel down to my inner elbows. My blood was different now, two of my *Truhtein's* arteries nestled within my flesh, granting me Teuton blood and all of its privileges. The blood-transfer was a sordid ritual, impossible by scientific standards.

Philipp had told me that afterward, my blood type would change from O to AB. The universal recipient, the blood that absorbed all other types. Thankfully, the mystic qualities of Teuton blood remained invisible to modern science, or else my people would be shut away in labs or hunted to extinction.

My people. So insane, to imagine an ancient Germanic conclave as my people. What would they think of a brown-eyed witch of stone, a child of immigrants? A maiden whose father had sold her to pay a bad debt?

"I'm not strong, Philipp," I muttered at my reflection, wondering if he could hear me from the unreachable realm of his heaven. "I'm not strong without you. I'm trying so hard. But I can't find my way alone."

Carefully, I leaned my forehead against the mirror's cool surface and closed my eyes, wallowing in my grief. But then my element detected the presence of another Teuton spirit approaching the house, and I stiffened in dread.

Chapter Two:
Choices

Pitch black darkness rivaling that of a moonless night. That unusual sense the blood-transfer had granted me identified which Teutonic element intruded upon my solitude, the sturdiness of my stone readying me for defense in an instant. Leaving the bathroom behind, I scurried toward the hallway on silent feet, preparing to meet the man who approached the front portico.

Although my mastery of my magic was not refined enough to recognize his spirit by his element alone, I knew my guest had to be Lenz. Even after Philipp left this world, the invisible shield of dark energy he had cast over his property long ago held strong, the generator hidden in an old root cellar producing sufficient voltage to power the entire house. The shield repelled anyone who harbored sinister intentions. A nearly flawless security system.

As I wound my way through the downstairs passageways to the vestibule, it occurred to me to wonder exactly how long Philipp's spells would last now that he was dead. The electricity and internet had not yet gone out, but I suspected I would have to learn all about connecting this place to the city's power grid at some point. And what about the house itself, and all of

Philipp's investments? I had not checked his accounts once this entire week.

I was a failure. Not the shining star my *Truhtein* envisioned.

When I reached the front door, I paused to draw a deep breath, pulling myself up straight. A Teuton priest of darkness awaited me, a man my *Truhtein* trusted without reservations. Lenz Schneider, a retired private investigator, had played a pivotal role when we broke up the child pornography ring in Nürnberg three years ago. He had tracked down other survivors who had already come of age, asking them to testify against the criminals who plastered our tortured bodies all over the dark web. Each fiend languished in prison now, my anonymity intact.

Philipp and Lenz had protected me from having to face them again in court, from dealing with government officials who would demand I be sent to school, to the care of unknown guardians. Yet here I stood in blue gym shorts and a soiled tank top, my hair uncombed, my feet bare, my heart stuttering painfully, seeking a reason to continue on after its trusted partner departed this world. Lenz deserved better than this. I ought to make coffee.

"I can sense you in there, Zehra." Lenz's reedy voice prompted me to jump, my fingers stretching forth to unlatch the deadbolt. "I've brought a loaf from the bakery."

I cracked the door, casting my gaze over Lenz, where he stood several paces back from the threshold. Attired in dark jeans, a black trench coat, and a flat hat, he looked fully prepared to start a new investigation. His irises were as black as coal, and his hands held a papery bag that smelled like heaven. Raising bushy gray eyebrows, he presented the bag to me, a silent message.

"Thought the bakery didn't open until six," I said, the earthy scent of warm Vollkornbrot reminding me that I ought to eat. I opened the door wider.

"If you know the owner, you can call in the occasional favor."

"Come inside." I nodded in the general direction of the kitchen, stepping aside so Lenz could enter. "I'll make some coffee."

I darted further into the house without waiting to see if he would follow, this time flicking a couple light switches along the way. My element had receded from my blood into my spirit as I relaxed in Lenz's presence, my vision returning to its normal state. Odd that stone would grant me the ability to see in the dark, but maybe all earthen elements were like that. Maybe they prepared a Teuton mage to explore caves and mines.

Lenz rattled off a few comments about the weather and the local soccer team while I busied myself with the coffee pot. The bright kitchen lights made me feel exposed after three and a half days of huddling in my master's private suite. My hands shook as I retrieved a pair of mugs from one of eighteen over-head cabinets. Philipp's downstairs kitchen was enormous, containing three convection ovens, two refrigerators, a deep freezer, three dishwashers, an extensive wine rack under the dry bar, and enough dishes and place settings to serve a hundred people. All vestiges of his late father's extroverted nature. Philipp never staged one party in the five years I had known him.

Of course, that may have been because he wished to keep my presence in his house a secret. He had rescued me from my previous master—the producer of child porn—right after I turned thirteen. Philipp's plan was to educate me, help me make my own way in the world once I grew up. And he had done just that. But to those on the outside, he appeared to be an elderly mogul who kept an underage Turkish girl as a servant.

So I had stayed hidden for all this time, a status that suited me. Lenz was the only one of Philipp's friends who knew I existed and what I meant to Philipp. He retrieved butter from the fridge and honey from a cabinet while he chattered on about a soccer player who recently sprained his knee. Lenz's insistence upon serving himself irritated me, but I had no authority to demand he settle down. I eyed him from where I stood before the counter, pouring two mugs of piping hot coffee.

Lenz had divested himself of his trench coat and hat, both of which lay upon the bar, his plaid flannel shirt typical attire for him. Tousled gray hair that matched his eyebrows ringed his bald crown, his fingers extracting the loaf of Vollkornbrot from its bag to set it atop a serving plate. I had not seen him retrieve the plate from a cabinet, my usually keen senses dimmed by my grief. I really needed to get it together. Turning back to the counter, I breathed out a quiet sigh, then lifted both mugs to carry them to the bar. Lenz had already laid out the cream and sugar.

After handing Lenz his mug, I plunked myself onto the bar stool beside the one he occupied, turning my attention to the slices of bread he had cut from the seeded loaf. I shut my eyes for a second to inhale its warm fragrance, then laid two pieces upon the plate before me. Coffee could wait; my stomach wanted food. Impatient, it growled as I took up the small container of herbed butter.

"You're not doing well, are you?"

Lenz's query cut me to the core. He had ceased his casual chatter when I handed him his mug, and now his hazel eyes pierced me from where he sat blowing on his coffee. Concern evident upon his features, he took a single sip, holding my gaze as I spread too much butter over the slices on my plate.

I felt as though a vise squeezed my heart. *Keep it together. No crying,* I ordered myself. Taking a single bite of buttered bread, I forced myself to chew slowly, not wanting to overdo it after four days of intermittent fasting. Then I admitted the truth, dropping my gaze from Lenz's to the brown slice in my hand. "I've been drinking."

Lenz exhaled heavily, setting his mug onto the bar. "He was my friend, too, Zehra. More than a friend. I'm not sure it's fully hit me yet, even though I've spent the past three days getting his affairs in order."

"What?" The word fell from my lips before I could squelch it. While I had floundered in misery and alcohol, Lenz had conducted business like a mature adult. A quality I had yet to attain, apparently. I hunched my shoulders, embarrassed.

"He made me the executor of his will years ago," Lenz went on, fingering a half-eaten slice of bread on his plate. "You're lucky he was an only child with no children or ex-wives, or gold diggers would have invaded this property already. He left you all of his assets, aside from what he donated to charity and the investments we maintained together. Everything, including this property, granted to Frau Zehra Saliha Liebig. His will records your chosen surname."

The implications of what Lenz declared prompted me to gasp. "He planned this," I realized, tugging my full mug of coffee toward me, its warmth not touching the chill in my soul. "My *Truhtein* planned to die giving me Teuton blood."

"I'm not sure if 'planned' is the right word," Lenz said, his tone sympathetic. I poured a bit of creamer into my coffee, glancing at him while I waited for him to explain. The older man took a bite of honeyed bread, his thick eyebrows coming together.

"Philipp's COPD started progressing late last autumn. He told me in March that his doctor gave him six months to a year, at most."

"I didn't know that." I thought about how strained my master's breathing had grown during the winter. He coughed and wheezed for a good twenty minutes each morning before making his way to the shower. Neither of us had spoken of his worsening health, denial my trustworthy raft.

"He preferred to bear that burden alone. I doubt he would have told me if he didn't need me to set his affairs in order afterward. But the last time we spoke, before I conducted the ritual for you, he told me, 'Wuotan will require one of our lives, since Zehra and I are opposite genders. I don't want you offering that demon some ransom in an attempt to save us both.' He made me promise not to deviate from the light, but I'll admit I was tempted. I didn't want to lose my dearest friend, or the lovely young lady who challenged him to become the best version of himself."

Lenz cleared his throat and focused on his slice of bread, while I sat reeling from the sacrifice my *Truhtein* had made for me. I had read in multiple volumes that blood-transfers tended to be deadlier if the recipients were not of the same gender. But I had convinced myself that it would be different for us. That my master and I were strong enough to live, despite Wuotan's foul schemes.

"Then . . . my *Truhtein* chose to die . . . to spare me." Tears welled in my eyes but I blinked them away, trying to concentrate on the magic within my spirit, to center myself. Philipp had died to give me this gift of stone. It was time for me to stop mourning him and put his gift to good use.

"Philipp believed in you," Lenz noted as I drank from my mug, the gears in my brain starting to turn with possibility, perked by the caffeine. "He believed that you would bring light to this world, use the privileges of Teuton blood to help those shackled by evil and greed. I haven't archived the record of your blood status yet, but once I do, the local witches will certainly want to connect with you."

The idea of meeting other Teuton females sent my magic running for cover. The solidness of earth had started to weave through my blood and augment my senses, but now it contracted back into my spirit. "I haven't really . . . practiced all that much yet," I confessed, embarrassed again. "Am I going to turn into a gargoyle whenever I separate my spirit from my body?"

That particular Teutonic talent was one I longed to hone. Philipp had used it often to gain intel on traffickers and their clients. His dark energy always buzzed around him in solid waves of electricity whenever his spirit went on the hunt. But my element was stone, gray the only color it had manifested thus far.

"A gargoyle. Really." Lenz raised his eyebrows at me and burst out laughing.

His amusement awakened my own, a grin breaking across my face for the first time since Monday. "I'm stone. That means gargoyle. How exactly is my body supposed to *breathe* like that?" I needed to set my mind at ease about this before I set out on my first spiritual journey—to infiltrate the place where my father ran his trafficking scheme. Where my mother remained bound in servitude.

"Your body doesn't need to breathe when your element preserves it. Life flows in a Teuton's blood and element, along with their spirit. And the lungs of your spirit can breathe anywhere, even up in space. Spirits don't need oxygen to sustain them. Since you're stone, you'll be able to travel through castle walls and Alpine crevices without trouble. Useful talent."

Lenz mirrored my grin and took up another slice of bread, topping it with a spoonful of honey. I blinked at him in a daze as I thought about what he had said. "So when I'm in spirit form, I'll be able to walk through walls?"

"Not just *through* them. *In* them. You'll probably be able to sink down into the earth itself, should you wish to do so. It'll come naturally to you, because your element stems from the earth. One thing to remember—" Lenz took a bite of bread and chewed it thoroughly, studying my expression before finishing "—is that most Teutons, aside from wary priests, don't think to look for spirits within walls."

Resolution reared up inside of me, my brain compiling countless ways my stone could assist me in freeing my mother and bringing my father to justice. While I could not disrupt camera feeds or electrical barriers like Philipp could, my stone would allow me to unfasten physical locks, shift the bars in windows, and conjure weapons from the magic of my blood and spirit. All things I had not yet attempted. Once Lenz left, I would go to my bedroom for the first time since Monday morning, sit down at my desk, and make a list of the spells I needed to practice. I would have to dig out some of Philipp's ancient tomes to guide me along the way.

"I can see the wheels turning in your brain." Lenz's voice extracted me from my reverie. I shook myself and reached for my coffee, realizing I had been staring off into space for more than a minute. When I met my companion's gaze, he asked, "What have you got for me?"

That phrase initiated the mindset shift I needed dearly. I could still mourn Philipp while pressing forward with our investigation into my father's business. He worked with a band of traffickers who called their operation "Befreiung," which meant "liberation" in German. They offered their services to refugees from the east—usually vulnerable women and children—shackling their clients into forced labor and prostitution. Philipp and I had not yet shared our findings with Lenz, for we had yet to uncover sufficient evidence to press charges.

But Lenz knew we had something cooking. And I would need his help if I wanted to do more than simply steal my mother away.

"You know how the child porn ring we broke up had no connection with my father at all?" I shifted to face Lenz directly, setting my coffee mug down and taking up a fresh slice of bread. He nodded once, and I buttered my bread without really looking at it. "Well, my *Truhtein* found something a couple months ago. Something that might explain what my father actually does for a living. Even though he wasn't in deep with the porn, some of his associates have their hands coated in filth."

I told Lenz the basics of what Philipp and I had found thus far. Most of it hinged upon transactions on the dark web. My master had been a whiz with code and computers, his element granting him insight most mortals never attained. One of many reasons I had wished to claim some type of energy myself. Luckily, Philipp had schooled me extensively throughout the past five years, though I found it much easier to study financial trends than to stay ahead of online criminals.

I was still unsure whether I wanted to do this for the rest of my life, or call it quits once my father's business collapsed. There had to be other, more satisfying ways to help those in need.

"So your plan is to break your mother out of Befreiung's compound," Lenz said after I finished my report. I bowed my head in acknowledgement and took a sip from my mug. Lenz's next statement almost made me spit out my coffee. "How do you know your mother isn't involved? That she even wants to be free?"

"My mother cares about protecting her children," I responded, leveling a glare at him from over the rim of my mug. "My father had to hold her back when he sold me to that rapist. She was crying, fighting. I saw him hit her."

Lenz's lips parted, his distrust shifting into something else. "Are you sure she's still alive?" he asked in an undertone.

I drained my coffee and smacked the mug onto the bar. Raising my chin, I looked Lenz square in the eyes and said, "She is. My *Truhtein* scouted out my father's compound in spirit form just last week. Now it's my turn to do it."

Chapter Three:
Peculiar Craving

On Saturday morning, I showered and put on a pair of flared jeans and a purple long-sleeved blouse, then wound my hair into a basic braid. Today, I intended to start practicing with my elemental magic, out in the back garden beside the pool where my late master and I had planned to marry. Nervous anticipation seemed to braid my spirit into a knot in my chest, but I refused to allow my doubts to hold me back. I no longer had a strong partner to support me, which meant I must defeat all antagonists myself. Even those that lived in my own mind.

Frau Zehra Liebig had inherited an expansive house and grounds, so I must complete daily tasks whether I liked it or not. Before I delved into my newfound Teutonic gifts, I embarked on a solo trip to the nearby grocery store. I knew where it was from studying one of Philipp's local maps, but terror slid its claws down my spine as I strode along the driveway to the front gate. An aged stone wall adorned with creeping ivy surrounded the Liebig property, the wrought-iron gate one I had not stepped through in five years.

A cool spring breeze caressed my cheeks as I neared the gate, the sky a lovely light blue flecked with wisps of cirrus. A robin called out from one of the two oaks that framed the gate, nature's beauty inviting me forward, along with a deep-seated instinct that told me I must emerge from my isolation today. A weird instinct, but not one I thought to question. I halted before the gate's lock, narrowing my eyes at the iron mechanism holding it shut. Could I loosen the lock through the power of my stone, without using the key tucked in the pocket of my jacket?

I sensed the intrinsic camaraderie of the stone wall and even the iron before me, although my spirit detected a definite difference there. Interesting. Metal and stone were not the same element. I knew that, but it was odd to *feel* it whispering to my inner self. Glancing from the lock to the trees that lined the far side of the street beyond the gate, I realized I was stalling. Trying to put off my entrance into the unknown as long as possible.

"This isn't going to get any easier the longer you wait," I told myself, scuffing my boots on the asphalt beneath me. Plunging my left hand into my coat pocket, I unearthed the gate key. When I pulled the gate open, I sensed my *Truhtein's* energy shield sliding gently over my skin. His element knew I was no threat. In fact, I felt like his spirit was sending me a blessing, granting me the tenacity to meet all trials the world tossed my way.

"I love you, Philipp," I whispered, shutting my eyes as I stepped through the shield and onto the sidewalk that ran along the street. The Liebig property stood on the southern edge of Erlangen, forest springing up all around it except to the northwest. That was the direction I needed to walk—past a collection of houses and shops and over two sets of railroad tracks until I reached the grocery store. Taking a deep breath, I exhaled slowly, listening as a variety of vehicles passed by along the road. I could do this.

Reopening my eyes, I closed the gate behind me, sending Philipp's energy one final brush of regard. Then I struck out toward civilization, my senses on high alert for potential dangers. This was a safe and quiet neighborhood, even though it lay along a main road. Still, I would not let my guard down.

Other Teutons might notice the stone in my essence and grow curious, especially since I did not look like a stereotypical German.

I should have hidden my brown eyes behind sunglasses.

As I progressed further into the southern section of Erlangen, I thought back to the letter Lenz had given me before he left yesterday. My *Truhtein* had compiled a list of hired people and companies that maintained his property, along with the schedules each employee kept. Groundskeepers, pool maintenance and cleaning, a chauffeur, even a buyer of groceries. All personnel I had never met before, since I used to cower in my bedroom whenever Philipp had company.

The groceries I determined to obtain myself. I already kept the house clean and organized; it would not be an added burden to choose ingredients for meals. Just a little over a kilometer's walk twice each week would let me keep the pantry and refrigerators stocked. I could even take the bus, if I got brave enough. Driving was not in the cards for me quite yet. On several occasions, my master had set me behind the wheel of his Jaguar so I could traverse the driveway, from the garage to the front gate to the section that circled the marble fountain.

But I had yet to get beyond second gear.

Shops and businesses began to crop up among the houses and apartments lining the street, as I neared the bridge over the first set of railroad tracks. Along the way, I passed other pedestrians about their daily activities. A mother pushing a baby in a stroller, a young man jogging, an elder walking his German shepherd. Each acknowledged me in their own ways, and my tension began to dissipate. My stone had identified no other Teutonic elements yet. Philipp had told me around three thousand Teutons lived in Erlangen, but maybe this southern neighborhood leaned more mundane.

Just as I started to believe I could actually accomplish my mission without any misfortunes, I caught sight of a Döner Kebap stand situated between a florist's shop and a laundromat. My fists clenched of their own accord, my stone filtering from my spirit into my blood in reaction to my dismay. My former handler used to eat Kebaps—seasoned lamb drenched in garlic sauce and wrapped in flatbread—while shooting scenes. The stench of his breath would waft over me when he ordered the male performers to take me harder, to make me hurt.

Keep walking. Keep walking, and don't think about it, I told myself as my heart thrummed erratically in my chest. *The grocery store is just another couple streets away. Just have to cross one more set of railroad tracks. Nobody in that shop is going to hurt you. If they try, they'll learn not to mess with a stone witch.*

Working hard to steady my breathing, I reached the second set of railroad tracks, checking both ways before I crossed. My ludicrous reaction to the Kebap stand shamed me, provoking demons that amplified my uncertainties. *You went from sweet treat to trash. Swallow, you little bitch. Show us those big salty tears.*

"You're not what they said. You're not what they said," I repeated under my breath, fixing my gaze on the grocery store's entrance. "You are worthy just as you are. Strong and dedicated. A shining star."

I envisioned my beloved *Truhtein* walking beside me as I stepped through the sliding doors, grabbing a shopping basket and heading for the produce section. I really needed to get this task over with so I could focus on delving into the depths of my stone magic. Maybe once I could conjure weapons using sorcery alone, these wretched memories would loosen their grip on me. Five years under Philipp's care should have been enough to free me completely. Most days, my demons only came for me in my dreams.

A Döner Kebap stand had pushed me over the edge. Ridiculous.

I dug my grocery list from my jacket pocket, glancing over it quickly to make sure I had not forgotten anything. Fresh fruit and vegetables were my top priority. After that came heavy cream and cheese. Milk could wait until my next trip, since I had to carry everything home myself. I could gather enough to fill two reusable shopping bags.

Stuffing my grocery list back into my coat, I eyed the selection of citrus fruit—navels, blood oranges, grapefruits, limes, lemons. I began depositing items into my basket at random, chagrined by the thudding of my heart. It should have calmed down by now, but it continued to patter swiftly, a strange yearning opening like a rose inside my chest. Another shopper eased up to my left side and I sidled toward the grapefruits, tossing two into the basket I balanced upon my left hip.

A third grapefruit glanced off the corner of the basket and dropped toward the floor. I gasped, but before I could fully react, the lean male beside me reached out to snag it with his right hand, a half-second before it would have smashed upon the ground. "Got it!" he exclaimed in a deep voice.

I turned my full attention upon him as he straightened, and our eyes met. His were an enchanting cobalt blue that reminded me of the winter sky. I judged him to be close to my age, probably a college student, clad in plain blue jeans and a worn leather jacket that would have fit in at a rock concert. His brown hair parted down the middle and pulled back into a ponytail, its true length remained a mystery, since we faced each other directly. He raised his eyebrows in interest, holding out the grapefruit for me to take.

Just how long had I eyeballed this guy in silence? I mentally shook myself and accepted the fruit from him. "Good job," I said, awkwardness descending upon me. I ducked my head and prepared to move on to the apples and pears. Something unusual tingled inside my spirit, slowing my retreat.

"You seem familiar. Have we met before?" the young man asked, his voice surprising me all over again. How could a guy who looked no older than twenty sound like a scholarly mage who sang bass solos with the local choir? I narrowed my eyes at him, an expression he mirrored. I thought I saw a spark flicker along the edges of his irises—a trace of element magic.

"We haven't met before. You're thinking of someone else. Have a good rest of your day." Words tumbled from my lips as I darted away, setting my sights on the vegetables. Apples could wait; the young man was a Teuton. And I was wholly unprepared for that sort of encounter.

"Okay, then." I heard him breathe out a sigh as I planted myself beside an older woman rooting through heads of lettuce. Hopefully he would not pursue me, especially since my current companion was an outsider. His regard had awakened my own magic, its mysticism sharpening my vision as I looked over the lettuce. I picked out the freshest head in seconds and added it to my basket.

The older lady checked her shopping list and moved on to the celery, while I glanced toward where my element told me the young Teuton male lurked. He was looking over the pears, reaching out to add two to his own basket. He looked over at me when I paused before the peppers, a strangely wistful smile appearing on his smooth face. Was he trying to flirt with me?

Why did I feel stirrings in my chest, as though my heart wished me to cast myself into his arms? Philipp had told me about Teutonic mating traditions—the ritual wedding, the spiritual heart-bonds priests formed with their chosen ones, the elemental binding that occurred whenever Teutons had sex. Not once had my *Truhtein* ever alluded to any sort of instinctual lust, but my hormones conjured blissful images in my brain. Images of myself in that young man's arms, my hands tangling in his sienna locks.

I needed to get away from that man. I sincerely hoped my magic would not react this way to every single Teuton male I had yet to meet. Silently ordering my stone to return to its rightful place within my spirit, I sailed away from the produce section in search of the dairy products.

We don't have time for romance, no matter now desperately you want to get laid, I rebuked my stone as it receded into my spirit. Frustration lingered along my nerves, and I rolled my eyes at myself. Fated mates did not exist in the realm of Teutonic magic, but the arousal in my blood implied otherwise. I would have to put my vibrator to work tonight.

I walked back toward the Liebig property on the opposite side of the street, keeping my distance from the Kebap stand. My stone grew more and more restless the further I went, as if it really and truly wanted me to run back and find that tantalizing young male whose eyes glimmered with flames. Was his element some type of fire? Thank goodness it had not been dark energy; then I might have thrown myself at him in a desperate bid to raise Philipp from the dead.

By the time I passed through my *Truhtein's* shield into familiar territory, I was an emotional mess. My master and I should have survived the blood-transfer's torture and joined our spirits in ritual marriage that same night. Then, he would have finally permitted me to please him, to shower him with all of the adoration I had harbored deep within my heart for so many years. Dark energy and stone, twin souls, true partners.

But now, my stone magic pined for a mystery man with a ponytail. And in my dreams that night, a powerful Teuton priest cradled my heart in his hands, his sonorous voice inviting me to my rightful place at his side.

Chapter Four:
A Spiritual Expedition

Two weeks later, I sat cross-legged on a smooth rock beside the decorative pool in the back garden, trying and failing to grant my element full sway over my body to set my spirit free. Out of all possible uses for elemental magic, this was the one I needed to perfect first. Once I could separate my spirit from my body at will, I could infiltrate my father's compound and learn whether my mother wished to escape from beneath her husband's authority.

I could also find out if any of my younger siblings still lived —whether they, too, were trapped in the shackles of crime. I was the eldest of four, my younger sister a mere infant the day my father sold me to the porn producer. Time had blurred my memories of my brothers, Faruk and Murat. Had my father roped them into his business, or sold them for labor?

The past weeks had not gone smoothly, overall. While I had achieved small victories—like cooking meals for myself and revisiting the grocery store without facing that odd pull toward a long-haired Teuton male—my stone magic refused to cooperate with my wishes. I spent far too much time consulting various tomes for guidance, the old version of *Der Weg Teutonisch* at the top of the list. Written in the dead dialect of

Teutonica, the ancient spells for each Teutonic rite lay plain on its pages, including one that allowed a Teuton priest or witch to pull another Teuton to the spiritual realm through their element alone.

That did me no good, since I had yet to figure out how to send *myself* to the spiritual realm. I had tried meditating, centering myself on that mystical essence deep within, summoning my stone into my blood while sitting in Philipp's suite, on the concrete floor of the laundry room, in the grass where my *Truhtein* and I used to play bocce with Lenz, on the rocks that lined the waters of the pool. While watching colorful fish swim beneath the surface, flowered lily pads floating here and there, the same terror would stop me every time, just as my veins began to solidify into actual stone.

Whenever my element stole the air from my lungs, I found myself trapped within memories from my time as a slave. Aside from setting me before bright lights and cameras while adults battered me, my former handler rented my body out to clients. Disgusting males who paid for private sessions with "the exotic cutie" they had seen in videos. Three of those clients choked me every time, though my handler made them stop before they left any marks on my skin.

Now, when my stone cut off my breath, ghostly fingers constricted around my throat. Then I would lose focus, my magic ebbing into my spirit.

After failing to release my spirit from my body for the sixth time that Friday morning, I groaned and rose to my feet, pacing the circumference of the pool while trying to shake off the panic that chilled my body. "I'm doing exactly what *Der Weg* says you should do," I muttered, casting my gaze over the oak trees that shaded the pool, spring's growth ornamenting their branches. "Letting my stone expand from my spirit to my blood to my body. I *know* I'll be able to breathe just fine once my spirit leaves my body. *Why* can't I do this?"

My frustrations welled up as tears. I collapsed upon the dark gray lip of the pool, my fingers reaching out to stroke the smooth stone. Its presence granted me a strange comfort I had never sought before I gained Teuton blood. For the past thirteen days, I had tried to do what I had watched my *Truhtein* do many times. I remembered how his dark energy would coalesce around his body, its magic growing stronger and stronger until he resembled a pure glow of violet-black electricity.

Then he would speak to my mind, caress my cheek with his spirit to assure me of his safety. *You'll be doing this yourself one day, Zehra.*

Neither Philipp nor I had expected my past trauma to inhibit me. Why could I hear my demons in my head right now, telling me I was worthless and weak? Why was it so easy to believe their lies, rather than what Philipp had taught me? *You are not what they say. You are strong and resilient, a shining star. You are worthy just as you are.*

Lenz had come by on Tuesday to collect print outs of what my *Truhtein* and I had uncovered about Befreiung in recent months. He planned to continue investigating alongside me, but I begged him not to infiltrate the compound until I could do it first. In response, Lenz mentioned that Philipp's funeral had come and gone on Saturday the 10th, an event he had expected me to attend.

Since I feared to appear at a church among so many people —most of them Teutons—I had not attended. I had never been to a funeral before, and the prospect of breaking down in tears in front of a crowd terrified me. The public need not gawk at my fragility; and thus I must mourn Philipp in private, safe from the judgment of confident witches. Instead of appearing at his funeral, I had seized onto an uncanny instinct that sent me to the grocery store. The place where I found myself lusting after a mysterious Teuton male.

Lenz's disappointment was obvious in his expression, though he held his peace on the subject. He told me Philipp's urn had been placed in the Liebig family crypt, something that did not sit well with me. His remains should not rest alone in the dark; they needed to be in a place of honor in his home. German law required ashes to be interred in a cemetery, though. More reason for me to walk this world in spirit form—to liberate Philipp along with my mother and siblings.

Sometimes, serving the light demanded a nimble dance along the edge of what society deemed acceptable.

Watching a crimson goldfish weave its way through the waters before me, I mulled over just how to defeat the panic that gripped me when I could not breathe. Philipp had said the moment of transition lasted three to four seconds at most. Then a Teuton's spirit would propel itself into the sky, all discomfort forgotten. Maybe I should try holding my breath for five seconds without tapping into my elemental magic. I had not tried that yet, because it seemed too simple.

Master the simple tasks first, then move on to what's more complicated. Philipp had reminded me of that principle whenever I struggled to learn a new skill. Like swimming. He had me practice the strokes while sitting beside his indoor pool first, gradually progressing until I could traverse the deep end. I had yet to summon the courage to swim underwater or jump off the diving board.

If I practiced holding my breath, I might be able to do all of that. Would it be harder to keep myself afloat, now that I claimed the element of stone? I grinned at the thought. Without question, I would have to integrate into the local Teuton community sooner or later, so I could share silly ideas like that with witches close to my age. Lenz was a loyal friend, but I did not wish to expose all of my doubts to him. He was not my *Truhtein.*

If you integrate with the Teuton community, you might meet another male who could become your real Truhtein, I realized. *One who could cradle your heart in his hands. Like the fiery priest from your dreams . . . that long-haired guy from the grocery store.*

As foolish as my dreams had become recently, at least my latest imaginary companion showed no intentions of hurting me. So I decided to think of him while I situated myself upon the stone, shutting my eyes and taking one deep, lingering breath before forcing myself to hold it. I counted to five in my mind while picturing the face of that long-haired Teuton male, his irises the vivid cerulean of a pristine lake. *You can do this. You can do this.*

I practiced until the sun stood directly above me, until no vestiges of fright crept along my nerves while I held my breath. It helped to envision that young man beside me, encouraging me to reach for the magic innate in my blood. Whether I would ever get the privilege of meeting him again or not, I sent off a silent prayer of thanks to his spirit, for chasing my demons away from my dreams. I had eaten the grapefruit he saved for me last Friday, a warm sensation coddling my heart as I enjoyed its juicy tang.

While I cooked a one-pot stew for lunch, I mused on my attraction to that mysterious young man, wondering whether my fascination with him grew out of the emptiness of my heart. For years, I had longed to marry Philipp as his equal. Seeing his spirit dissolve before me in Wuotan's bloody river shattered me in ways I never imagined possible, especially after so many males destroyed me during my childhood. My wary heart opened itself to my *Truhtein* when he proved interested in educating me and helping me heal, gently brushing off my attempts to lure him into a physical relationship. He wanted me to make my choices as an adult, not a child trained to lust after meaningless sex.

Less than a week after Philipp's death, my heart started yearning for a male I did not know, a Teuton of fire who corrected my faux pas with a grapefruit. Was my heart just trying to fill the void my *Truhtein* had left? What was it he had said before I scurried away? *You seem familiar.* Impossible. I had not appeared in public since my father sold me.

Unless . . . .

Had that long-haired Teuton male seen my videos?

I almost bit my tongue at the thought, my heart dropping down into my gut. "Couldn't be," I told myself in a whisper, after swallowing a tentative bite of celery and potato. "There's no way anyone would connect the adult Zehra to how I looked as a child. I have boobs now. Curves. Blackheads. Not the same."

Working hard to nix my latest uncertainties, I sealed the rest of the stew into containers to store in the fridge and freezer. After cleaning up where I had eaten at the dry bar, I squared my shoulders and struck out for the back garden once more. First, I would practice five more times, making sure I could still hold my breath for five-second intervals without panicking. Then, I would invite my stone to take me.

With that tiny, hopeful corner of my heart fixated on Mr. Fiery Long Hair. I wondered if he was really a Teuton priest, like my dream world companion.

This time, when I sat upon the stone lip of the fish pool, I sensed a readiness running along my nerves, as if my stone magic wanted me to seize its glories at last. But I settled into a cross-legged pose first and practiced holding my breath, visions of my fiery priest blocking the terror from my mind. And when I reached deep within and called my element to the fore, I shut my eyes as stone hardened my limbs from my fingers and toes upward. It felt *right* this time, my heartbeat steady.

Before I realized what was happening, my spirit broke free from my body. My eyes opened of their own accord, the fresh spring breeze filtering through the locks of my hair, which swirled around my face. I had braided my hair today. But now . . . now the breeze itself whispered to my consciousness, inviting me into its domain. Surprise shivered through me when I looked down at my hands.

They were translucent, my beige skin casting a silvery light. I wore a robe of gray that matched the stone where my body sat, my bare toes peeking out at me from down below. Even my *clothing* appeared translucent. Nature's life seemed to embrace me, the power of the earth welcoming its child home.

I did it, I thought, exhilaration brightening my outlook. My spirit hovered a few centimeters above the ground, not far from where my mortal body sat beside the pool, encased in dark gray stone. With a victorious smile, I tilted my head back, curious about how the city would look from high above. I had never been afraid of heights, and my *Truhtein* had assured me that a Teuton spirit could not get hurt if it fell. As an earthen element, the ground would simply swallow me up and eject me as good as new.

Determination swelled inside me, reinforcing my intent, and I rocketed into the atmosphere, the trees dotting the Liebig property shrinking beneath me. Thrill bubbled in my chest, and I began to giggle. Coming to a halt about thirty meters up, I spread my arms and spun around, my hair and robe whirling in the breeze. This was what it meant to be a Teuton. Utter freedom, perfect unity with the forces of nature, the wonders of magic and light purifying my soul.

Taking a moment to observe the layout of Erlangen, I noticed wisps of elemental magic rising into the sky from a variety of places. A flicker of spiritual red fire caught my eye to the west—a sizzling shield protecting something near a two-story house in the old section of the city. *Wow,* I thought to myself, realizing Philipp was not the only Teuton who used his element to defend his property. I glanced beneath me, tracing the edges of my *Truhtein's* violet-black shield, a proud smile curving my lips.

Focusing again on the magic in the air, I realized that I could sense each Teuton spirit occupying my city. From this distance, I could not pick them out individually, but I caught glimmers of mystical life occupying many of the buildings below. Red fire, metal, wintry wind, water, molten rock, air, lightning. There seemed to be quite a few Teutons at the large corporation my *Truhtein* used to run as CEO, people he likely once called his coworkers.

I love all of you. Keep reaching for your dreams. I sent the mental blessing out along with a breathy kiss, then shifted my attention to the Autobahn that ran north to south. I needed to follow that eight kilometers north to the compound where my father ran his business—a seedy motel halfway between Erlangen and Bamberg. He and his cronies at Befreiung maintained the motel as an actual motel, while using the buildings further back from the street for dark purposes.

While I could have drifted in the right direction as a spirit, I was not entirely sure whether I could find the motel from high above. No point in wasting time; it was nearing three p.m. So instead, I dove toward the interchange below me, my eyes scanning the vehicles in the left lane. Those drivers would probably stay on A73 long enough, and I knew what exit I needed.

This might be a little crazy, Zehra, I told myself as I zeroed in on a bright red Mercedes zooming through Erlangen without a care. *Keep your thoughts to yourself. You don't need to cause a wreck.*

My anticipation had built so high, I thought my grin might stretch too wide for my face. Narrowing my eyes, I leaped atop the Mercedes' roof, sinking my feet into the metal just enough to secure my spirit in place. Wind whipped at me like knife blades, the air's power somehow strengthening my magic. *WOOOO!* I yelled in my mind, raising my fists into the air.

If being a Teuton spirit was always this exciting, I might fall into a new and otherworldly addiction—leaving my body behind to grasp a surreal freedom. *Can't have sex as a spirit, though,* I reminded myself, absurdity quivering my ethereal form. *I'll have to make sure I can do this whenever I want, memories or not.*

The Mercedes' driver changed lanes shortly after I saw the sign indicating the exit I needed. A jarring experience, but now it was time to leave the car behind. I yanked my feet out of the roof—a scratchy sensation—darting into the sky again and reaching out to grab at the wind's currents, letting them pillow me. Once my spirit had slowed into a casual drift, I headed right, seeking the single-story motel with its aging sign advertising rooms with cable TV.

I found it several minutes later, its outer façade resembling the pictures my *Truhtein* had taken with his hidden camera. The size of a thumbnail, that camera was one of the only items Philipp ever dared to bring on spiritual expeditions. Not too many people would notice it floating through the air, or situated upon the brim of Lenz's flat hat. I knew where Philipp kept that camera, but I had not yet built the courage to use it myself. My childhood had given me a distrust of cameras. I noticed each one in the grocery store and on traffic lights.

A semi-disguised camera sat upon the motel's sign, facing the street. Again, I felt a touch of annoyance about my earthen element. If I claimed some type of energy, I could take out every camera on this property and set my mother free this very day. As it stood, I would have to find her first. And plan.

My stone detected no Teuton spirits on the property, thank goodness. But I sensed several ordinary humans inside the motel's front-facing building, others in the compound behind. That second building looked abandoned, tan paint peeling away beneath its blocked windows. The compound's walls were made of brick and stone, two familiar materials. Maybe I should try that trick Lenz mentioned. Stuff my spirit into the outer wall and study what lay inside.

Today, my primary purpose was to reconnect with my mother. Fate appeared to be on my side. While I hovered above the compound, pondering the best way to identify her among the ordinary humans—outsiders—in the buildings below, I noticed a woman exiting a back door of the main motel. She spoke a couple words I did not catch to someone inside, then walked toward the compound, her bearing indicating exhaustion.

The acute vision standard to all Teuton spirits told me instantly that I looked at my mother. Clad in an airy dress of dull orange with matching head covering, her lips pursed in what might be resignation, her deep brown eyes the same ones I saw in the mirror. Pain gouged my heart as I watched her. She often wore dresses, but the hijab was new. Had my father courted more radical forms of religion in recent years? Or did he consider his wife a mere servant?

I drifted down to ground level, following several steps behind her. Glancing around the parking lot between the two buildings, I saw four cameras recording all activities in the lot. Though I knew that no technology could record a Teuton spirit, shivers ran along my limbs at the prospect of being noticed. There were no Teutons in this place right now, and outsiders could not see spirits. I reminded myself of that as my mother unlocked a door at the right corner of the compound.

I had never laid eyes upon Philipp's spirit until we met in the bloody river, after all.

My mother paused to glance behind her before shutting the door, her gaze passing through me as if I did not exist. I would have to speak directly to her mind, once I could catch her alone. I suspected she performed housekeeping duties for the motel, and now she would have to cook dinner for her family. And make sure my siblings did their homework, if my father actually sent them to school.

Steeling myself, I eased my spirit forward until my palms touched the brick wall beside the door. Could I really drift *through* the wall, like Lenz had said? It was time to find out. Taking a deep breath, I pushed myself forward, my element tingling within me as the bricks enveloped my spirit. Blinking, my eyes widened at the innate energy weaving throughout the wall. I slid my fingers through the bricks at my sides, testing the mortar that held them together. Certainty arose in my soul, telling me I could break this entire wall into pieces if I wished to do so.

No. *I don't want to destroy you,* I whispered silently to the bricks around me, fearing they might have caught the direction of my thoughts. *Can you lead me to my mother's room?*

A silver cord appeared within the wall to my right, the bricks' essence sliding against me in what felt like reassurance. I smiled and followed the cord, realizing I had a new ally in my quest to bring my father to justice. Maybe the stones of this compound did not agree with Befreiung's dark deeds.

Maybe they remembered Philipp.

The silver cord guided me into a sparsely-furnished bedroom before I could explore that idea further. I knew Teutonic elements were sentient to some degree, but the tomes I had read declared they never communicated in words. But now, I hovered a centimeter above the floor with the wall at my back, gazing down at my mother, who knelt upon her prayer rug with her head bowed.

She did not voice her prayers aloud. She never had, my entire life. I ran my gaze over the contents of the room—one queen-sized bed, a desk with computer and chair, two bureaus, a trash can, and a full-length mirror on the back of the closed door. There was also a mirror on the ceiling over the bed. That implied my mother had to offer erotic services to my father's clients, or his business partners.

I clenched my ghostly hands into fists, resentment roiling through me. Looking at my mother's submissive posture, I decided to interrupt her prayers. I no longer worshiped her god, anyway. Anne, *can you hear me?* I directed my thoughts to her alone, my brain taking a second to switch from thinking in German to Turkish. Anne, *can you hear me? It's Zehra. Your daughter.*

A tremor raced over her body, and she did not raise her head. "Are you . . . an angel?" she murmured so quietly I could hardly discern the words.

Sorrow gripped me as I recognized that she believed me dead. *Not an angel. Just Zehra. Your oldest child. A girl who escaped her handler years ago.*

My mother's body quaked again, and she wrapped her arms around her bowed head. Concealing her face from my sight. Or were there cameras in this room, too? I cut my gaze toward where the walls met the ceiling, searching for them, and my mother whispered, "Oh, Zehra. My precious child. You shouldn't be here."

There it was. A lens hidden within the brass border of the mirror overhead. That meant my mother never enjoyed real privacy. She must not want her captors to read her lips as she talked with me. Fury darkened the gray robe that cloaked my spirit. My mother should not have to live like this.

Well, I'm here whether I should be or not. I've become more than the Zehra you remember. I'm going to get you out of here, free you from Baba's *cruelty.*

Sobs shook my mother's shoulders, though she muffled their noise as best as she could. I knelt beside her, reaching my right hand out to stroke her head. *That's me trying to comfort you,* I told her, since she had likely never interacted with a Teuton spirit before. *I know this is all new for you, but I promise I can get you out of this place. You'll never have to submit to a man again. I'll take you to a home where* Baba *and his partners will never find you. And I'll free all of my siblings. Faruk, Murat, and Leyla.*

My mother blotted her nose on her left sleeve without lifting her head from its submissive position. "Oh, Zehra," she breathed, her voice even quieter now than it had been at first. I bent my head low to catch her next words. "It's not as easy as you think."

She straightened her left leg, poking her foot out from beneath her orange skirt. There, around her bare ankle, sat a band shimmering with a potent sorcery I recognized.

Dark energy.

Chapter Five:
An Unforeseen Pivot

Wrath darkened my robe into a black that resembled an onyx stone. *There's a Teuton working for* Baba, I growled, reaching a finger out to judge the anklet's strength. To mortal eyesight, it would look like a standard piece of jewelry. But the violet-black threads pulsing around it revealed its true purpose—a shackle. Dark energy prickled along my fingertip.

"He works with one sorcerer," my mother whispered, her voice breaking. My plans to liberate her and my siblings had grown infinitely more complicated.

I can sense the magic in this anklet, I told my mother, having run my finger along its length from one side of her foot to the other. *It's not causing me any pain. I'm guessing that's its purpose, though? To shock you if you do . . . what?*

My mother cowered, muffling her voice in the folds of her dress. "If I stray more than a hundred meters from this place, it cripples me. All of the . . . working women here . . . have an anklet. For control."

I sat back on my heels, the cement floor's similarity to stone offering my element a needed boost. I would have to figure out how to break this shackle off of my mother's ankle without hurting her. Lenz might have some insight, especially

37

if we went over everything Philipp had told us about his dark energy. With his final words, my *Truhtein* had declared me strong. Was stone strong enough to vanquish dark energy's power?

Do my siblings have anklets, too? Though my ultimate goal was to break my father's business apart like the child porn ring, I wanted to get my mother and siblings out first. They needed to start afresh, to heal.

My mother sighed, lifting herself into a sitting position. She glanced around the bedroom, as if hoping I might be visible, her countenance creased with grief. Pushing herself to her feet, she stretched with a groan, then tugged the base of her hijab around her throat. "They do not. I have to start dinner. It's my duty to feed Kemal and his partners. You need to get out of here, Zehra. The sorcerer will be here for dinner. He always is. And he'll know how to find you."

Nervousness ran through my spirit. *Are all of them still alive?*

My mother paused before the mirror on the back of the door, retrieving a small container of face powder from a pocket of her dress. "Faruk is lost," she said, her tone bitter as she dabbed at her forehead. "He graduates in June but already works for one of Kemal's partners. Murat is unsure. I do what I can to guide him, but I fear Kemal will poison his mind, too. He is ambitious and gifted."

Finished with her makeup, my mother opened the door and started down a short hall toward a kitchen at the far end. The hallway reminded me of one from an old war movie—gray walls, ceiling, and floor, with bare bulbs glimmering above each door. Most of the doors were shut, but I sensed ordinary humans in several chambers. I wondered if one of the rooms belonged to Murat. I needed to talk to him. Did he even remember me?

The fact that my mother had not yet mentioned my baby sister, Leyla, did not escape my notice. I hovered in the doorway to the kitchen, watching her grab pots from a cabinet and set them upon a stove that looked fifty years old. Anne. *What about Leyla?* It scared me to ask the question, but I had to know.

My mother halted before the stove, her hands gripping its edge as she shut her eyes. "Leyla's dead," she whispered, her sorrow touching my spirit.

I stifled a mental cry of pain, my robe dulling into a muddy gray. An instant later, the door at the far side of the kitchen swung open, fresh air wafting inside on the heels of a broad-shouldered man in a dark suit. My mother choked out a gasp as the man advanced on her, ominous energy radiating from his aura.

"Dear little Arzu has been playing with her anklet, hasn't she?" the man charged in German, his gravelly voice scratching at my spirit. My eyes widened, unable to make out his face, though he wore no hat. He took my mother's chin in his hand and twisted her head around to face him. "What exactly does she hope to accomplish doing something like that, hmm?"

"Get out of here!" my mother screeched in Turkish, her words not for her tormenter, but for me.

"Now she's getting feisty! Looks like someone needs a lesson." His right fist came forward to knock her square in the eye. Anger swept over me, awakening an instinct to protect, no matter the consequences. I snatched a napkin holder from the table beside the door, the first weapon I found.

"I'll get more from you tonight than boring old meatballs," the looming man sneered at my mother. She whimpered, on her knees before him, her trembling hands cupping her injured eye. Channeling all of my fury into my arm, I lobbed the napkin holder at her tormentor, paper fluttering to the floor.

It hit him square on the head, and the magic obscuring his features wavered. A strangled sound escaped his lips and he whirled to face me, dark energy igniting in his irises. In that moment, I realized my mistake. Terror consumed me, and my element squelched itself. For a perilous second, my spirit seemed to funnel its way into a stone vent with a compelling undertow.

Then my physical eyelids shot open, showing me the fish pond in the Liebig garden. Exactly where I had started this journey. Goosebumps rose along my skin, and I pressed a hand against my racing heart. What had I done?

"Have to admit, you make an elegant gargoyle, Zehra."

I jumped to my feet and spun around to see Lenz sprawled in the grass with his back against an elm tree. He wore his typical attire of plain jeans, trench coat, and flat cap, a hardback book resting in his lap. He favored me with a sly grin that faded at the panic in my expression. Before I could stop myself, I ran at him, my body quaking with sobs. Lenz stood up in time to catch me, tucking me into an awkward embrace while I bawled aloud. I felt like a complete failure. My mother would doubtless face punishment for my thoughtless act.

Now that evil Teuton male of dark energy knew what my spirit looked like. I might never be able to infiltrate Befreiung's compound again.

Lenz did not speak while I wept, but he eased us both down onto the grass, his right arm firm against my shoulders. Bit by bit, the whole story burst from my soul, my tears running dry. I wiped my eyes on the light blue sleeve of my blouse, shame settling upon me like a rock-filled backpack. I had meant to gain intel from my mother without making myself known to others in the compound. But my urge for revenge dominated my reason, spurred on by my love for her.

As I began to compose myself, I suddenly realized I managed to grasp and throw a physical object with my spiritual hand. I knew that was possible. Philipp carried his tiny camera on spiritual expeditions, after all. It had been easy; I did it without thinking twice. I also managed to insert my feet into a car's roof and my entire self into a brick wall.

Teutonic magic did not seem quite so inaccessible, now.

"Okay," Lenz said after I finished relating the entire story, his arm sliding away from my shoulders. "We both admit you made some mistakes, but let's look on the bright side first. You've learned that your mother is alive and willing to leave her husband, once we work out how to safely remove her anklet. Your younger brother, who has no anklet at present, is a second candidate for rescue. Do you plan to shelter them here on this property, once they're free?"

"This is the safest place, as long as my *Truhtein's* energy shield holds. I can clean two guest rooms for them to use. And lock up anything important." While I trusted my mother without reservations, Murat was a stranger. A thirteen-year-old now, I last saw him as a toddling youngster. My mother called him ambitious and gifted, which meant I must secure all of Philipp's—now my—online accounts, as a precaution.

"They likely don't have access to their passports or birth certificates," Lenz noted, gazing out toward the pool with a thoughtful expression. "Which means they will have to stay with you until we can bring the authorities down on Befreiung."

"I know." I sank my fingers into the grass, searching for the earth below, a silent request for mystical comfort. "Do you think you could scout out the place a little more? I have to go back to keep my mother informed of what we're planning. And I need to talk to Murat, find out whether he wants to get out, too. But I'm kind of nervous after what happened in the kitchen. That big Teuton looked straight into my eyes. He knows what I look like. And he knows I'm female."

"I can do some surveillance starting on Monday," Lenz responded. "I can lurk in the shadows as a spirit, take note of when people come and go. I'll try to get a magical read on the anklets, too. See if they have any backup spells that come into play if they're forcibly removed. Since the dark energy didn't harm you when you touched your mother's anklet, I expect your stone could break them. Along with metal, yours is the strongest Teutonic element where brute force is concerned."

"My *Truhtein* said I'm so strong," I whispered, my chest tightening.

"He knows. He knows you can do this. And I'll be here to help you every step of the way," Lenz promised, lifting his book from the grass and placing it in his lap.

I glanced at the hardback's title. "Sherlock Holmes. I've read that one. Just how long were you waiting for me to return to my body?"

"Ah, I got here right after three o'clock and found you meditating in gargoyle form. Figured I'd get some reading done in the meantime. Got a few things I need to ask you." Lenz eyed me from beneath the brim of his cap, his visage unreadable.

"I've been eating every day. Cooking meals. Cleaning, feeding the fish. Got to the spiritual realm for the first time this afternoon." I rattled off a bunch of basic activities, figuring he meant to check on my welfare. While Philipp's absence left a gaping hole in my heart, I thought back to my encounter with Mr. Fiery Long Hair more and more. If I visited the grocery store tomorrow morning, I might run into him again.

"Tell me something. Have you sensed anything unusual meddling with your heart lately? A deep, abiding pull toward a Teuton priest you don't know?"

I did a double-take, my eyebrows coming together at my companion's query. "What?"

Lenz's hazel eyes darkened with magic, as if he wished to read the depths of my soul. "When you reached the spiritual realm today, did you transform reality around you to send you straight to your father's compound? Or did you take a minute to observe this city from high above, sprinkling your blessing upon every Teuton within its borders?"

My breath caught in my throat. How did Lenz know? "I—"

"Could you sense every Teuton in this city, if you concentrate on the magic harbored within your heart?"

I had done that very thing just an hour ago. "Can't . . . can't everybody?"

A knowing smile appeared on Lenz's lips, and he cleared his throat. "How much did Philipp tell you about the Keyholder and Lady of a Teuton city?"

My forehead wrinkled. "They're the honorary rulers of modern-day Teuton cities," I said, thinking back to the histories I had read about such individuals. "*Leitaeri* and *Leitalra*, which mean male and female leader in Teutonic dialect. In the Middle Ages, Keyholders opened and closed the city gates every day. My *Truhtein* was friends with Erlangen's *Leitalra*, Frieda Dahlhausen."

"They were good friends," Lenz agreed, leaning back against the tree while tapping his fingers upon the cover of his book. "The former Lady Erlanga, God rest her soul, departed this world on the same day you gained Teuton blood. A sage woman of the light, she chose to give her life for the good of the Teutons under her jurisdiction. A noble sacrifice . . . like the one my dearest friend gave for you."

Lenz's eyes locked with mine, a thousand implications seeming to lurk within their depths. I shook my head once, trying to keep up. "Lady Erlanga . . . the one who was my *Truhtein's* friend . . . is dead?"

He nodded. "And that means the mystical soul of this city must choose a new female avatar, a young maiden to ascend as the next Lady Erlanga. If I'm not mistaken, I believe she has already made her choice."

I scooted away from him, my fingers digging into the earth. "No. You're not saying . . . you think it's *me?* You think *I'm* the new *Leitalra* of Erlangen? But I just became a Teuton three weeks ago! I'm Turkish!"

"Race and creed don't matter. You were born in Erlangen, weren't you?"

My heart rate increased, a cold sweat breaking out across my skin. "At the forest hospital," I murmured, clutching the earth below like denial's firm cord. Was *this* why I felt the need to send a spiritual blessing to every Teuton I sensed in the city, while I drifted overhead? Had I lost control over my ultimate destiny? Was I doomed to marry Erlangen's Keyholder, a man I had never met before?

Was *this* why my heart seemed uneasy whenever I wallowed in misery over Philipp's absence?

"It's somewhat unusual that you've been chosen," Lenz went on. I barely made sense of his words, my emotions in turmoil. "For over two centuries, this city's soul has chosen a maiden who has lived outside of Erlangen's borders for a significant amount of time, an effort to extend charity and hospitality to all. You, Zehra, bring another feature to the table entirely. Different cultures, experiences from the darkest side of humanity. You could break apart the prejudices that linger among our people, open our community's hearts to what's truly important."

"Wait." I raised one palm toward Lenz, shaking the dirt off of it as I worked to organize my thoughts. "You are positively *sure* that I'm the new Lady? Why?"

"Because you met the young Keyholder in the grocery store on the day of Philipp's funeral. He's been asking all the priests in the city if they know a Teuton witch of stone with sable hair and brown eyes ever since." Lenz grinned.

Horror overtook me, and I choked on my breath. Mr. Fiery Long Hair was the Keyholder of Erlangen—or in layman's terms, my fated mate. If this city's soul had truly chosen me. That warmth I sensed in my spirit during our brief encounter might mean more than my foolish hormones acting up.

"What did you *tell* him about me?" I shrieked.

Lenz held up both hands in a mollifying gesture. "No need to panic. I barely told him anything. Just that I know who you are. Pulled him aside privately to give him the news. I didn't mention your name or your relationship with Philipp."

I pushed out a heavy breath and rubbed my forehead. "I don't have time for this. I don't have time. We have to get my mother and Murat out before I worry about some weird connection with a guy I don't know at all. I can't really be the Lady of Erlangen, anyway. This has to be a misunderstanding."

Lenz shrugged and rose to his feet with a grunt, stuffing his book into his trench coat. "Misunderstanding or not, this isn't something you can just run away from. The Keyholder is expecting you at Pritzl tomorrow afternoon at four o'clock. If you don't agree to meet him, I'm not sure how long he'll resist the urge to hunt you down and claim you. Here."

Chapter Six

Henning Glossner

My entire body trembled with nervous anticipation on Saturday afternoon when I struck out to keep my appointment at Pritzl, a family-owned pub nestled in a cozy neighborhood not far from the Liebig property. I knew next to nothing about the place, except that its owners stocked a type of peach Schnapps my *Truhtein* and I used to enjoy whenever I achieved a new goal. Since I cracked the code of the spiritual realm one day earlier, I planned to order a bottle in celebration, whether Mr. Fiery Long Hair—the Keyholder of Erlangen—approved or not.

While I did not appreciate Lenz putting me on the spot, I knew I would have to face the Keyholder sooner or later, if only to learn whether he, too, believed this city's mystical soul had chosen me to embody her essence. Yesterday evening, I had searched my heart, trying to determine if it could really be true. According to Lenz, I met all the criteria required to become this city's *Leitalra*.

I had been born in the forest hospital downtown on April 5th, 1986. Three weeks ago, I became a Teuton witch by blood alone, through the harrowing ritual that drowned and burned my spirit in Wuotan's infernal river. And as of right now, I claimed no Teuton mate.

This would never have happened if Philipp had survived the blood-transfer. We would have married that very night at twilight, with Lenz binding our blood in the most absolute way possible. But my *Truhtein* went into the ritual with the intent of giving his life for me, not merely his blood. A starry-eyed maiden, I never imagined one of us would not greet the dawn afterward.

I wondered if Philipp knew that his aged friend, Frieda Dahlhausen, planned to relinquish her life in some noble manner that very day. Had my master decided to die to grant me the opportunity to take her place? In Philipp's eyes, I was worthy and strong. A fitting *Leitalra* for Erlangen's Teuton community.

Imposter syndrome held a firm grip on me as the daffodils adorning Pritzl's window boxes caught my attention the closer I drew. Their vibrant blooms shone like the sun, which hid behind a layer of clouds. The prospect of losing control over my destiny upset me, but I could still free my mother and Murat and anyone else mired in Befreiung's network while representing Erlangen's mystical community. Before he left yesterday, Lenz spoke a truth that brought light to my world, like the growing daffodils defying the afternoon's gloom: "Out of all eligible witches in this city, Erlanga's soul found *you* worthy to carry her torch. Not any of the females who grew up posturing amid their peers. You."

I repeated his reassurance to myself in my mind when I reached the pub's main entrance, gathering the courage to step inside. With time, I might be able to confide in this young Keyholder, like I had in Philipp. This could be the moment when my goals and dreams began falling into place. Assuming I found the courage to bare my shattered heart before an unknown young male.

Inside, I paused for a second so my eyes could adjust to the low light, neon signs advertising brands of alcohol luring my gaze to the bar. It stood along the wall opposite the door, one security camera situated among a collection of wine bottles.

Several male patrons sprawled upon the barstools, watching a soccer match on a grainy TV. A bartender dressed in traditional Bavarian attire favored me with a welcoming smile from where she stood near the short stairway that likely led toward the kitchen and restrooms. I nodded back at her and stepped further inside, counting eighteen tables sprinkled across the floor. Only three were occupied at this hour.

My stone magic tested the pub's atmosphere, sensing no Teutons present as yet. Disappointment clasped my heart, but I shoved it aside and headed for a two-person table near the stairwell. It was barely three-thirty, and Lenz said I was to meet the Keyholder at four. Even though Germans were notorious for being early, I had taken it to an extreme, too antsy to remain at home any longer.

A male waiter appeared with a drink menu after I situated myself with my back to the wall, giving me a view of the entire pub. He noted that the kitchen would not open again until five, but Pritzl served a limited snack menu in the meantime. I managed to order the bottle of Schnapps I wanted, then asked for the snack menu, so I would have something to do while awaiting my mystery companion.

A shiver of accomplishment ran through me after the waiter departed, and I grinned to myself as I set my purse onto the floor. That was the first time in my life I had ever ordered anything from a restaurant. Despite the nervous tremor in my voice—which the waiter may not have noticed—I handled the task well.

I relaxed a bit and ran my gaze over the pub's other patrons. One middle-aged gentleman nursed a glass of wheat beer in the far corner; he was probably a regular. A group of four young females, likely college students, chattered around another table, a mostly empty basket of soft pretzel bites in their midst. A couple that appeared to be in their thirties sat nearest to the exit, gazing into each other's faces while they shared a quiet conversation.

All at once, the males gathered at the bar started hooting, prompting me to check the score on the TV. I could not read the numbers from where I sat without using my element to enhance my vision. The pub was dimly lit, so no one should notice. I invoked my stone magic into my irises for a couple seconds, sitting on my hands in the process. Chelsea had just scored. They were up by two.

The waiter brought my bottle of Schnapps along with two glasses, "in case your friend wants to share," he said as he opened the flask. I glanced over the snack menu while he poured the blushing pink liquor into my glass, deciding I would wait for the Keyholder before ordering any food. I ate some leftover stew for lunch, so my stomach had not yet begun to complain.

Not long after the waiter left, the main door opened to admit a lean young male whose lengthy hair rustled in the breeze. My eyes widened of their own accord, for my spirit recognized him instantly. He secured the door behind him, then shifted his attention to me. I caught a gleam of cerulean fire in his irises as he sauntered my way, a shy smile curving his lips.

He wore the same leather jacket he had at the grocery store, his hair draped carelessly over his shoulders, a hint of awkwardness in his posture as he made his way around the tables to where I sat. Warmth spread throughout my core while I watched him approach, my thoughts racing back to how he looked in my dreams. His fire was blue. I knew that for sure now, my hormones splashing my muses with how wonderful it would be to bind my stone with this man's fire.

You don't know him, Zehra, I reminded myself when he halted before my table, thrusting his hands into his jacket pockets. *No matter what Erlanga's soul tells you to do, you can't offer him your heart on a silver platter. Not until you know he's a good man.*

"Is this seat taken?" the young man asked in his unusually deep voice, his eyes now absent of magic as he studied my face.

Was he making a joke? Surely he could feel the attraction between us, just like I could. Deciding on a whim to throw my knowledge in his face, I responded in the Teutonic dialect. "Unfortunately, that seat is reserved for this city's *Leitaeri.*"

His eyebrows arched in what looked like a mixture of surprise and respect. "Well, good thing I brought these along, then," he answered in standard German, retrieving an antique ring of sizeable keys from his right pocket. He plunked them onto the table, then pulled the chair out to sit down.

I gawked at the keys, their inherent magic arousing peculiar sentiments within me. My spirit recognized their power, but I felt no need to recoil. My heart assured me this man and I were equals, guardians of the essence that bound the Teuton community of Erlangen together. There was no escaping it anymore. I was the Lady, the *Leitalra*. This city's honorary matriarch.

"Have you ordered anything to eat?" the Keyholder asked, running his gaze over the snack menu I discarded earlier. I jerked as his voice extracted me from the spell the city's keys had cast upon my mind. Heat rose in my cheeks. Nice to know a ring of ancient gate keys could drive me loony.

"I had stew for lunch," I heard myself saying, pushing my chair back a few centimeters. My right foot nudged my purse, and I looked down at it.

"I'm going to order the basket of soft pretzel bites. You can have some if you want. I haven't eaten yet today, so I'm ravenous at this point." My companion laid the menu down and eyed my bottle of Schnapps.

"It's not healthy to go this long without eating." My opinions kept tumbling out of my mouth at random, whether they ought to or not. Now I was rebuking the Keyholder's eating habits. What was I thinking? I hardly knew him.

"Yeah, I know. It's been a busy day. Still sorting out my Omi's affairs." The young man placed the city's keys back in his pocket, then worked his way out of his jacket. Our gazes met for a second, and he seemed to read the confusion in mine. "Your predecessor, that is."

I caught my breath. "Oh. The late *Leitalra* was your grandmother? I'm so sorry." Sympathy washed over me, my spirit sensing his grief.

"My great-grandmother, actually." The waiter reappeared before the young man could go on. I held my peace while he ordered the pretzel basket and a glass of Kellerbier, observing his manners. He spoke politely to the waiter and met his gaze, not giving off the impression of arrogance at all. A Teuton leader who knew humility. Attraction swelled in my heart, and I clenched my legs together in an attempt to squash my need. *Keep your head on straight, Zehra.*

When my companion finished his order, I stretched one hand out toward him. "If there's anything I can do to help you with your Omi's loss, please tell me. I know a little about sorting people's affairs." A fact I did not particularly like, but true nonetheless. I had recently scheduled someone from the pool care company to come by next week to change all of the filters and perform maintenance.

A wavering smile appeared on the Keyholder's face, and he dropped his gaze to his hands in his lap. He did not reach out to touch mine. "The priests on the council would say we ought to get married and complete our bond. The best help you can offer, as this city's *Leitalra.*"

I straightened in my chair and yanked my hand back, chagrined. "Doing that seems a little too shallow to me, though," the young man went on, wincing at my reaction. "Like I'm using you as a bandage against my loss."

"Is that what most Keyholders and Ladies do?" I asked, repulsion tainting the peace I felt in my companion's presence. "Get married right after their partner dies? Did you and your Omi get married after you took the keys?"

The young man grimaced and looked toward the stairwell. "No! That would be gross. It's a medieval tradition, anyway, not something that really applies in today's world. Keyholders and Ladies don't have to marry at all, no matter what the city bond tells them to do. I'd rather get to know you as a person first. If you'd like that."

He cast his gaze toward me again, shyness evident in his expression. I did not know what to say, my hormones and magic urging me to embrace him while my past warned otherwise. The waiter returned with a frothing mug of beer before I organized my thoughts, so I used the quick break to mull over how much of myself I should reveal. The Keyholder wanted to get to know me as a person, but he gave off a naïve vibe. He had doubtless grown up cherished by his family.

He would not be able to comprehend my background or my motivations at all. It would be best to keep the full truth under wraps for as long as possible. He might reject me if he knew I was raped as a child. Thus far, he had not paid much attention to my breasts, even though I wore a snug blouse that emphasized their shape. Nor had he taken my hand when I offered it. Maybe this Keyholder had no interest in me sexually.

Maybe he preferred males. Or children. I swallowed hard, trying to stifle those thoughts before they polluted my hopes. *He's innocent, and you're not. Keep your true nature hidden, and don't judge him.*

My companion took a slow drink from his mug, then brushed a stray lock of bronze hair over his shoulder before meeting my gaze again. "I'm such an idiot. I've been going on about marriage and tradition when I don't even know your name. I'm Henning Glossner, and you can call me Henning. I'm the only child of Robin Glossner, master plumber. I've been his apprentice for about three and a half years, and I'll take the journeyman exams in July. I'm twenty and I've held the keys of this city since December 2002."

He sat back and rested his hands upon the table, looking expectant. I considered all he had said, knowing I could not reply in kind whatsoever. He had held the keys for a year and a half, so he accepted them at age eighteen. Young and sweet, but maybe not as naïve as I initially thought. To claim a city's keys, a Teuton must pass the initiation for the priesthood. Philipp told me that involved torture of body, spirit, and mind.

I pulled my glass of Schnapps toward me and studied its contents. "It's an honor to meet you, Henning. I'm Zehra."

"Zehra. What a lovely name." I took a huge gulp from my glass as Henning spoke, prompting his eyes to widen. "Uh . . . that's pretty strong stuff."

I swallowed the liquor, savoring its fruity taste, then narrowed my eyes at my companion. "Are we in the U.S. now? If so, you can't be drinking that, either." I set my glass down and pointed at his beer.

Henning's forehead wrinkled, emphasizing a crooked scar above his right eyebrow. "Sorry, I was just surprised. Hoping you're not secretly an alcoholic."

I frowned. "I'm not. This is my favorite drink, and I'm celebrating."

"Right." My companion appeared perplexed.

"Got to the spiritual realm for the first time yesterday," I explained.

Comprehension dawned in Henning's ocean-blue eyes. "You're a Teuton by blood alone," he murmured, admiration evident in his tone.

"I am." I ran a hand through my hair as the waiter reappeared carrying two plates and the basket of pretzel bites. They came with three types of mustard, two of which looked spicy. My mouth watered. Maybe I was hungry after all.

Henning offered me the basket after the waiter left, speaking a few generic sentences about the blood-transfer. I laid a handful of pretzel bites onto my plate and selected the cup of spicy Löwensenf, nodding along while he spoke. The first bite erupted upon my taste buds, tingling my nose. Henning had started describing a blood-transfer he witnessed while he studied for the priesthood. I cringed when he mentioned the deathly smell of artery blood.

"Sorry, I'm going on again, aren't I? You already know all about the blood-transfer." My companion appeared embarrassed, dropping his gaze from mine to dip a pretzel bite into the cup of plain mustard. I chewed on another spicy piece, ordering my mind to stay in the present, not to fall back into those harrowing memories of Wuotan's bloody river. With Philipp's spirit vanishing before my eyes.

"Did your friend survive?"

Henning's direct question brought me up short, especially since he spoke the German word *friend* in feminine form. Of course he assumed my donor was female. If I told him the truth, he might get jealous of Philipp. I wiped my fingers on my napkin and folded my hands in my lap.

"No," I answered, holding his gaze. "And I'd rather not talk about it."

"Okay. That's fair. I'm so sorry about your loss, Zehra. Sometimes as priests we forget the human aspect of rituals like that one." The young Keyholder held a hand out to me across the table, an offering of support that mirrored my earlier gesture.

For some reason, our discussion of the blood-transfer had shuttered my emotions, rendering me unwilling to accept his comfort. While I still sensed that bonded attraction pulsing in my heart, my reason had reasserted itself, grinding my initial lust into ash. "You said before that the priests on the council want us to marry," I reminded him. "Do they have any other expectations I need to be aware of? Are they going to force us to come together?"

I eased my glass of Schnapps toward me and took a sip, studying Henning's countenance. His brown eyebrows had come together, and he chewed on his lower lip as he thought about my query. Taking another bite of pretzel, he glanced at my face, then toward the main entrance, then swallowed.

"They don't have the authority to force anything upon us," he replied, his left hand moving to scratch at his neck. "They'll want to meet you in person as soon as you're comfortable with that, but I'd suggest you ask Herr Schneider to file the record of your blood-transfer, first. There's been a lot of . . . rumors floating around . . . since my Omi's death. Since none of the 'expected' maidens sensed Erlanga's soul making her home in their hearts."

Henning drew back from the table, his pallor revealing his opinions of our people's gossip. The idea of presenting myself to the city council prompted dread to creep its way down my spine. I pushed that prospect from my mind and focused on how my companion had referred to the sole Teuton I trusted. "'Herr Schneider,'" I repeated, rolling my eyes. "Wow. I'll let him know."

The Keyholder lifted another pretzel bite from the basket and fingered it, brushing off my remark about Lenz. "There's also the matter of the *Herzestein*." His deep voice grew serious.

"The what?" I had never heard that word before, though my brain translated it without difficulty. Heart stone.

"An enchanted crystal that each *Leitalra* uses as a vessel for her magic and experience, throughout her years representing Erlangen," Henning explained, switching from standard dialect into Teutonica and lowering his voice. "Not very many people know about it. It's a secret guarded by the Lady and Keyholder. In times of transition, like now, the new *Leitalra*—you—will need to absorb the gifts my Omi left for you, the gifts harbored within the *Herzestein*."

I withdrew from Henning's intense gaze, thinking back to every tome I had ever read about Teutonic sorcery. "No books say anything about a magical crystal except for Prince Otto's time travel stone. I've never read about a heart stone."

Henning's lips quirked into a grin. "*Der Weg Teutonisch* isn't the most thorough record of—"

"*Der Weg* isn't the only book I've read." Annoyance rose to the fore within me as a shield against my insecurity. I hated being in the dark about anything. Before I could stop myself, I started spewing out knowledge again, stone altering the hue of my vision. "I know how to survive a blood-transfer, remember. And how to perform one. Even the spell to summon Wuotan."

"Wait. *What?*" My companion looked stricken.

I rolled my eyes at him again and shifted my gaze to the doorway, through which a couple around our age had just entered. "Erlanga's soul obviously wanted an avatar well versed in Teutonic magic, not some ignorant maiden dependent on a priestly master. So she chose a Turk."

"You're Turkish?" Henning sounded entranced. "Did you know there's a Kebap stand right by the grocery store? They've got the *best* lamb in the city!"

Chapter Seven

Investigations

Dark memories resurfaced from the depths, polluting my dreams that night and the following week. The progress I had made under Philipp's guidance crumbled at my Keyholder's carefree reaction to my heritage. Now, when sleep took me, my former handler marched into my world, his breath reeking of Kebaps as he stripped away all of my protection. Then faceless males would ravage my body, spotlights emphasizing every second for the cameras.

Of course Henning would think of Döner Kebaps, once I mentioned I was Turkish. Anyone would. He had no idea what the thought of those wraps did to me, how I had started walking a longer path to the grocery store so I would not have to see that stand beside the laundromat. I had to shoulder this burden alone, because it made no rational sense. My trauma rendered me pathetic, a fool.

I would have shut myself into Philipp's private suite for the entire week, like I did right after his death, had I not scheduled someone to take care of the pool, fountain, and fish pond. The man came on Monday with his assistants, and I met them on the portico, paying for their services with a few mumbled phrases. Once they finished their duties, I checked all of the property's security measures again, both physical and mystical, before returning to my *Truhtein's* suite and pulling all of the curtains closed.

I tried staying awake as long as possible each night, rereading a pile of books on Teutonic magic and scouring the dark corners of the internet for details on Befreiung's business practices. But eventually, exhaustion would win the fight and the handler would come, sticking his fingers deep inside of me and thumbing my clit until my body shuddered in unwanted pleasure.

You long for it. A masochist at heart, like all exotic cuties. Rabid whore.

How could I ever be good enough for the Keyholder when a lighthearted remark could ruin me?

Lenz called the house on Wednesday evening, stating that he had updates to share regarding his investigations of Befreiung's compound and motel. I had completely forgotten that he planned to stake out the place as a Teuton spirit starting on Monday. In a voice shaking from disuse, I asked him to come by in the morning. He promised to bring a loaf from the bakery and said that sometimes, just taking a shower could help ease depression. When I hung up the phone, I shut my eyes and whispered a prayer to Philipp's ghost. His dearest friend knew I was struggling. I needed to take Lenz's advice and get in the shower, then try to snatch a few hours of dreamless sleep before greeting him at dawn.

Lenz arrived at six a.m. on Thursday, his familiar presence granting me a respite from my demons. I had spent half the night crying in Philipp's bed, begging my Keyholder to return to my dreams and chase my tormentors away. Sometimes I believed I could feel his concern filtering into my heart along the bond we had not yet sealed, but that was likely my overactive imagination. The earthy scent of warm Vollkornbrot helped center me when I led Lenz to the kitchen and switched on the lights. It was time for business now, not frivolity.

Once we settled onto our usual stools at the dry bar, mugs of steaming coffee and sliced bread laid out before us, Lenz gave me the rundown of what he had learned thus far. He observed the motel and grounds during the day on Monday, then on Tuesday evening and night, and again on Wednesday afternoon. He had noted who had come and gone and when, along with the types of energy shields active on the property.

"The Teuton seems to have channeled much of his magic into the camera systems and the anklets," Lenz said, taking a sip of his coffee. "There is one powerful shield protecting a section of the compound's basement, but nothing cast over the property as a whole. Nothing like what Philipp set up here."

I frowned while I chewed on some buttered bread, trying to work out what that might mean. "Maybe that Teuton's not strong enough to cast a wide shield. Or maybe he doesn't know how. But I bet the place he's protecting underground is where they keep their cash."

"Cash, drugs, servers, passports, records of business transactions. Anything that would nail the company and identify all of its employees and customers can likely be found in that basement. Gaining access won't be simple. I didn't touch the shield or run my darkness across it for fear of alerting its master, but it's built to repel spirits along with mortal humans."

"We need to get my mother and Murat out first. Then we can worry about how to break into the basement. They might be able to help us with that."

Lenz eyed me seriously, darkness creeping into his irises. "I spoke to your brother on Tuesday and Wednesday, while he was working on his homework. He currently believes I'm a *cin*."

That term prompted me to stare. "A *cin* is kind of like a djinn."

"Yes, that's what I found out when I looked it up." Lenz grinned, seeming entertained by Turkish concepts of magic. "The kid has a strong sense of right and wrong, despite your father's attempts to corrupt him. He knows the women in the compound aren't there voluntarily. And he's seen your father hurt your mother. He's tried to stop him, but then he gets beaten instead."

Pain lanced my heart, but I covered it by taking a sip of coffee. I feared to ask the question hanging over me, but I could not evade it forever. "Did you . . . talk to my mother . . . at all?" I cleared my throat and set my mug down, my gaze focused on my plate. How had that evil Teuton punished her?

"I did." Lenz's voice sounded strained. I tensed, preparing for the worst. "You sure you want to hear this?"

"Please," I begged, moisture forming in my eyes. I blinked it back, trying to focus on my element, asking my stone to soothe me.

"I spoke with her very, very briefly on Monday morning, while she did some housekeeping in the motel. The Teuton—she called him Remmi—invoked a strong shield in the walls surrounding her bedroom. To keep you from contacting her. He . . . had his way with her that night . . . and he bled her, among other things."

My fists clenched and hardened, my element reacting to my distress. "That means he knows everything. He knows she talked to me. And he knows I'm a witch now." I slumped forward onto the bar and buried my face in my hands.

"It's going to be complicated, moving forward with that knowledge," Lenz said with a sigh. "The longer we take trying to pull off the perfect rescue, the more likely Remmi will discover our plans and react accordingly. I'm not sure just how much your father knows about Teutonic magic and what it's capable of doing. And I also don't know if Remmi is a priest. I've never heard of him, and I sent my spirit into the clouds whenever I saw or sensed him approaching the property. We could probably break your mother and brother out on our own, but I don't think we'll be able to crack that basement shield without help."

I rubbed at my eyes, trying to blur out the mental image of that burly brute sinking his teeth into my mother's neck. That was blood magic, a type of Teutonic sorcery I had not yet explored. Any Teuton could sift through a person's memories by drinking blood from one of the carotid arteries—the channels that connected the brain and heart, the two vessels that stored human experience. Philipp had told me Teuton priests bled their partners often, to deepen trust and intimacy. But for that horrid Remmi to tear my mother's secrets from her?

My father must not love her at all.

"How do you think we can get them out?" I asked in a dead voice, taking up a new piece of bread along with the container of butter. I kept my gaze on what my hands were doing, unable to face Lenz's pity. "Without my *Truhtein*, we can't disable the cameras. I might be able to hack into them and change what the lenses are showing, but I've never done that without help."

"I think our best bet right now is to watch the place for an entire week and make note of everyone's schedules. Both of us. We could do it in twelve or six hour shifts, whichever you think would be easiest for you. Starting today."

I turned my neck to meet Lenz's gaze, his solemn eyes studying me as if he was not sure I was up for the challenge. Since Henning's gaffe revived my darkest demons, I doubted my capabilities myself. But failure was not an option. Not with my mother's safety and my brother's sanity on the line.

"You go at seven, and I'll switch with you at one," I said, knowing I had to cook some meals for myself and possibly visit the grocery store first. "Then I can talk to Murat, let him know some of what's going on. Hopefully Remmi isn't wicked enough to bleed a thirteen-year-old."

"Seven to one for me, and one to seven for you." Lenz nodded once, running a finger down the side of his nose. "Do you mind if I make the crossing here? That would be easier than running back to my townhome first."

"Do it. You can sleep here if you want. I can get a bedroom ready."

Lenz agreed to this, though he said he would pack a suitcase when I switched with him and bring all of his notes along with his personal paraphernalia. I swung into motion, racing upstairs to change the sheets and clean the bedroom closest to the front staircase for Lenz's use. He had stayed there often while he and Philipp hunted the child traffickers. Although our paths would not cross much throughout the next week, the idea of having him in the house with me gave me an odd sense of security.

Maybe Lenz's elemental darkness could scare my demons away.

On my way to toss the old batch of sheets into the laundry, I found the elder Teuton in the lounge, resting in the dark gray armchair to the right of the marble fireplace. He used to sit there when he and Philipp got together, while my *Truhtein* occupied the matching seat to the left. Lenz gazed at his watch. I shifted the pile of sheets in my arms and glanced at the grandfather clock. Two minutes till seven.

"My meeting with the Keyholder . . . didn't go quite like I'd hoped," I said, unsure how to express my doubts on that subject. I longed for Lenz's advice, but we had no time to discuss the specifics.

His hazel eyes sought out mine, where I stood in the doorway with my arms full of laundry. "The young *Leitaeri* told me you left him abruptly after throwing fifty Euros down to cover your bottle of Schnapps."

They had already talked. That figured. I chewed on my bottom lip and tore my gaze away from his. "When he found out I'm Turkish, he mentioned Kebaps." My heartrate increased just by saying the words, and I took a shaky breath.

"My dear girl." Understanding radiated from Lenz's aura, though my stone sensed his darkness rising to the surface. "Do you want me to explain it to him?"

I shook my head. "Please don't. I know I have to tell him everything, and it has to be me that tells him. I'm just not ready yet. He wants you to file the record of my blood-transfer, though." I glanced at Lenz's face to ensure he understood.

"Very well. I'll see you at one. Don't be late." Before I could respond, a veil of blackness encompassed his body, its mystical essence pulsing with power. Lenz had gone to do his duty; now I must do mine. I left his mortal form in the lounge and turned my steps toward the laundry room.

~*~

When I sent my spirit into the ether ten minutes before one o'clock, I found the transition much easier than before. After facing my worst enemies during the past few nights, it seemed laughably simple to permit my stone to stifle my breath, to bind my physical body in elemental strength. It took me several tries to change reality around me through intent alone—the fastest way to travel as a spirit. I had to envision the compound and motel exactly how they looked when I drifted above, willing myself to appear there from where my spirit hovered in the lounge.

But eventually, the spring afternoon arose before my eyes, a gentle breeze swirling my gray robe around me. Triumph warmed me from deep within, and I spun in midair, letting the air's currents toy with my wispy hair. A smile broke across my face when I caught sight of a hawk riding a thermal far overhead. It was truly liberating to have no body weighing me down.

Philipp would have loved to see you like that. Lenz's mental voice crept into my thoughts, reminding me that I was here to do a job, not float along the breeze. I saw his spirit balancing atop an oak that grew behind the compound. Even my enhanced vision could not cut through the darkness that shrouded him, waves of obsidian hair swaying atop his crown like spectral flames. His eyes were pitch black pits, soulless voids, his youthful face glimmering with vitality in contrast to his dark element. In his right hand, he held what appeared to be a broadsword made of solid darkness, sunlight glinting off its blade.

Well, that's creepy, I thought, shuddering even though I knew Lenz would never hurt me. He looked like a sentinel from hell's gates.

Thanks. Just showing off a bit. Lenz flipped his sword around his hand as if it weighed nothing. An instant later, it disappeared.

I eyed my companion in bemusement, realizing he had conjured the weapon from his spirit alone. *You need to teach me how to do that.*

Your Leitaeri *can teach you.* Lenz drifted away from the tree toward where I hovered above the compound's roof, gesturing once at the motel. *Your mother's still cleaning the rooms down there, if you'd like to catch her alone. Your father and his associates—including Remmi—drove off in a flashy Bentley just before noon. Likely about to close another deal.*

Okay. I'll see what I can find out about the compound after I've talked to my mother. And I'll make sure I don't touch any energy shields or anklets. Going to try to have a heart-to-heart with Murat once he's home from school. I looked down at the motel across the parking lot, my spiritual senses stretching forth to locate my mother.

Be careful, Zehra. I'll come relieve you at seven. Going to pack a bag and get some rest. Lenz looked up at the sun, then nodded at me.

There's pasta in the fridge. And two types of soup in the process of freezing. Don't eat those yet. Lenz placed his palms together and gave a short bow, which prompted me to snicker in my mind. His spirit grew hazy, about to vanish, and I called after him, *My* Truhtein *did see me like this.*

I wondered whether Philipp watched me now from his heaven, while I eased my spirit toward the earth, my element detecting exactly which types of stone made up the parking lot's aging asphalt. I hoped he was proud that Erlanga's soul chose me to represent her, even though I gave the Keyholder a bad first impression. Once Lenz and I managed to free my mother and Murat and bring these criminals to justice, I could open up to Henning and learn whether he could accept me for who I was. I had no wish to involve him in this mess.

My mother seemed harried when I found her, in the process of changing the sheets in a room that faced the street. The scent of semen was heavy on the sheets, proving what sort of motel Befreiung used as its front. My mother jumped when I spoke to her mind, her brown eyes darting this way and that, as if searching for me . . . or for one of her handlers. I launched into my apology straight away, shame choking my mental voice as I begged her forgiveness for striking out at Remmi. If I had left when she asked, the brute may not have bled or raped her.

The fading bruise on the left side of her neck infuriated me. I caught sight of it just before she shifted her hijab to conceal it. That Teuton wretch had bled her without bothering to heal the wound. I would make him pay for this.

"Zehra, I love you very much, but you shouldn't pry into Kemal's affairs," my mother murmured after I fell silent. "You know he struggles with addictions. He provides for us the best he can."

If that were true, then Leyla would still be alive, I countered.

Chapter Eight:
Culture Clash

By Thursday of the following week—the first week of May—my mind and body were utterly exhausted from sleeping in four hour shifts. I would never make it in the navy or as a private eye, apparently. Lenz seemed unfazed by the schedule, his spirit's darkness seething with liveliness whenever we relieved each other. It occurred to me toward the end of our stakeout that Lenz loved doing stuff like this, collecting information on criminals and potential leads.

Meanwhile, I spent the early morning hours fighting boredom, watching working women drifting from motel room to motel room, renting out their services to clients. They turned their earnings over to Remmi in the back parking lot before sunrise, his sinister voice and sometimes his hands molesting them in the process. They were not permitted to keep a single cent of their earnings, and none seemed to speak German very well. I judged most to be from Eastern Europe, but the two youngest appeared to be Arabic. They wore hijabs.

Which meant their religion condemned them to hell, since they sold their bodies to be ravaged by males. One of many reasons I had given up on God, until Philipp introduced me to another version of faith. His deity offered grace to women society had broken, a trait that deeply resonated with me.

The afternoon shift proved much more fulfilling. I spoke with my mother only once. She made it clear that whether Lenz and I intended to rescue her or not, it was too dangerous to share any details with her. Remmi did not bleed her often, but the option remained on the table anytime she dishonored him. "Kemal fears I'll grow unfaithful to him if the sorcerer drains my blood during sex. He'd rather Remmi use a needle," she told me.

That revelation startled me. I had never read anything that implied Teutons might bleed a person using a needle instead of their teeth. Philipp never mentioned that concept to me, either. But when I reported it to Lenz that evening, he nodded gravely. Priests had created a special variety of needle in the 1800s for the purpose of bleeding dark truths from criminals. Lenz suspected Remmi would have trouble obtaining that sort of needle, since he may not have earned his priestly robe.

I spent most of the afternoons building a relationship with my little brother, Murat. He had grown from a precocious toddler into a cunning young teen, his wide brown eyes filled with curiosity whenever we talked. It took me about an hour to convince him I was neither *cin* nor ghost, but an enhanced version of his long lost sister, Zehra. He believed it when I rehashed a hazy memory of tossing a ball with him and Faruk years ago, when our family lived in an apartment in Erlangen's city center. The ball had gotten away from us and bounced down a fire escape. Faruk had chased after it and set off the alarm. Our father had beaten all three of us.

Murat remembered that incident, and he even recalled me trying to shield him from our father's wrath. His confession dimmed my robe into a darker gray as sorrow overtook me, my spirit hovering above where he sat on his bed cradling an algebra textbook in his lap. *I'm so sorry I let* Baba *send me away. I failed you,* I whispered to his mind.

Murat's black eyebrows came together behind his glasses. "*Baba* sold you, didn't he? Like he did to Leyla." Realization dawned upon his countenance.

He did. My spiritual teeth sliced through my lip without finding purchase. Not a useful thing to do as a spirit.

"*Anne* thought you were dead. She never heard from you again."

I would have come back sooner, if I could. I'm so sorry. I apologized again, even though I knew I had no choice at the time. Without me, Faruk had stepped onto the dark path, and Murat had to bury his goodness deep inside. He longed to help people rather than hurt them, channeling his desires into his studies. He was a whiz with science and wanted to work at a hospital once he grew up.

On our second afternoon together, Murat admitted he knew how Leyla had met her end. Until that point, I had not truly mourned my younger sister's loss, for I hardly knew her. But Murat's story chilled me down to the core of my soul. Our father had handed Leyla over to a mafia boss with a fetish for choking children.

My baby sister died while being gang raped on a yacht, her body dumped in the Adriatic Sea. "I'm not supposed to know about it," Murat muttered, wiping his eyes on the sleeve of his polo shirt. "But I heard *Baba* telling one of his buddies. He said, 'Better not ring up a debt with that boss again, or you'll have to hand over one of your prizes.'"

That was how our father referred to his working women, refugees seeking asylum in one of Europe's most welcoming nations. Instead, Befreiung led them to shackles, rendering them mere 'prizes.' Murat hated keeping everything bottled up inside. He had been trying to hack into Remmi's anklets so all of the women could escape. He believed the anklets were powered by a computer program.

Then, I had to explain the idea of Teutons and Teutonic magic. Murat knew our mother called Remmi a sorcerer, but he guessed the man's methods relied on technology. It took me several afternoons to convince him that elemental sorcery was real and not inherently evil. By Wednesday, our final scheduled meeting, my brother agreed to shift his focus to the cameras and standard security systems. I told him his "cin buddy" and I would free both him and our mother as soon as possible, but we needed access to the basement vault to bring this trafficking ring down.

Lenz joined me as I rested my spirit atop the compound's roof on Thursday morning, weariness muddling my thoughts into mush. He advised me to go sleep, pledging to watch the working women pay Remmi and return to their quarters, before crashing himself. *We need to go over everything we've learned and come up with a plan, but I think that'll be easier if we wait until we've gotten some rest,* he determined, his pitch black eyes sweeping over my spirit.

Murat's going to try to access the cameras, I thought in the middle of a yawn, my spirit's lungs craving oxygen even while the night air flowed through me. *And try to find out if there's anything else protecting the shielded vault aside from Remmi's dark energy.*

We don't want to involve him too much, considering his age, Lenz observed with a wince. *I have some ideas. We'll talk about them later tonight.*

I returned to my physical body shortly thereafter, then wobbled my way to Philipp's private suite, not trusting my legs to climb the stairs to my own bedroom. Before slumber took me, I vaguely noticed that the blue numbers on my *Truhtein's* digital clock read five fifty-six. Lenz had come to relieve me long before seven. A true friend, just like Philipp had always said.

~*~

To my surprise, I did not wake again until after four p.m., my demons having left me in peace for once. Rolling out of bed with a satisfying yawn and a stretch, I headed for Philipp's bathroom. My brain was in the process of emerging from its fatigue, making a list of tasks I needed to accomplish. Shower. Fresh outfit. Braided hair. Brushed teeth. Check on Lenz. Feed the fish outside. Prepare a hot meal to enjoy while discussing how to free my mother and Murat.

Right after I finished dumping a final handful of flakes into the pool before the waterfall, smiling at the blue orfes, koi, and goldfish reaching up to snag my offerings, my spirit sensed a familiar presence encroaching upon my solitude. The numinous bond surrounding my heart flared to life, directing my attention to the branches shading the pool. My stone filtered into my blood, invoking a silvery hue upon my vision while augmenting its precision.

"You might as well join me down here, instead of sneaking around in the branches," I called out, recognizing my Keyholder's blue-fired spirit. "Not sure it's polite to spy on your *Leitalra*."

Henning's spirit manifested on the smooth stones that encircled the pool, a hint of awkwardness evident upon his face. My lips parted in silent wonder while I looked over his ethereal form. It was far more striking than Lenz's. Pure cerulean fire encased him from neck to the ground, licking flames in darker shades of blue springing from his head to drape his shoulders and back. His pale face and hands cast a radiant glow, his smoldering eyes reminding me of the gas flames on one of my *Truhtein's* three convection ovens.

Marveling at my Keyholder's appearance prompted me to wish all three of the ovens ran on gas flames. Also the dryers. And the main heating system. But my *Truhtein* had claimed an energy element and preferred to run his property in kind. I was lucky he maintained a gas line on the grounds at all. It fed a single stove and three ornamental fireplaces inside.

I'm sorry I surprised you. Henning spoke to my mind at last, his fiery gaze fixed upon my face. *I've been wanting to reconnect since . . . our meeting at the pub . . . but I didn't get your number.*

He dropped his gaze to the pool, tracking the course of several fish. Heat rose in my cheeks and I looked at the fish myself, settling into my usual spot and folding my legs. "I'm sorry I left you there without an explanation," I breathed in a quiet voice, hesitant to reopen that subject. I was not ready to tell him about my background. Not until I got a clearer picture of his own.

Henning shrugged and set his spirit down beside me, leaving a fair patch of space between us. He dipped his pale, fiery feet into the pool's waters, creating a puff of steam. The fish swam around his feet as they dispersed from their feeding area, seeming to sense his presence. His element doubtless warmed the water.

I didn't mean to make assumptions about you, Henning said, clasping his hands in his lap and gazing toward the oaks across the pool. *It's still kind of a shock for me, discovering that Erlanga's soul chose a Teuton by blood alone to embody her essence. Makes me feel unworthy, to be honest.*

His apprehension touched my spirit, and I looked up at him, surprised at the direction of his thoughts. "You're feeling unworthy when you've been a Teuton all your life. I've been worried what people will think when they find out who I am. A foreign Lady who learned most of the magic from books, not teachers."

That was not entirely accurate, but at the moment I had no tutor. Lenz had not stepped into Philipp's position after our friend passed away. Whenever I mentioned it, he repeated that it was up to my Keyholder to guide me. I suspected Lenz held himself apart for fear I might fall in love with him. Philipp had warned me about that years ago—that females often grew enamored with Teuton priests due to the nature of their magic. Something my father must also know, since he did not permit Remmi to bleed my mother frequently.

A Lady who learned how to summon Wuotan in the process. The Keyholder raised an eyebrow at me, his expression wavering between amusement and uneasiness. *Most Teutons consider that dangerous, you know. Only Teuton priests are legally allowed to invoke demons. Priests exist as a go-between, a safeguard against Wuotan's deceit. Our former demon lord prides himself on his allure. He tries to lead females astray every now and then, to remind Teutons of his power.*

"Just because I know how to invoke Wuotan doesn't mean I've actually done it," I clarified, resentment churning in my blood at the memory of Philipp dying in that demon's infernal river. "And he won't get anywhere if he tries that with me. He took something very precious to me."

Henning's fiery eyes narrowed, lowering from my face to my chest for the first time. *You're referring to your blood-transfer?*

Confidence arose within me out of nowhere, and I yanked the front of my blouse down to the top of my bra, revealing the two scars arching upward from my heart. The scabs that had marred my skin had fallen away, the scars upon my arms, legs, and abdomen gradually fading. But according to everything I had read, those four lines around my heart would remain forever as a symbol of Philipp's gift.

"I paid a terrible price to gain Teuton blood and this stone magic," I said, as Henning's eyes widened at the sight of my scars. "Becoming *Leitalra* of Erlangen was never part of the plan. I had a life before this. Goals. Dreams. All of it torn away from me."

Herr Schneider filed the record of your blood-transfer after an extensive delay, Henning noted after a pause, averting his gaze from my scars to my face. His mien grew severe. *I know now why he hasn't been forthcoming whenever I've asked for information about my new* Leitalra.

Anxiety tingled along my nerves. "What do you mean?"

My Keyholder did not respond right away, and I dropped my hand from the neck of my blouse, rolling my shoulders in an attempt to banish my nervousness. I knew he was about to mention Philipp, but I could not fathom why his eyes burned holes in my spirit. Could I talk about my beloved *Truhtein* with this young male fated to take his place? Would I be able to defend myself—and him—without breaking down in tears?

Why did I need to defend us both? The disgust spilling from my Keyholder's spirit indicated I must. But *why?*

The record of your blood-transfer listed Herr Philipp Alexander Liebig as your donor. Retired CEO of the largest, most lucrative corporation in this city and all of Franconia. A Teuton magnate of dark energy with mystical blood of ninety-three percent, a tycoon notorious for wealth and reclusiveness. Proprietor of the extensive woodland property where we currently sit.

I blinked at Henning, bewildered. "Are you saying my *Tru* —Herr Liebig—shouldn't have offered his blood to someone like me?" I had to cover the Teutonic word *Truhtein* with a fake cough. It would not be prudent to refer to Philipp as my 'master' in front of the priest who held the keys of Erlangen. The man destined to become my lifelong master, whether I liked it or not.

Henning's blazing eyes darkened, his spirit still seething with disgust. *Herr Liebig cast an impressive shield over this property, as I'm sure you know. I was surprised it let me pass. How long has he been hiding you here, shut away from the world? Did he employ you as a servant?*

Horrified, I leaped to my feet, stone hardening my skin. "How . . . *dare* you!" I squeaked, my anxiety destroying the strong stance I wished to convey. "Philipp Liebig saved me from a terrible fate, one that haunts me to this day, and you come here implying he locked me away as a *servant?*"

Shock broke across Henning's attractive face, the fires of his robes altering from their vivid light blue to deep cobalt as he rose to his feet himself. *You were intimate with him.*

A strangled cry erupted from my throat. "How could you assume something like that?! Philipp Liebig treated me with *respect!* I wasn't his whore!"

You do realize he was known in the local community for his relationship with Herr Schneider. Henning's statement sliced my heart with a jagged blade, his translucent lips pursed in what appeared to be pity.

"Lenz was Philipp's best friend. They didn't have a 'relationship,'" I retorted, doubt slinking its way into the dregs of my mind. Every moment I had witnessed Philipp and Lenz together marched before my eyes on replay. I had never seen them kiss or exchange any intimate gestures. They laughed and joked a lot, shared knowing glances, patted each other on the back after a job well done.

Had they been more than just friends?

Was *that* why my *Truhtein* had never accepted my offers of romance and passion? Why then had he vowed to marry me once we were both Teutons?

How many other young females did Herr Liebig keep on this property? My Keyholder directed his gaze toward the house, a short walk from the pool. *I can sense Herr Schneider's darkness on the second floor. Do you plan to seduce him next? Hoping to succeed now that you have Teuton blood?*

I took several steps back, my thoughts scrambled. "*What?*"

You have to understand how this looks to me, to literally anyone who's never set foot on this property. You're a young girl no one knew existed until Erlanga's soul laid her claim upon you. Until a Teuton priest with a shady background filed the record of your blood-transfer, which happened the exact same day my Omi died. Seems a little convenient, don't you think?

I wrinkled my nose at my fiery companion, appalled by his accusations. Crossing my stone-stiff arms, I growled, "April 5th was my eighteenth birthday. I'd have done the blood-transfer sooner if my *Truhtein* allowed it, but he—"

Your . . . Truhtein? Henning's jaw dropped, his ghostly countenance cracking in pain. *You called Herr Liebig . . . your master?*

"A title he earned with honor and dignity," I spat at the fiery priest before me, furious that he insisted upon assuming the worst. "That man gave his blood and his *life* for me, and I watched his spirit *die* in front of me in Wuotan's river. He called me strong in his last words, and I refuse to let you dishonor his sacrifice."

You . . . you've formed a trauma bond with Herr Liebig. Henning stared at me, a look of comprehension appearing on his face. *You believe he loved you when he kept you hidden away from the world, sealed beneath this shield. Have you even seen your passport? Does Herr Schneider let you leave this place without his permission?*

Fury unearthed itself from the depths of my soul, crushing all of my gentler emotions beneath its supremacy. The rocks lining the pool quivered, my element awakening them from their sleep. "Get out," I ordered the Keyholder, my clenched fists transforming into solid stone.

Henning's spirit drifted over the pool, and he lifted his palms in defense. *Zehra—*

"Get *out!*" I shrieked. Channeling my magic and my fury into a single dark gray stone quivering centimeters from my feet, I lifted it into the air through the power of my spirit alone. Then I chucked it at that cruel priest who wished to taint my memory of the one who saved me from an empty, meaningless life.

The dark stone passed directly through Henning's ethereal chest, smoke wafting from it as it arced toward the far side of the pool. My Keyholder gaped at the hole my weapon created in his spirit, his blue fire quickly fleshing it out again. But then his form flickered like an image on an outdated TV. An instant later, he vanished.

My magic withdrew into my spirit, my skin warming from stone into flesh while I stood gawking at where Henning had disappeared. I had thrown a heavy rock through my *Leitaeri's* spirit and ordered him to leave. He may have dishonored my *Truhtein*, but what I just did to the Keyholder of Erlangen was far worse.

What was wrong with me?

Chapter Nine:
An Indulgent Heart

"Every time I try to have a conversation with my Keyholder, I screw it up," I told Lenz several hours later, while we sat at the dry bar eating chicken pesto over rigatoni. Preparing the meal eased my fury at Henning's accusations, but distance prompted me to doubt myself. "I know Henning's my fated mate. I've sensed it in my heart, the certainty that I belong with my Keyholder. But now he thinks my *Truhtein* shackled me here and that you helped him do it."

I had managed to relate most of our conversation to Lenz, my violent reaction to Henning's final charge encumbering me with remorse. *You've formed a trauma bond with Herr Liebig.* I knew all about trauma bonds. That was one sort of bond I most certainly did *not* form with Philipp. My beloved master had never hurt me once.

"I know you're not ready to share your entire background with him quite yet," Lenz observed after chewing on a bite of chicken, staring across the kitchen toward the hall. "But you're going to have to tell him *something*. And if he refuses to listen to your version of the truth, you know there's one way around that."

Lenz raised a bushy eyebrow at me, the overhead lights shining strangely off his bald crown. I knew what he referenced, the mere idea inciting me to recoil. "You think I should let my *Leitaeri* bleed me? Let him see every one of my flaws, how those terrible men destroyed me? And how desperately I loved my *Truhtein* and still love him to this day?"

Lenz's nostrils flared as he exhaled, his expression cagy. "Being honest with him first would be better. It makes sense that he came to those conclusions about your situation. Evil priests have misused their authority over young maidens throughout Teuton history, even in recent decades. A former *Leitalra* put an end to that practice in Erlangen during the 1800s, officially at least. But your Keyholder knows some priests defy the laws. He wants to make sure you're not being manipulated, that his Lady is free and unbound."

Aghast, I ogled Lenz. "Henning thinks you're manipulating me."

"I'd probably better move back into my townhouse, now that we've finished with our stakeout." Lenz pulled his glass of mineral water toward him, glancing at me before taking a swig. "Just our luck I happened to be here when the *Leitaeri* came by today. Should have crashed at home."

I reached out to touch Lenz's sleeve, anxiety creeping up my spine. "Do you think Henning might send some of the priests on the council to question you? Are you sure you'd be safer there than here under my *Truhtein's* shield?"

"They can interrogate me all they want. They don't have enough evidence to bleed me." Lenz quirked a smile. "I'll have to share our plans with Herr Burkhardt and Herr Ehrlich, though, when we move past getting your mother and brother out. Like I said before, we'll need Teutons with connections to the local police once we're ready to break into that basement vault. We have to be one hundred percent sure its contents will reveal felonies before we do it."

He would know. I turned back to what remained of my pasta, telling myself I could trust Lenz's judgment. This was his specialty, and as I started eating again, he said he had a few sources he planned to tap in the upcoming week, to try to trace the flow of Befreiung's goods and cash. Neither of us had witnessed any transports of human beings during our stake-out, so my father's business was probably not the primary source in that area. They might conduct such exchanges at some other location rather than at the motel.

My thoughts returned to Henning while I ate, disquiet darkening the peace the city bonds wished to grant my restless heart. I needed to speak with him again, tell him just enough about my past so he could understand why I idolized Philipp Liebig. Erlangen's mystical ties urged me to allow Henning to replace my *Truhtein* in my heart, to offer him my unwavering loyalty and trust.

"No Keyholder can take Philipp's place," I murmured to myself, using my fork to push two noodles around my plate. At first, I did not notice I had spoken aloud . . . and referred to Philipp by name in front of his dearest friend.

"It wouldn't be right for him to take Philipp's place," Lenz said in a gentle voice. "No one can take his place in your heart or in mine. I'm afraid I might have tried to get *you* to take Philipp's place for me, without realizing it. You're the Lady of Erlangen, this city's elegant matriarch, not a retired CEO with a longing to bring criminals to justice. If you want out once we've freed your mother and brother, I can finish investigating Befreiung on my own."

I met Lenz's gaze, his candor impressing me. "I probably should start working on my relationship with my Keyholder, after we've gotten them out. This whole thing has been a nice distraction, but I can't keep running away from destiny. I *do* want to help, though, as much as I can. But I'll have to guide my mother and Murat toward recovery. That'll take up a lot of my time, especially since I'm not fully healed, myself."

Lenz murmured his approval through a mouthful of pasta, then mentioned a few things he noticed about the anklets during his investigations. He suspected my stone was powerful enough to literally break them, especially since an earthen element could absorb and disperse the destructive qualities of dark energy. I half listened as I finished my pasta, thinking back to Henning's statement that haunted me the most. *You do realize he was known in the local community for his relationship with Herr Schneider.*

I was not ready to confront that topic with Lenz, but now might be my last chance to do so. Especially if he had to field queries from the council once he left the Liebig property. I gulped down some cool mineral water and silently prayed for courage, then shifted in my stool to face my companion directly.

"Lenz," I began, my tone prompting him to give me a questioning look. "Did you and my *Truhtein* . . . have a . . . physical relationship?"

Heat flooded my face as I spoke; I wanted to crawl under a rock. The priest beside me wrinkled his forehead, a slow smirk appearing on his face. "Quite a few people have thought that over the years. Because society expects all males to have this uncontrollable urge for sex, like mindless beasts."

I blinked at him, unable to fabricate a response to that. Lenz snickered, then went on. "I had a wife once, long ago. She didn't want me to bind her heart, and I respected her wish. She left for Las Vegas after three years of an empty marriage, taking our daughter with her. Haven't seen them since. Decided I'd rather hunt criminals than females. Philipp's choices always made rational sense, unlike those of my ex-wife."

A nostalgic expression passed over Lenz's face and he took up his glass, a wistful smile on his lips. He had been hurt by a woman and swore them off in lieu of a career. I had been hurt by men and treated them warily to this day, though I ached to experience love along with passionate sex. My body and hormones craved union with my Keyholder, my past assuring me I could satisfy his needs.

"So did you two ever . . . ." I let it hang, my curiosity piqued regarding my *Truhtein's* true preferences. He had told me many times that he wanted me to make my choices as an adult, not a sullied child. Philipp also said he despised stifling his dark energy in order to mate with outsiders. Therefore, we must wait until I was a Teuton in full, able to match his element's destructive power.

I had begged him to take me the night before our blood-transfer, but he had refused, tears gathering in his eyes at my fervor. I had pleaded for the privilege of pleasing him in other ways, but he softly promised, *Tomorrow night, my shining star. Tomorrow night, you can claim me forever.*

"We had our moments," Lenz admitted at length, his gaze cutting away from mine to trace the bottle of water standing between our plates. "But our friendship was rarely physical, Zehra. Just days before your blood-transfer, he told me he had never wanted anyone as ardently as he wanted you. You captured Philipp's heart and rendered him helpless in your grasp, willing to grant you his life so you could thrive. Never doubt Philipp's love for you, no matter what people say."

Before Lenz departed that night, he wrote down Henning's address, suggesting I visit him in person so we could talk through our misunderstandings. I appreciated his counsel, but I feared to confront my Keyholder in his territory after tossing a stone through his chest. Especially not in my physical body.

As a spirit? That was a different story.

~*~

Henning lived with his parents in a two-story house that backed up to the larger set of railroad tracks I crossed every time I walked to the grocery store. Their home was a half kilometer from the Liebig property, just a street away from Pritzl. Once I pinpointed its location from high above on Friday afternoon, the gray robe of my spirit melding perfectly with the low-hanging rain clouds, I understood why Lenz had thrown us together at the pub, why we first met at the nearby market.

His family had lived here since Henning was a little boy, according to Lenz. The two of us passed our teen years within a quick bike ride from each other, never imagining Erlanga's soul would unite our dissimilar destinies.

I studied the house from above for a few minutes, the dampness in the cloud around me giving my spirit a sensation of weightiness. My *Leitaeri* had followed the rules of propriety when he visited me; he had remained on the grounds, not intruding into the house. But yesterday it was not raining. And my spirit detected an enticing vibe thrumming from inside Henning's home, something that summoned me to scrutinize its source.

My stone magic sensed no Teutons in the house below or anywhere else in the vicinity. Either this neighborhood leaned mundane, or everyone was at work. There was no point in hanging around outside, even though I knew Teutons should not invade others' privacy while in spirit form. I wanted to know more about this fiery young priest who held the keys of Erlangen, without accidentally sticking my foot in my mouth in the process. Now was the perfect time to do it.

So I descended into the small yard behind the house, taking quick note of a detached shed, raised beds of herbs and vegetables, and a sad-looking trampoline. That last was doubtless a relic from Henning's childhood. I wondered if he hoped to have children of his own one day and dance with them upon the trampoline.

I ground my spiritual teeth at the thought, ordering my mind not to go there. Instead, I passed through the back door into a utility room, then pulled my silvery eyelids over my eyes as I sent my spirit up to the second floor, seeking out that odd enchantment whispering to my heart.

Finding myself in what had to be Henning's bedroom, I paused in the center of the room to look around at its contents. It was not a particularly large chamber, much smaller than my own quarters in Philipp's mansion. It seemed that Henning had learned to put every space to good use. His window faced the street out front, blue and violet tulips blooming in the flower box. Thick navy blue curtains framed his window, inviting the rainy day's glimmer to brighten the room.

Posters covered every centimeter of his walls. Some depicted Hollywood movies—like *The Matrix* and *Lord of the Rings*—while others appeared to portray metal bands, judging by the harsh fonts. Somehow that seemed fitting, considering Henning's long hair. A CD tower stood in one corner and I frowned, thinking I may need to expand my tastes in music. Philipp had preferred music from the '60s and '70s. Black Sabbath was the only metal band I knew.

A bureau with a mirror stood beside the door to the hall, a cobalt blue trash can set next to it. A bookshelf decorated with crystals took up the entire wall to the left of the window, a properly-made single bed pushed against the room's right wall. The pillows sat at the end closest to the hallway, implying that Henning might gaze out the window when lying in his bed instead of watching for unwanted company. Interesting. His parents must respect his privacy.

Suddenly I realized an all-black cat lay wrapped in a hole at the center of my Keyholder's bed, its golden eyes staring straight at my face. *Well, hi kitty,* I said to its mind. Its round eyes must be able to see my spirit, even though normal human vision could not. Its ears perked up when I spoke, its nostrils quivering.

I grinned and drifted toward the cat, stretching my fingers cautiously out. *Sorry I probably don't smell like much right now. Do you see Teuton spirits a lot? Do your humans pet you while they're spirits? I had some kitty friends when I was a little girl.*

The cat sniffed at my fingertips, then yawned and settled back into its hole. Taking that as an invitation, I stroked its head, avoiding its whiskers in the process. *You're a beautiful kitty. Is Henning your favorite human? I'm trying to figure out just who he is, and I haven't given him a good impression yet.*

I sighed and straightened, turning my attention from the snoozing cat to the Keyholder's desk. Positioned before the window, it hosted even more crystals than his bookcase, many of them glistening in the low outside light. Floating closer, I saw an extensive pencil collection, along with a sketchbook and folder stuffed with drawings. Intrigued, I flipped the folder open, wondering whether Henning had artistic talent or if he drew simply to pass the time.

To my surprise, the first sketch I encountered portrayed me clad in the airy blouse I had worn at our last meeting—

yesterday. The sketch did not seem finished, my eyes snapping in anger even drawn with pencil. My full lips curved downward, my eyebrows crimped in frustration, my braid peeking around the back of my neck. On the top right corner of the page lay a plea in sprawling handwriting. *How can I convince you to trust me?*

"Are you here to answer my question?"

Henning's deep voice tore my attention from his drawing. A shocked cry burst from my mind as I whirled my spirit around, gaping at the young man who stood in the doorway. How had I not sensed him coming? My Keyholder favored me with a rueful expression, his basic polo and trousers indicating he had come straight from work. What was his occupation? Plumber, right, he was a plumber. So was his father, Robin Glossner.

A dingy baseball cap sat atop his head, his long hair tied back in a ponytail. A band name in a font I could not read decorated the front of his cap.

He eyed me in silence for what seemed like forever, while I stared back, no answer arising in my mind. At length he shrugged and said, "You know it's kind of illegal for you to be here without permission."

You came onto my property without permission yesterday. The retort fell from my thoughts before I could stop it. Henning had visited the Liebig grounds, which was entirely acceptable. But here I was, creeping through his bedroom, looking at his private drawings.

"Touché. I guess we'll call it even? You're welcome to stop by anytime, as long as Lumpi approves." He turned his gaze to the black cat on his bed, who had reached a paw out to stretch and display its claws. Lumpi blinked at Henning, whose countenance softened in respect.

Some of my uncertainty evaporated when I witnessed his obvious affection for his cat. As he stepped forward to stroke its head, I turned my attention to the plain blue polo hiding his chest from my sight. *Are you okay . . . from the stone I threw? I shouldn't have done that.*

My Keyholder glanced over his left shoulder to smirk at me, from where he crouched to pet Lumpi. "There's a giant hole in my chest now, thanks to you. Of course I'm okay. It's not that easy to harm a Teuton spirit."

My lips quivered, fighting a smile, and I eased my spirit away from his desk. *Sorry I looked at your drawing. It's pretty lifelike.*

"Couldn't get your face out of my mind, after what happened yesterday. It's true, by the way. What I wrote on that page. I want you to be able to trust me."

Henning got to his feet and turned toward me, brushing his hands off on his gray trousers in the process. Remorse radiated in waves from his fiery spirit, while shame welled up in mine. *I'd like that, too. It's hard for me to trust someone I don't know, especially when he . . . .*

My thoughts trailed off and I looked down at my hands, knowing that I had to at least try to explain my relationship with Philipp Liebig. That would clear the air for sure, assuming my Keyholder was open to the truth. I sneaked a glance at him through translucent eyelashes, our heads almost on the same level since I hovered a handbreadth above the hardwood floor.

"I misjudged you yesterday. I know I did. Can you help me understand?" Henning's tone reflected the yearning in his essence. He stuffed his hands into the pockets of his trousers and met my gaze, cerulean fire glinting in his irises.

Lenz warned me people would assume the worst about my Truhtein *and me,* I began, deciding to be as honest as I could be while holding my worst secrets close. *Philipp Liebig saved me from a horrible situation. He helped me see that I'm worth something, despite—*

I had been about to say, *despite the fact that I have breasts now,* but I cut that thought off. Straight men liked breasts. Only beastly males raped children. My earlier worries resurfaced as I reminded myself of what Philipp taught me. After a pause, I said, *The first time we met, when we were in the fruit section, you said I seemed familiar. Can you tell me why?*

A blush appeared on Henning's cheeks, but he held my gaze. "I think it must have been Erlanga's spirit nudging my heart. I'd never seen you before, but when I looked into your eyes and sensed the strength of your stone, I knew. And I got all tongue-tied. Couldn't think of how to explain."

He snorted quietly at his own expense and my shoulders straightened, relieved of their unspoken burden. Henning had not seen my videos. I was a mystery to him, an enigma his choice to accept the city's keys insisted he solve. Not an exotic cutie hammered by depraved males.

Philipp Liebig taught me what it means to be a Teuton. I decided I was brave enough to do the blood-transfer right after we brought the child trafficking ring down, the one based in Nürnberg. You heard about that, right? It was all over the news a couple years ago. I raised my eyebrows at Henning, expectant.

His jaw dropped, and his right hand extracted itself from his pocket to point at my spirit. "*You* played a part in taking that ring down? You and Herr Liebig?"

And Lenz, I appended. *It was our plan to keep rescuing people trapped in situations like that after I gained Teuton blood. I was hoping to be energy like my* Truhtein. *But fate had other plans, I guess.*

I glanced at my spirit's slate-gray robe, still stunned that my Teutonic magic chose to manifest itself as solid earth. "Did you hope to be dark energy, too? Like the shield around your property?"

Henning's decision to refer to the Liebig grounds as *my* property prompted my back to straighten further, the truth of the matter vividly clear. Philipp had no direct relatives, and I chose to trade my last name for his. My passport and the record of my blood-transfer called me Zehra Saliha *Liebig*.

It was up to me to carry on Philipp's legacy.

I'd hoped to be lightning, actually, I answered, ordering myself to keep up with our conversation despite my abrupt epiphany. *I was my* Truhtein's *shining star, so it was kind of weird to wake up as stone instead.*

"You ever feel like you've been thrown into the deep end without knowing how to swim?" Henning queried, his expression thoughtful. "Like you didn't realize you chose something a lot bigger than you ever imagined?"

Yes, I replied instantly. *Every single day.*

"Then we've got something in common." Grinning at me, my *Leitaeri* pulled the city's keys from the left pocket of his trousers. He ran his fingertips over each key, their power far more than symbolic as it threaded through my spirit. I looked toward Henning's desk, pinpointing a delicious aura surging from an oblong crystal poised amid its companions.

My lips parted and I stretched my right hand out, enchantment sparkling along my fingers, beckoning to me. *Is that the stone you mentioned? The one that holds the wisdom and experience of the previous* Leitalra?

"The *Herzestein?* Yep, that's it. Figured it'd be happy sitting with the rest of my crystals, until my new Lady is ready to absorb its gifts."

I tilted my head at the crystal, its magic creating rainbows along its surface. It seemed to be of a turquoise hue normally, not exactly fitting in with the others of its kind. Most of Henning's crystals were of blues, reds, and purples. *Are you sure it's safe to just keep it laying there on your desk? Can any Teuton absorb my predecessor's gifts, or just me?*

"Your everyday Teuton wouldn't notice anything unusual about it, especially since I've collected crystals for years. You and I are the only people who can sense its magic. It's the greatest legacy my Omi could have left you."

A bit too trusting, but maybe Teutons rarely pried into their Keyholder and Lady's private affairs. I had not noticed any supernatural security over this house, anyway. "I need to get going, Zehra. I actually came back to grab a tool for the job my Papa and I are working on. You can keep looking through my drawings if you want. I'm an open book, because I want my *Leitalra* to not be afraid of me."

Tearing my focus away from the *Herzestein,* I looked back at Henning, the gentleness in his gaze touching my heart. *I'm not afraid of you. Just cautious. But I need to get going, too.*

My family's coming for a visit soon, and I've got to finish getting their rooms ready.

Lenz and I planned to break my mother and Murat out next Friday, while my father worshiped at the mosque in München. I had started preparing two upstairs bedrooms for them, but I had far more to do to ensure they felt safe with me. My Keyholder offered to help out and I politely declined, assuring him that I had it under control. Then he asked if I would be interested in meeting some of his family and friends at some point soon, maybe at the outset of June.

Not long afterward, I transformed reality around me to send my spirit back to my bedroom, where my body awaited me in statue form. In my hand, I held a sketch Henning had made of the city's keys, his fire magic embracing their brass— a union of flames and stone. He had written his phone number at the top corner of the drawing, along with an encouraging note: *Always open to sharing my heart with my magnificent Leitalra. Henning Glossner.*

Chapter Ten:
A *Leitalra's* Sway

Friday, the 14th of May 2004, dawned with misty fog cloaking the grounds, a fresh scent of dew in the atmosphere as I brought the fish their food. I had not slept well the previous night. Nightmares of Wuotan's bloody river mixed with brutes choking me on camera chased me from slumber, convincing me to rise just after four a.m. I prayed silently to Philipp's God on my way to the fish pool, begging for the grace and success I could never earn. Today, I must stride onto Befreiung's property with impossible courage to lead my mother and Murat to freedom.

My strength could not fail me today. I had gone through one batch of coffee already, barely forcing myself to eat one of the croissants Lenz brought yesterday, when we discussed our plans one final time.

I had spent most of the week preparing the Liebig mansion for my family's arrival. Two adjacent bedrooms with a shared bathroom stood ready without a speck of dust, their balconies sporting lovely views of the back deck and gardens. I had paid the groundskeepers to beautify everything on Monday and Tuesday, and I visited the grocery store four times to stock the kitchen and pantry with foods my mother might find familiar and comforting. Lentils, grape leaves, lamb, flatbread.

I also made the tough decision to renovate Philipp's suite into my own quarters. Since I was the mistress of Liebig property now, I ought to act like it and claim the principal living space. I had moved my clothing, laptop, and favorite books into the master bedroom and begun the painful process of sorting Philipp's attire. I planned to donate most of his clothing to charity, but I wanted to find out if Henning would like any of it first. He and my *Truhtein* were about the same height, with similar build.

I thought over the plan again as I crouched before the waterfall to feed the fish. The usual ones arrived right away to snag flakes from the surface, while the golden tenches—bottom feeders—would clean up later. Lenz had enchanted a plain black hoodie for me to wear, along with black jeans and shoes with silent treads. Once I raised the hood to conceal my hair, his elemental darkness would hide my features from human eyesight and cameras.

I could not use the hood until I finished riding public transportation.

Truth to be told, the prospect of riding the train and bus by myself freaked me out more than any other aspect of our plan. When Lenz told me that it would be best if we traveled to the appropriate locale separately, I protested, my anxiety shooting through the roof. I had not ridden a train or bus in ages, and I feared other travelers might try to speak with me if I sat by myself. Lenz assured me I would be fine, since we intended to pull off the rescue during daytime hours. He advised me to bring a random book to help me blend in with commuters.

This past week, I had ridden the train to the necessary stop four times as a spirit, then transferred onto the bus that would deposit me a short walk from the motel and compound. Once I stepped off the bus, I must raise my hood and keep my head down while I walked to my father's property. I would have to approach the motel from the far side, so I could catch my mother at her housekeeping duties without passing by the lobby's windows.

Lenz would drive my *Truhtein's* black Mercedes to the neighborhood after switching out the license plates and filling the gas tank. He planned to await me in the parking lot of a nearby beer garden—one which sported no cameras. Both of us had verified that. He had also gotten us a pair of disposable SIM cards for our cell phones, so we could destroy evidence of our communication after my mother and brother were safe. I was supposed to call his number and let the phone ring twice just before I stepped in range of Befreiung's cameras. Then Lenz would block their lenses with his darkness.

That, of course, would alert anyone watching that something was amiss. But my father would be far away at the mosque in München, unable to intervene for at least a couple hours. Remmi would likely be elsewhere, for Lenz had tracked him the past two Friday afternoons to a retirement home in Bamberg. He seemed to be visiting his mother each time, which should delay his interference long enough for us to get my family out.

From what we observed during our stakeout, my father and Remmi were the key players at this particular compound. There were some hired minions of the mundane variety— some who delivered goods while others guarded the basement vault and occasionally patrolled the rest of the compound. Since I was supposed to meet my mother while she cleaned one of the front-facing motel rooms, I should not encounter any guards.

Murat should have no trouble getting out, either, since he said no one ever bothered him when he wandered outside the compound. He sometimes kicked a soccer ball around the back lot, though he admitted disinterest in the sport. Today, his job was to convince my mother he felt too sick to attend school, so he could be left alone to pack and prepare for my arrival.

Then, once the three of us reached my *Truhtein's* Mercedes, it was up to me to break the shackle off my mother's ankle. Lenz believed my element was potent enough to stifle the anklet's energy and snap it in half. I had practiced coating my hands in stone and breaking unnecessary objects every day this week. Still, I worried as I watched the fish enjoy their breakfast.

"This would be so much easier if I could do the whole thing as a spirit," I murmured to myself, musing on how skilled I had gotten at sending my spirit from one place to another in seconds. Out of all types of elemental magic, that was one I had mastered already, along with freeing my spirit from my body. The moments of breathlessness no longer petrified me whenever my element transformed my flesh into solid rock. "Then I could return to my body if something goes wrong."

I sighed through my nose and frowned, getting to my feet for a good stretch before heading back to the house. Of course, I knew why Lenz insisted I do this deed in my mortal body. As outsiders, neither my mother nor Murat could see my spirit. Also, I had not yet managed to break anything while drifting around in spirit form. And it would be too tempting to flee to my body and leave my family behind to face the fallout, if something went wrong. Just like I had done after smacking Remmi on the head with a napkin holder.

This time I would not fail my mother. She deserved a life of her own.

Right before noon, as I sat stiffly in the front parlor with a Mercedes Lackey novel in my lap, too distracted to absorb its plot, my ringtone prompted me to jerk to attention. Snatching my phone off the arm of the leather sofa, I flipped it open. "Zehra Liebig." My voice sounded small.

"Lenz here. Your father left for München an hour and a half ago. I tracked his Bentley all the way to Ingolstadt. Remmi just ordered lunch at the McDonald's drive-thru on the other side of A73. He's on his way north to Bamberg. Your mother and brother are on the property as expected."

"Okay." Lenz had observed everyone's comings and goings that morning in spirit form, as agreed. "You coming to get Philipp's car?"

"On my way. It's about time you head for the bus stop."

"On it. I've even got a book, like you said." I passed through the front door as I spoke, locking it behind me and securing the key in the left hand pocket of my jeans. I had stuffed my book in my hoodie's pocket, Lenz's darkness spell addling my spirit as I marched toward the iron gate. The bus stop was a minute's walk from Liebig property.

"Zehra?"

"Yes?" I undid the lock upon the gate by directing my stone magic into its mechanisms and compelling them to loosen. Another trick I had been practicing.

"You can do this. Philipp believed in you, and so do I."

For some reason, tears threatened to well in my eyes at Lenz's sentiment. I took a deep breath as I shut and locked the gate behind me, then said, "Thanks," into the phone. I heard a dial tone. Lenz had already hung up.

I was on my own to meld with noonday commuters and tourists.

Help.

To my relief, none of my fellow travelers bothered me, like Lenz predicted. Most seemed thoroughly invested in their own matters, some reading newspapers or books, some texting, some herding children. By the time I exited the local bus at the village a quarter kilometer from Befreiung's compound, I had begun to believe everything would come together seamlessly. Although my muscles remained tense, my stone filtered lightly along my veins, ready to come to the fore at the first sign of danger.

I raised my hood when I stepped onto the sidewalk, then struck out toward the edge of town. I sensed Lenz's darkness enveloping me, granting my magic an extra boost. Smiling to myself, I stuck my hands in the pocket of my hoodie, sliding on a snug pair of black leather gloves. Tracing a finger along the spine of my book, I wondered whether it was wise to read fantasy novels in public, now that I was a Teuton. Would witchy reading material inspire outsiders to look twice?

Don't be silly, Zehra, I ordered myself, catching sight of the beer garden where Lenz awaited me. *Lackey's griffons aren't anything like elemental magic. You still look like a human female, and scientists can't detect the enhancements in your blood. Thank goodness.*

I scoured the beer garden's parking lot as I passed, noticing my *Truhtein's* black Mercedes parked beneath a shade tree. Lenz had backed into the spot, likely to make a quicker escape once my family and I piled into the back seat. Even with my magic sharpening my vision, I could not see anything inside the car. Lenz had darkened the windows with his element; they were not actually tinted.

Turning my attention back to the sidewalk before me, I jumped at the sound of my cell phone ringing. My eyebrows came together, for that was not part of the plan. I was the one who was supposed to call once I reached Befreiung's territory. My right hand began to tremble with apprehension as I dug my phone out of my pants pocket. "Zehra Liebig."

"Lenz. Wanted to give you a heads up that we have a slight problem."

The silvery veil did not lift from my eyes. "Oh?" My voice cracked.

"One of your father's minions is taking a rather long smoke break in front of the lobby. Not sure if he's going to patrol the area after he's done. But you might want to keep your mother inside until he returns to the compound."

Dread began to wreak havoc with my composure. "Can you distract him? Or would that make things worse?" Lenz must have arrived long before me, since he had time to observe the current situation as a spirit. He probably saw me get off the bus and returned to his body to make the call shortly after.

"I actually put a suggestion or two into your brother's head. He's chomping at the bit to sneak out. Has a schoolbag stuffed to the brim."

That sounded about right. Murat probably packed every schoolbook he had, without thinking about extra clothing. I would have to do some shopping for both him and my mother once I knew their sizes. Taking a steady breath, I prayed again for courage, recognizing the trees and brush on the edges of Befreiung's property fast approaching.

"Okay. I'll try to stay incognito. What room's my mother in right now?"

"Room 101. The farthest one from the lobby."

I halted centimeters from where the front-facing camera would record my presence. "I'm here. It's time for you to take out the cameras."

"Done. I'll cast an extra shadow over you, too. Be swift, Zehra."

Lenz ended the call, and I gritted my teeth as I moved closer. At the edge of the front parking lot, I left the sidewalk behind, walking as swiftly toward Room 101 as I could without running. I noticed a stocky male leaning against the brick façade at the far end of the motel, smoke rising from the cylinder in his mouth. His gaze was toward the highway, opposite the village.

Convenient.

My mother's housekeeping cart stood before the door to Room 101, which was propped open, the sound of a vacuum cleaner scratching at my eardrums. I glanced at the smoking male once more before pushing the door all the way open and slipping inside. He had not seen me.

My mother's horrified gasp grabbed my attention as I eased the door shut. Quickly, I reined in the magic altering my vision and lowered my hood, hoping Lenz's elemental darkness would reveal me at the same time. "*Anne*, it's Zehra. I'm here to rescue you," I blurted in Turkish as she switched off the vacuum.

Her eyes bugged and she placed a hand over her mouth. "Zehra?"

"Yes, it's me. Your oldest daughter, Zehra. The one who's wanted to free you for years now." My mother's brown eyes grew damp with tears, and she stretched one shaking hand toward me, stepping out from between two double beds. I longed to embrace her, but now was not the time. I raised one palm to delay her.

"We have to get out of here as soon as Murat comes," I said, refusing to allow my emotions to take hold. We stood just an arm's length apart, her eyes studying my countenance, then passing over my braid.

"So that's why he pretended to be sick this morning." My mother nodded, a hint of a smirk twitching her lips for an instant.

"You knew he was faking it?" It figured my brother was a poor actor.

My mother sighed and set her hand upon her hip. "It's an *Anne's* job to know when her children are plotting something devious."

A laugh escaped me despite the seriousness of the situation. "One of *Baba's* buddies is out front smoking. Murat's going to distract him so we can get away."

"Really, Zehra? You shouldn't encourage your brother. He imagines himself far more mature than he actually is." My mother rolled her eyes toward the ceiling, her demeanor hinting at a mixture of pride and maternal frustration.

"It wasn't my idea."

"You have a plan to do something about this, right?" She lifted the hem of her maroon skirt, revealing the anklet above her loafers. My element still flowed freely through my veins, on high alert, detecting the defensive magic woven upon my mother's shackle.

"I'll get it off as soon as we're away from here. I promise." Straightening my spine, I allowed my element to alter the color of my irises and met her gaze.

My mother's lips parted. "You've become a sorceress yourself!"

"I've become a Teuton witch," I corrected. "I'll tell you all about it once we're out of here. You're okay with this, right? You don't actually want to stay here?"

I braced myself as I spoke, fearing my mother might prefer to remain in a familiar place, despite her husband's cruelty. But she pulled herself up straight in response, resolve sharpening her appearance. "I would have left him long ago if it weren't for my children. I've faced hardship before and can do it again, as long as you and Murat are with me."

The door swung open, preventing me from casting myself into my mother's arms and sobbing like a little girl. Murat stood on the threshold, hefting a bulging backpack. "We need to go *now*," he panted in German, his black hair mussed, his glasses crooked. "Told Herr Ludolf . . . something weird . . . in the basement."

Of all of the lies he could have told to get the smoker off our backs. I reached out to take our mother's hand, urging her forward. "Let's go."

Outside, my mother tugged her hand free from mine to stop at the cart laden with towels and pillows. "I've got my bag here," she said, extracting a bulky purse from down below. My brother scampered toward the sidewalk, not pausing.

"Hurry," I begged her, jogging to catch up with Murat. He glanced back at me and I pointed in the direction of the beer garden.

We reached the parking lot a minute later, my brother still panting from exertion. I beckoned him toward the Mercedes, but our mother's pained cry halted me. She clenched her teeth and shook out her left foot. "It's hurting her!" Murat hissed, his face blanching as he grasped our mother's arm.

I took her bag from her and leaped for the car, gesturing frantically for Lenz to unlock the doors. Yanking the passenger door open, I tossed the bag to the floor and said, "Pray to God I can break that anklet."

Darkness seethed in Lenz's eyes. "I'll help her get comfortable in the back seat. Concentrate on your magic, Zehra. Call your power forth and claim it."

Lenz got out and opened the door behind the driver's seat, my brother supporting our mother as she hobbled for the car. Sweat drenched her face, lines of anguish deepening on her forehead. Working hard to stifle her cries.

I shut my eyes for a moment, focusing on the solid earth inside of me. Its strength hummed within my spirit, impatient for an outlet. Mouthing a silent plea to Philipp's ghost, I channeled my element into my hands, turning my fingers into hard stone beneath my leather gloves. I could do this. I could do this.

Coming around to the other side of the car, I knelt before my mother. She had parked herself in the back seat with her hands braced upon the doorframe. Lenz drew my brother aside, giving me space as I took hold of her ankle. My mother bit her lip to smother a moan, and horror overtook me when I saw how the anklet tortured her. My elemental vision pinpointed currents of dark energy sinking into my mother's flesh, shocking her nerves. A very deliberate attack.

No. My mother did not belong to a depraved Teuton male. She deserved to choose her own destiny.

I clutched the shackle between my fingers and thumbs, pressing them together while deflecting the energy's assault from my mother to me. I grunted when its power fought to restrain mine, my stone hardening in response. I crunched my fingers harder into the anklet, angry that it refused to break. My element had destroyed small stones, steel rebar, and two cinder blocks earlier this week. How could a tiny anklet prove tougher than all of that?

"No mere Teuton sorcerer can defeat your supremacy. You are the *Leitalra* of Erlangen. Set your daughter free."

Lenz spoke in Teutonica, the phrases dripping from his lips like an incantation. A new force awakened within me, one that gathered every Teuton soul in Erlangen beneath her protective sphere. The Lady could defend outsiders, too. They made up the whole of her city. *My* city.

Bending my head close to the offending anklet, an order fell from my lips in Teutonica, my voice resounding with the knell of past centuries. "*Set my daughter free.*" In less than a second, the anklet shattered to pieces, transforming into dust upon the asphalt. A crisp breeze wafted into the parking lot, carrying the traces away.

Dazed, I stared into my mother's eyes as she shifted down to the opposite end of the back seat, gratitude pouring from her aura. Lenz helped me climb into the car beside her, Murat scrambling in behind me and stuffing his backpack onto the floor between his legs. None of us spoke for a while, my gaze locked with my mother's.

Somehow, the potent sorcery of Erlangen's *Leitalra* had emerged from deep within my heart, the city's soul imbuing my spirit with accomplishment. *No mere Teuton mage can defeat the collective strength of our departed warriors. You symbolize justice and light. Never forget that,* Erlanga's soul whispered to my mind.

Once Lenz got us onto the Autobahn, my brother broke the silence. "So are you my sister's partner or something?" Murat narrowed his eyes at Lenz's flat hat.

"I'm your *cin* buddy," the elder Teuton answered, sounding amused.

"You look like a secret agent. Not a *cin*."

Chapter Eleven:
Sharing Burdens

Humor burst to the surface amid my tornado of emotions, and I started giggling. "What? He doesn't look like a *cin* at all!" Murat pointed out, defensive. I laughed harder and slumped against my mother's breast. She wrapped me in her arms, our long-awaited embrace.

"You may call me Lenz, young man. And you are correct. I'm not a *cin*. I'm a Teuton like your sister."

"Oh! You're the same thing as Zehra and Herr Remmi? Why didn't you tell me that?"

Tears leaked from my eyes as I continued to snicker, my magic retreating into my spirit after an entire day on high alert. My mother began to hum a Turkish lullaby, doubtless sensing my fatigue. Lenz continued to chat with my brother, noting that he intended to drive in a wide arc on the highways before returning to our home base, just in case anyone happened to follow us.

Lenz called the Liebig property "our home base." That felt right to me—the place where my *Truhtein's* energy shield protected all inhabitants from danger. At long last, I need not fear for my mother's safety. We were together, and I would never allow another evil male to take advantage of her.

That evening, my mother insisted upon preparing dinner for all four of us, after she and Murat unpacked what little they had brought. I helped her cook Turkish *manti*, a lamb-stuffed dumpling entrée I remembered from childhood. We crafted spicy tomato sauce to pour over the pasta, topping the dish off with flakes of mint and chili. We ate around the dry bar at my insistence, keeping to the tradition my *Truhtein* established. Family meals were served at the bar, the formal dining room reserved for special occasions.

Lenz departed after dinner, admitting through a yawn that he could use a long nap. He asked me to inform him once my mother and brother felt ready to disclose what they knew about Befreiung's business. And he reminded me to make sure they stayed beneath Philipp's shield, in case my father sent Remmi on the hunt. "That foul beast shouldn't be able to track them, since outsiders' spirits all look the same to an element's sense. But it's best to be cautious until we can bring Befreiung's network down," he said.

I could not disagree, though I wondered whether I might be able to tell my mother's and brother's spirits apart, if I allowed my stone magic to study them long enough. Either way, I brought up another point as Lenz passed through the front doorway, one I was not sure he had considered. "We have to keep everything quiet since there's at least one Teuton working for Befreiung. Remmi might have plants among the community here, especially since my family used to live in Erlangen."

Lenz paused on the portico, scowling. "I certainly hope that's not the case, but it's entirely possible. I'll keep you informed, Zehra."

Late that night, after my little brother fell asleep, I knocked lightly on my mother's bedroom door. I had changed into the gym shorts and tank top I usually wore to bed, taking my hair out of its braid and brushing it out, readying myself to meet whatever demons wished to haunt my dreams tonight. But first, I yearned to speak with my mother one-on-one, to open my heart about the trauma I had faced and the ways I worked toward healing.

My mother's soft voice bade me enter. I found her standing before the table between her room's two armchairs, boiling water in a hot pot for tea. I had placed the hot pot and coffee maker in her chamber for moments like this, along with all the ingredients for tea and coffee. She looked over her shoulder and smiled at me, her hijab discarded for the night.

She had brought only one spare outfit with her, since she did not want her husband or Remmi to make assumptions about what she kept in her bag. Thus, she sported the same maroon dress she had worn while cleaning Room 101 for the last time, her bare feet free of shackles. Traces of gray sprinkled the hair that brushed her waist, the signs of age upon her gouging my soul. My mother was only thirty-eight years old, but her husband's lifestyle had worn her down.

We made small talk while she steeped the tea. Once we settled in our chairs with wildflower-scented mugs warming our hands, I asked my mother how much she knew about Teutonic magic. She had experienced the worst from Remmi, but I could not guess which gifts he had used against her.

It took almost a half hour for my mother to share all of her experiences with me. She hesitated at first, not wanting to burden me; but I assured her I could handle it, that struggles were better shared than carried alone. That was one of Philipp's lessons I had taken to heart, though I still wavered about revealing the whole of my past to my Keyholder. We had spoken on the phone twice since I sneaked into his room. While Erlanga's soul urged me to claim him as my mate, I feared Henning would consider me tainted, after he learned how my former handler had wrecked my body.

I longed to ask my mother for advice on how to handle my connection with Henning, but tonight I needed to educate her about Teutonic magic. She knew that Remmi could see her past experiences and thoughts in her blood, and she knew of the dark energy that answered his call. She had never heard the term "Teuton" until I mentioned it, so I gently built on each topic she understood, outlining the history of the Teuton people and their connection with the elements.

"So you're saying Remmi is a descendant of an ancient Germanic conclave blessed with magic by an otherworldly being. And that these sorcerers—Teutons—produce children who wield similar powers. A mother of fire and a father of water might have a child of fire or water." Frown lines creased my mother's forehead as she finished her tea and set her mug onto the table.

"Correct. There are actually twenty-four Teutonic elements, so parents of plain or natural fire and water could have children of natural fire, black fire, yellow fire, red fire, blue fire, light, water, ice, snow, or mist." I had researched all possible elemental combinations extensively throughout the years.

My mother shook her head slowly, looking lost. "And all Teutons, no matter what element they wield, can see someone's secrets if they drink their blood." She winced, her left hand reaching up to touch her neck.

"The blood has to come from one of the carotid arteries in order for a Teuton to read memories. Because those arteries carry blood from the heart to the brain, the places where all memories are stored." Another basic fact I had memorized long ago. Weird, when considering it from a scientific standpoint, but true nonetheless.

"Have you ever drunk someone's blood?" My mother cringed back in her chair. Apprehension darkened her earth-hued eyes.

"I haven't. It kind of grosses me out. It's usually the priests who do stuff like that, anyway. It's part of their training."

"But you don't think Remmi is a priest."

"Lenz has looked for his records without finding anything. We think his real name isn't actually Remmi. All of *Baba's* minions use code names, right?" I raised an eyebrow at my mother, curious.

"They do. Even Kemal goes by Mohammed. I don't know any of their real names. Your *Baba* kept me in the dark about how his business operates." My mother rose from her seat and asked whether I would like more tea, since intuition told her our conversation had barely begun.

I caught a glint of amusement in her eyes and tucked my legs beneath me on my chair. "I don't mind, but I'll probably have to pee at some point. If you want to get some sleep, just let me know. We have all the time in the world to catch up on everything. It's safe here beneath my *Truhtein's* shield."

I explained the basics of spiritual magic while my mother boiled a fresh pot for tea, choosing a peppermint flavor this time from the variety of tea bags in the basket with the coffee. She seemed intrigued that a Teuton's element protected the body from harm while the spirit drifted free, no matter what sort of gift the Teuton claimed. "I hope fiery Teutons use fireplaces for that sort of magic," she said.

That prompted me to wonder where Henning had stashed his mortal body when he intruded on the Liebig property as a blue-fired spirit. It had not occurred to me to ask him that question. Countless uncertainties still simmered in my brain about the young male who held Erlangen's keys, subjects we ought to discuss in person. Like, how early in life had the keys called to him? What sort of intentions did he have for us going forward, as Keyholder and Lady?

Did he want us to complete our bond in marriage?

"So I have a pretty good idea of what Teutonic magic can do now, Zehra," my mother observed after we both settled in with steaming mugs of peppermint tea. "But you haven't told me how you became a Teuton witch yourself. I've seen your eyes change color and felt the strength of your stone earlier today. But neither of your parents wields an element, as I'm sure you know."

She raised her cup to her lips and blew on her tea, grinning at me while she waited to learn how her daughter seized gifts beyond the reach of ordinary humans. I mirrored her grin, deciding on the spur of the moment to lay it out bluntly. "There are two ways an outsider—a normal human being—can become a Teuton. The long way and the short way."

"You did it the short way."

My mother stated her conclusion as fact, without doubt. Now I must reveal exactly what that meant. Gathering my courage, I took a sip of tea, relishing its burst of mint. Then I met her gaze and began the tale.

"I did. It was the most significant step I took on my eighteenth birthday. To become more than just Zehra." I set my mug onto the table, then traced my fingers along the ends of the two scars stretching just above my tank top's neckline.

"I paid a terrible price to gain Teuton blood and the magic that comes with it. The ritual that gave me this gift also took my *Truhtein's* life. The man who owned this house and willed it to me at his death."

I explained a little bit about the mechanics of the blood-transfer, though I left out the worst parts when my mother's face took on a nauseated tinge. Then I told her about Philipp Liebig, the retired CEO who transformed me into an educated maiden with a drive to help those in need. I rattled on about my studies of history, math, economics, psychology, English, German, and Teutonica, all that shaped me into a survivor determined to create her own destiny.

Now that destiny included Erlangen's Keyholder. An odd twist, but one that might shine my light further into this world's darkness.

During a pause in our conversation, I set my empty mug upon the table, my insides warm and cozy thanks to the tea and my memories of Philipp. A remarkable man who opened a wonderful world to a battered child craving acceptance. My mother's next question threw a dart into my serenity, concern evident in her tone.

"You call Herr Liebig your *'Truhtein.'* What does that word mean?"

I wrapped my arms around myself, frost chasing away the warmth in my veins. Should I talk around the subject or confront it head-on? Would my mother judge me the same way my Keyholder did, when he learned of my relationship with an elderly tycoon? Nervous, I glanced at her countenance, fearing to grapple with the worst parts of my past. But that was why I had come to her bedroom in the first place, to get everything out in the open.

Please don't let her believe I'm bound for hell since I lost my innocence long ago.

Drawing a shuddering breath, I confessed, *"Truhtein* is a Teutonic word that means 'master.' When Philipp freed me from my previous handler after I turned thirteen, I had been trained to call my authority 'master.'" That time I used the Turkish word, which prompted my stomach to twist in distress. I had not spoken that word aloud in five years, except for when I screamed for mercy in my dreams.

A curse fell from my mother's lips, startling me. "Your 'handler,'" she repeated, her upper lip curling in contempt. "That man didn't buy you so you could help his wife with the housecleaning. Did he?"

I shrank down into myself, pulling my knees up and hiding my head behind them. "Is that . . . what he told *Baba?*"

"That was the excuse your *Baba* gave me. I didn't believe it. I wish I could have saved you, but I couldn't flee with four small children. I couldn't."

My mother sounded heartbroken, blaming herself for my awful fate. "You couldn't. I know. *Baba* was in debt and he never gave you any money."

"He's always in debt." My mother's voice shifted from distraught to irritated in an instant, and I sneaked a peek at her from around my knees. Her eyes blazed with disgust as she said, "He just won't stop gambling at cards and slots, no matter how many times I beg him. Even though he knows it's wrecked our family. That's where he met Remmi, the year after he sold you. At one of the casinos outside of Bamberg. He prays at the mosque on Fridays and then spends Saturdays chasing the jackpot."

"Hypocrite," I breathed when my mother paused, my body shuddering as I dropped my arms to my sides.

"Yes. He prays in hopes of earning forgiveness, but it's all a sham. I tried to leave him once, a few months before he sold your baby sister. Bundled all of my children on the train to Amsterdam." My mother wrung her hands in her lap, pain stenciled all over her face. Her gaze traveled past me from the bed to the bathroom doorway and back again, unable to focus for long.

"They caught us before we crossed the border," she murmured. My heart stuttered erratically and I braced myself for the worst. "Faruk had betrayed us all. He called his *Baba* while we waited to change trains. That was the first time Remmi drank my blood. He made the anklet for me right after . . . and then your *Baba* sold Leyla to the mafia boss. Punishment for my disrespect."

Before I realized what happened, I was beside my mother in her chair, my arms holding her tight against me. Stone filtered through my blood as silent sobs shook her shoulders, resolution building within me anew. "We'll bring *Baba* and Remmi to justice, along with all of their minions and clients. I promise."

My mother sniffed, blotting her nose on her sleeve and making an effort to pull away from me. I refused to let her go, combing my fingers through her hair as I laid her head against my chest. "Lenz has done this stuff for years. He's good at it. It'd be easier if my *Truhtein* were here to help, but we'll figure out how to get the evidence to imprison all of them. Even Faruk."

"The sorcerer has made it impossible to get into the vault where they store all of their documents. The Teuton." My mother corrected herself, lifting her head to meet my gaze. She looked at my face for a moment before her attention drifted to the scars marring my chest. Hesitantly, she brought her right hand forward to trace one and then the other with her fingertips.

"His magic is more potent than your stone. I saw how you struggled to break the anklet earlier today. If you and your partner try to access that vault, Remmi will catch you. He does terrible things to people who disobey him." My mother gazed at me again with pleading eyes. She wanted me safe and secure, a sentiment I shared about her.

She could never be truly free until my father and his associates languished in prison.

"Lenz and I aren't the only Teutons willing to take on Befreiung's minions." Confidence flooded my spirit alongside my element. Then I told my mother about my destiny as Lady Erlanga . . . and about my blue-fired Teuton Keyholder. Once I collected the courage to explain the situation to Henning, I knew he would help me bring that evil operation down. He might even have insight on how to channel my *Leitalra* magic to liberate the working women from their anklets, too.

Then we could ship Remmi off to rot in the Teutonic dungeon.

Chapter Twelve:
Community

As the weeks passed, I did all that was in my power to help my mother and brother transition to a healthier sort of confinement. Though I had freed them from my father's criminal organization, they could not leave the Liebig property. Like Lenz predicted, they were unable to obtain their birth certificates or passports before we rescued them, and my mother had no driver's license. It was up to me to buy them new clothing and other necessities, along with keeping the cabinets stocked with foods my mother preferred to cook.

While I focused on making my new housemates as comfortable as possible, Lenz watched over Befreiung's compound in the aftermath. Within a week, my father hired a fresh batch of minions to patrol the property, adding an extra layer of security. Lenz also detected the presence of another type of energy blending with Remmi's dark variety along the women's anklets and the basement shield. At least two Teutons worked with my father as he sought to expand his web to recapture his wife and son.

Murat and my mother gave anonymous testimonies to Lenz about what they experienced and witnessed under my father's control. He promised not to force them to appear in court if they did not want to, offering them the same protection he and Philipp granted me three years earlier. Although parts of their statements stoked my urge for vengeance, Lenz informed me privately that we still required hard evidence before we could involve the authorities. He would continue to investigate while I guided my mother and brother toward recovery.

~*~

Throughout the remainder of May and the outset of June, I spent more time with my Keyholder. We met for dinner at Pritzl on Friday nights to discuss what had happened in our lives each week. I also invited him to visit the Liebig property whenever his job or studies did not constrain him. Since he had welcomed me to invade his room anytime, I knew I should offer him a similar privilege.

Henning helped me refine my magical abilities during afternoons beside the pool, teaching me skills that furthered my confidence. With his support, I practiced extending my fingers into stone claws, identifying and summoning different types of rocks from the earth, and conjuring ethereal weapons from my element while in spirit form. We playfully sparred as spirits, obsidian blade against blue-fired saber, laughing as our magic enhanced each other's whenever our weapons clashed. At one point, I managed to do what Lenz had mentioned months before—I plunged my spirit into the ground as my Keyholder slashed at me with his flaming saber. The earth itself reinforced my spirit while I floated amid dirt, stones, pebbles, roots, and insects, delighted at the belonging embracing me as a Teuton witch.

Then I sent my magic out to track where Henning awaited me in the ether, erupting from the earth and snagging his ankles in stone fingers, dropping him to his knees. He lost his grip on his blue-fired saber, which vanished the second it hit the waters of the pool. *You cheated,* he thought with a smirk as he met my gaze, his ghostly ankles twitching in my grasp.

I grinned back. *Never underestimate an earthen witch.* Giggling in my mind, I released his ankles and drifted forward to plant a kiss atop his fiery hair, heat swirling into my core as our elements merged. Henning gaped at me and rose from where he lay upon the ground, but I shut my eyes and returned to my body before he could react to my gesture.

We shared more casual touches the more time we spent together, certainty building within me that my Keyholder was truly a good man, one worthy to fill the void Philipp's absence left in my heart. On the first Friday in June, while we enjoyed a dinner at the pub, Henning told me what motivated him to accept the keys of Erlangen. During his childhood, his great-grandfather taught him how to support other Teutons and help them along on their personal paths. Satisfaction refreshed his spirit whenever he steered someone past whatever roadblocks held them back from improving themselves.

"This city's soul has whispered to me since I was a kid, convincing me I'm the *Leitaeri* the Teutons of Erlangen need," he said after taking a drink from his mug of Kellerbier, his expression pensive. "I'll admit I was a little bit nervous about the fated mate aspect at first. I got used to supporting my Omi like an apprentice. Nothing romantic. I'd never felt romantic attraction at all, actually. When all of my buddies started trying things out with our classmates, I just concentrated on my studies and my drawings."

"And listening to the growling lords of metal," I put in, setting my elbow on the table to prop my chin up. I loved gazing at Henning's face, watching his emotions pour through as he shared his heart with me. A glimmer of cerulean fire highlighted the outer edges of his irises, luring me into his world. This man would steal my heart without the need for a city bond, soon enough.

Henning scrunched his nose and quoted a My Dying Bride song, his deep voice growling just like the male lead. I started laughing and waved my free hand at him. "Quit it, people are looking at you!" He had let me borrow a pair of CDs each week since the beginning of May, so I had begun to appreciate the differences in the metal genres. Doom metal was my favorite thus far, melancholy dirges that consoled my deepest muses.

"But I literally never felt romantic attraction to anyone at all. Or sexual attraction," Henning went on, bringing the subject back around. He spoke quietly now, a light blush coloring his cheeks. "Then I saw you there in front of the grapefruits and everything clicked into place."

Desire fluttered in my stomach, heat rising to my own cheeks. "I felt it, too. But I didn't know what was going on. I was too scared to let you know how much you influenced me that day." I stared at my mostly empty plate while I made my confession, then looked shyly at my Keyholder through my eyelashes.

He held his right hand out to me and this time I took it, our fingers twining perfectly. "You come to my dreams almost every night. But you know . . . we'll be able to actually share dreams together as spirits, if we complete the city bond." His fiery irises glittered with possibility.

A strong temptation, considering the demons I fought nearly every night. I squeezed his hand and released it, turning my attention back to what remained of my Jägerschnitzel. "I might be ready for that sooner than you think," I whispered, though I knew I must come clean about my past before we sealed our bond. He deserved to know how terribly my former handlers had ruined my body.

But I hesitated to tell him, fear of rejection still holding me back. Maybe I could break through that barrier after Lenz and I brought my father to justice. As yet, I had not opened that subject to Henning at all, though my instincts assured me Befreiung would fall if the Lady and Keyholder of Erlangen united to destroy it. On the second Saturday in June, Henning would bring a group of his friends to the Liebig mansion for a casual lunch, an event where I could mingle with the other witches in our community. Maybe if they accepted me for who I was, I could share my darkest truths with my fated mate.

~*~

That Saturday, I spent the morning in a flurry of activity, helping my mother and Murat prepare an extensive buffet for my Keyholder and his friends. This would be the first time Henning ever met my family, something that both thrilled and frightened me. I reminded Murat over and over again not to mention what his father did for a living, or anything about where he used to live. Anxiety stoked my elemental magic into unnatural prominence, casting a silvery veil over my vision. What would the witches in this city think, when they learned their new *Leitalra* was Turkish?

My mother insisted upon readying a mixture of Turkish dishes and German ones, in an attempt to appease all of our guests' appetites. She knew not to prepare Döner Kebaps under any circumstance, for I had explained my distaste for those not long after she came to stay with me. Instead, we made flatbread pastries filled with meats, veggies, and cheese; grape leaves stuffed with onions and rice; and baklava with filo, honey, and hazelnuts. Murat helped roll the grape leaves, declaring that he did not want his future wife to do all of the cooking.

"Good for you. You've raised him well," I told my mother while I stirred a pot of beef goulash. I was in charge of making the German main dish, one of many my *Truhtein* taught me to cook. Fashioning meals was one of Philipp's hobbies. It always soothed my grief to go through the motions of cooking, imagining his ghost working at my side.

The doorbell rang when I was in the middle of tossing a salad, and I glanced at the clock over the doorway to the hall before racing to admit our first guests. My element told me it was Henning himself, along with another Teuton of lightning. Had he invited his parents? No, he had told me they claimed light and water.

I paused before a mirror at the edge of the vestibule, making sure nothing crazy had happened to my hair and makeup while I worked in the kitchen. No strays visible, my eyeliner emphasizing the stone-gray color my irises refused to let go. My scoop-necked, patterned gray blouse appeared like granite to my elemental vision, my black jean shorts and sandals completing the confident vibe I wanted to portray. Maybe it would be smarter to let my stone enhance my vision throughout this occasion. Then I would not be the only brown-eyed Teuton on the property.

I took a deep breath and let it out, then stepped forward and channeled my magic to undo the front door's lock. Hiding my nervousness deep inside, I opened the door and smiled as my eyes met those of my *Leitaeri*. Cobalt blue enriched his already-gorgeous irises, his fiery aura silently reassuring me. Beside him stood a young female I judged to be close to my age, her straight brown hair in a pixie cut, her eyes a muted blue, her elemental lightning contained. She and Henning sported the same nose, so they must be related.

"Welcome to my home. Please come in, and I'll show you to the sunroom. That's where we'll be eating, once my family and I finish laying out the buffet." My voice sounded flat, like I was a butler inviting guests into someone else's mansion.

"This is *your* place?" The young female whistled, casting her gaze over the vestibule as she entered a step behind Henning. "What a catch!"

Henning jabbed her with an elbow. "Have a care, Kora. I won't stand anyone disrespecting my Lady, not even you." A frown line marred his forehead as he turned to face me, where I stood holding the front door's knob, chagrined by his companion's brazenness. "I'm sorry about her. She's my cousin, Kora Dahlhausen. I don't think she's ever been to a house quite like this one."

"Not since the Taubenball at Herr von Rische's castle," Kora put in, gazing toward the front staircase with an intrigued expression. Her bleached jean shorts crept partially up her ass as she turned in a circle, looking over every doorway. She stood a handbreadth taller than me, her crimson T-shirt hugging her breasts.

Shaking myself out of my daze, I closed the front door and set the lock again, this time with my fingers. I had never heard of a Taubenball or Herr von Rische, imposter syndrome eating away at my poise. How could I manage to get through this if all the witches yammered about events and people I did not know? They would start whispering that Erlanga's soul should have chosen someone else.

Henning placed an arm around my waist, his support granting me enough stability to do as I had said—lead them both to the sunroom. Once there, I invited them to grab drinks from the wet bar before the floor-to-ceiling windows facing the hydrangeas outside, grateful I had paid the landscapers to tidy the grounds earlier this week. Kora started grousing about some awful man with garlic breath who demanded she dance with him at the Taubenball, rolling her eyes as she bent to view the wine selection. Henning appeared bemused by his cousin's chatter, and I slipped out en route to the kitchen.

I should have invited Henning to come by himself.

To my relief, the rest of my Keyholder's entourage proved far more polite and cordial, likely because they already had partners of their own. I suspected Kora was on the hunt herself, but she would find no extra Teutons on Liebig grounds. While we all sat around the sunroom enjoying our food some time later, I held my peace and observed Henning's friends, taking mental notes on each one.

Bianca and Oliver Langguth were the only married couple, and they lived in the massive apartment building on the other side of the Regnitz River. Apparently they had met at the Taubenball, an event held in Nürnberg every five years where young Teutons sought mates. Bianca related the story of how an olive rolled off her plate while she built a salad at the ball ten years ago, and Oliver retrieved it before she could do so herself. Her husband shook his head in amusement when my brother howled with laughter at the story, stating that his wife told it to everyone they met.

"A sweet man named Oliver picked my olive up off the floor," Bianca said in a dreamy tone, her black curls bouncing as she turned her head to beam at her husband. "It felt like fate when we danced that night, even though it's nothing like what's happening between Zehra and Henning."

I nearly choked on a bite of goulash when she said that. The fact that the Taubenball took place in Nürnberg—the city where I was raped and videoed for five years of my childhood —had already set me on edge. While Bianca shared her romantic tale, I threw stones at the demons in my mind, the ones that informed me I could never appear at that event myself, for fear of running into former clients. Pedophiles.

Bianca's friend Gabi noticed my mortified expression and covered for me, admitting that she and her fiancé, Lukas, had reconciled at the most recent Taubenball. Now they were in the midst of planning their wedding and honeymoon, and the conversation shifted to dreamy destinations involving tropical beaches. The wonder of young love shone on both Gabi's and Lukas' faces. They sneaked kisses when they thought no one was looking.

Henning listened with rapt attention while his friends talked about beaches, seated on the cherry-hued leather chair that matched mine, a marble side table between us. My mother actually spoke up, reminiscing in broken German about a childhood visit to Cleopatra Beach on the Mediterranean. But I hardly heard any of the discussion, distracted by the date Gabi mentioned when she talked about the latest Taubenball. Friday, April 2nd.

Three days before my *Truhtein* gave his blood for me. Three days before the elderly *Leitalra* of this city gave her life for the Teutons under her jurisdiction. Had something happened at the Taubenball that made her sacrifice necessary? I sensed tension emanating from the spirits of the two younger guys occupying the narrow futon to Henning's left. Dennis, his childhood friend, and Till, a young man from a village near the Czech border.

Dennis and Till were romantically involved. None of the gathered Teutons seemed shocked or repulsed about that fact, even though I knew our people valued reproduction to preserve our magical heritage. The casual way everyone treated Dennis and Till gladdened my soul. If young Teutons were open to the homosexual community, maybe they could accept a Lady like me.

Then I remembered what Henning had said the first time he visited me as a spirit. The Teutons of Erlangen had believed

Philipp and Lenz to be a couple when they were not. At least not officially. My predecessor, the elderly *Leitalra*, had been close friends with Philipp. And Lenz had contacts among the Teutons who worked with local law enforcement.

If there was a place for gay Teutons, there was a place for Turkish Teutons. My hometown was Erlangen, not Nürnberg; I would not have to appear there if I did not feel comfortable doing so. I straightened my posture and laid my empty bowl upon the table, my gaze locking with Henning's as I took up a seeded rye roll from the small basket he had grabbed for us to share. He smiled, his blue-fired spirit caressing mine without touching.

Maybe this was where I belonged, after all.

Henning and I helped my mother and Murat collect the dishes when our guests finished eating, my mother shooing us away after we piled everything into one of the sinks. "You need to socialize with your friends. Murat and I will bring out dessert soon."

I took my Keyholder's hand to guide him back to the sunroom, proud of myself for making the first move there. Henning's fire warmed my earthen spirit as we strolled back to where his friends continued to chat, his deep voice restoring my confidence in myself. "Your mother is an excellent cook, I have to say."

"*Anne* wasn't the only one who cooked. I made the goulash and Murat rolled the grape leaves. We all worked together on the dessert." I grinned up at him.

"Ah-nay. Is that the Turkish word for mother?"

"Yes. And I'm sure she'd be honored for you to call her that." I pulled him aside before we reached the doorway to the sunroom and gave his jaw a quick kiss. "Thank you for accepting me as your *Leitalra*, even though I wasn't born a Teuton."

Henning touched his jaw, amazement breaking across his face. "Wow. Have to say you've attracted my attention, gracious stone witch."

I grinned again and tugged him toward the sunroom. "We'd better get back in there before someone senses us out here and comes to investigate."

After my Keyholder and I settled into our leather seats, Gabi cleared her throat and looked pointedly toward us. "I think it's about time we let Zehra in on the stupidest prejudices lingering among Teutons today. You two should be able to effect lasting change, since you're the *Leitaeri* and *Leitalra* of our community."

My eyes widened and I parted my lips, unable to form a reply. Luckily, my Keyholder put my thoughts into words. "Let's hear them. Prejudice doesn't belong in Erlangen." He slipped his right hand into the pocket of his khaki shorts to trace the city's keys, our shared authority sizzling along my spirit.

Gabi launched into a diatribe about how pointless it was that some Teutons still looked down on those of "low blood status." She referenced a test performed by priests to confirm that a newborn child—or an outsider coming out of the blood-transfer—claimed enough Teuton blood to control elemental magic. Anyone with blood at eighty-five percent or higher could wield magic, while those at eighty-four percent or lower could sense their elements but not invoke magic.

I had read about Teutonic blood prejudice in my *Truhtein's* tomes, but the concept was so ridiculous I had never given it much thought. All Teutons were equal in elemental power, so it made no sense to belittle someone on account of their blood status. Philipp's sacrifice had granted me blood at ninety-four percent Teutonic, a relatively high purity rate in the modern age. But Gabi and Lukas claimed blood at the lower end and had suffered ridicule for it, even though their elements were as strong as my stone.

Henning and I agreed to combat such outdated notions, my *Leitaeri* stating that blood prejudice was just an attempt to keep Teutons squabbling instead of working together to improve society. The others seemed to agree, and then Oliver spoke up, laying a supportive hand around Bianca's waist as he said that too many Teutons expected every female to bear children, even if they were unable.

Bianca's cheeks flushed with shame as her husband related the censure they had faced throughout their nine years of marriage, since his wife had yet to hold a successful pregnancy. They were about to try IVF alongside some sort of witchy mysticism, in an attempt to awaken her womb. Bianca confessed in a halting voice that she sincerely hoped she could carry a child this time around, for her barrenness often left her feeling empty. A rock dropped into my stomach at the topic, my earlier nervousness resurfacing.

"Henning won't have to worry about that if he marries my sister." Murat's boisterous voice carried across the sunroom as he appeared in the doorway holding a tray of baklava. "Our *Anne* had four children. But there's only three left now."

Chapter Thirteen:
Baring My Soul

Kora's loud gasp rang out as the sunroom fell silent, my little brother dropping a bomb no one expected, myself least of all. My awareness blurred and I wrapped my arms around my body, unable to put words together to salvage the lighthearted gathering as it shattered to pieces around me.

"Poor, sweet boy! What happened?" Through hazy vision, I watched Kora step toward Murat, her hands extended in a gesture of sympathy.

"Bad men murdered her. My *Anne* cried for a month." My brother sounded detached, as if he dealt with the tragedy through dissociation. Like me. Kora knelt before him and took the tray from his hands, cooing nonsense I could not hear. I needed to get it together, ask Murat to run back to our mother.

"Murat . . . ." I forced his name through my teeth, my entire body shaking.

"Her name was Leyla." While I could not discern what Kora said to him, my brother's voice continued to resound in the room, ruining what remained of my self-control. I sank to the floor and pulled my knees up to my chest, my quavering body rocking back and forth, my eyes unseeing.

"Zehra." My name slinked around me like veils of silk, my Keyholder's fiery presence granting me a lifeline in an ocean of emptiness. How had Murat's careless words vanquished my defenses? Why had I not begged him to keep silent about his family altogether?

There was a commotion around me, but I could not make sense of any of it. Trapped in a prison where the worst demons from my past clawed into my cell to drag me before a merciless judge. Teutons wanted all females to reproduce. That was what Oliver had said.

The *Leitalra* of Erlangen would be expected to bear children.

"*Truh . . . tein . . . .*" A plea for my beloved master fell from my lips, my grief taking shape as a tortured sob. Voices murmured around me and strong arms lifted me from the floor, bundling me in fire's supportive heat. Squeezing my eyes shut, I allowed my pain to consume me, my element rising to the surface, creating tears of solid earth.

Memories I had long stifled tormented every part of my inner self, my stone weeping on my behalf as I sought some source of comfort. Philipp was not here to reassure me that my past could not dictate my present or my future. He had died to grant me Teutonic magic, a vital defense against those who sought to smother my voice. But my childhood slavery reared its ugly head in moments I could not control, grinding my hopes back into dust.

Philipp could not save me or repair the damage done to my body and mind.

Could I manage to tear my way free from this inferno and explain myself to my *Leitaeri?* I sensed his spirit holding mine close, his arms embracing me as my *Truhtein's* never would again. How had Henning picked me up off the floor with my element front and center? Stone was not too heavy for him?

Would he reject me once he knew how broken his *Leitalra* truly was?

Eventually I managed to pry my eyelids open, my silvery vision recognizing the walls and furniture of the master suite. Philipp's suite. My suite. Henning had carried me to safety, sealed away the outside world while I regained control over myself. He had sat us both on the bed, his arms holding me securely against him. He did not speak, but his spirit caressed mine, offering wordless solace.

I blinked a few times and glanced down at my lap. A pile of tiny pebbles lay there in colors from the usual gray to tan, cream, black, and even jewel tones. My forehead wrinkled and I reached up to rub my right eye, bemused that I felt no pain in the socket after crying literal rocks. I did not know that was possible. But wait, I had seen energy sparking in Philipp's tears on several occasions. This must be one of many advantages— or drawbacks—of being a Teuton.

Henning still had not spoken one word, likely waiting for me to do it first. Terror raced into my blood as my rational mind reasserted itself. I had no choice but to tell my Keyholder everything, after breaking down in front of him and all his friends. Now he knew "bad men" had murdered my little sister. How much more had Murat divulged before our mother came to quiet him?

How could I explain?

I stirred in my Keyholder's embrace and he loosened his arms, allowing me to edge away from him. The pebbles on my lap spilled between my legs as I shifted, prompting me to expel a soft snort. "Rocks."

"You made a nice collection of rocks," Henning said after a pause, his right hand moving forward to touch the small of my back. I chanced a look at him out of the corner of my left eye, hoping for a clue about how he processed my collapse. Did he view me as weak? Insane?

To my surprise, Henning's eyes smoldered with what looked like devotion. He offered me a shy smile. "At least you don't leak little gas flames whenever you cry. Don't have to worry about burning anything."

I turned away from him, a feeble laugh quivering in my chest. "I'm sorry."

"Fiery Teutons get used to it after a while. But if you're apologizing for crying in front of me, please don't. I'm so sorry about your sister. I didn't know."

He sounded devastated. I ran my fingers through some of the pebbles bunched between my legs, asking my element to ground me and give me the courage I did not feel. "Thank you. It's not just that. There's so much you don't know . . . about me and my family."

"You don't have to tell me right now if you're not ready." Henning traced his fingers along my waist, his gentle touch soothing. "But I'm here for you whenever you need to talk. Or cry. And it's not just the city bond making me say that. You fascinate me, Zehra. I've never admired any witch more than I admire you. Not even my Omi."

I sniffed as moisture gathered behind my eyes again. Hopefully this time I could keep my stone contained; I did not want to be sweeping up pebbles for the rest of the day. My demons whispered in my mind, hissing that my *Leitaeri* would not admire me once he knew the truth. That he would wish Erlanga's soul had chosen any other witch.

But I had to get things out in the open to stave off any rumors that might arise thanks to Murat's revelations. *God, please help me be honest with him. And Philipp . . . please stand by my side if Henning won't,* I prayed.

"Remember when I told you . . . Philipp Liebig . . . rescued me from a terrible fate?" I continued running my fingers through the pebbles, focusing my gaze on their colors, not on my Keyholder.

"I remember." Henning had begun to knead circles upon my lower back, releasing a small portion of my tension.

I dug out a diamond-looking pebble the size of a nail's head, ordering myself to focus on what Philipp told me. My past did not matter. I was resilient, a shining star, capable of creating my own destiny. A brilliant light in the darkness.

"When I was thirteen, my handler decided to sell me. His clients didn't want my body anymore. My videos weren't making enough money. I was turning into a woman. And his clients preferred little girls. Not women."

Henning's hand froze upon my back. I could tell he was holding his breath. I chewed on my inner cheek and fingered the sparkling crystal my tears had formed. My spirit sensed

Henning's repulsion along with an emergent anger. *You can tell him. He's not angry at you. He's angry at what they did to you.*

"He was just about to sell me to someone who produced porn of teenagers. But then Philipp came along . . . and offered twice as much money. The first time I saw Philipp, I thought I was being sold to the Playboy mansion. I'd heard talk about that place. I was so scared. But then he brought me here and set me in a room upstairs. A really basic room. To detox me from the alcohol. He didn't want sex. I tried to give it to him so many times. I didn't understand. I thought he wanted little girls, too. I didn't understand why he bought me."

Salty tears dripped from my eyes, my stone confining itself within. "Philipp worked hard to change the way I viewed myself, the way I viewed the world. He showed me the kindness. The beauty. The path to recovery. He wanted to make sure I could take care of myself . . . so I'd never fall into the hands of evil men again. He kept me safe when we brought my handler to justice, along with all the others who worked with him. He and Lenz kept my testimony anonymous. When I turned eighteen, Philipp gave me his name and his blood, a new start."

My rushing river of confessions ended abruptly, my fingers pressing the crystal tight against my palm. Tears fell like rain onto my patterned gray blouse, my eyes squeezed shut once more. I had gained a new life and lost the man who made it all possible. Henning wrapped his arms around me again, and this time I leaned my face into his chest, the warmth of his fire comforting me.

"Your *Truhtein* gave you a priceless gift. I understand now why you love him, Zehra. I'm so sorry I misjudged you at first. I wish he could have survived the ritual, so you could have had the marriage you longed for."

"His ashes are still in his family crypt," I choked out, sorrow shattering me anew. "They should be here with me, in our home. I hate German law. His ashes should be here with me."

"Hmm." Henning's nose was buried in my hair, his voice humming against my brain. Our closeness stirred yearnings hardly appropriate at a time like this—or any time, for that matter. I had not yet told him the worst parts of my past. The parts that made me an unworthy *Leitalra*.

Blinking my tears away, I sighed and remained where I lay against his chest. "Lenz and I rescued my *Anne* and Murat from my *Baba*—my father—just last month," I said, skirting the issue for the moment. "He works with a group of human traffickers not far north of here. He sold Leyla and me to pay gambling debts. His biggest addiction. That's why he got into the dark side of business, to try to stay on top of his losses."

Henning exhaled heavily into my hair, then raised his head, his strong arms my anchor. "He may be your father, but he sounds like a crook."

"He's a terrible person," I responded instantly. Any latent love I may have had for him had evaporated long ago. "Even before, when he was a custodian at the university, he beat my mother. And all of us. Even Leyla. I saw him shake her once when she wouldn't stop crying. A little baby."

Henning murmured a curse on my father's behalf. "Lenz is trying to uncover enough evidence to break my *Baba's* organization apart, like we did with the porn ring," I went on. "But that took years. And we had my *Truhtein* then. He was good at tracing stuff on the dark web. I miss him so much."

"The three of you brought that ring down in 2001, right?" I nodded. "You were fifteen and did all of that after surviving the worst abuse ever. Gosh, Zehra. No wonder Erlanga's soul chose you to represent her."

I had not thought about it like that before. "I feel so unworthy sometimes. I can't understand why this city's soul didn't choose a born Teuton."

"If anyone's worthy to take the reins of a Teuton city, it's you. Never doubt that. I already respected you, but now I'm just . . . blown away."

Pulling back from his embrace, I met his gaze, astonished by the admiration pulsing from his fiery aura. I almost believed I sensed Erlanga's soul speaking to my heart, a gentle reproof. *Your* Leitaeri *is a good man, and that's why he accepted the responsibility of Erlangen's keys. It's his duty to guide and protect you.*

"I really appreciate you being so kind," I managed to say in a trembling voice. "It's hard for me to be honest about my past, because my handler trained me to believe I'm a worthless whore. And my religion . . . my former religion, because now I worship Philipp's God . . . my former religion taught me that raped women go to hell, not heaven. I believed I was damned for so long."

Henning reached his right palm out, his expression so tender. "Thank God your *Truhtein* opened your eyes to grace."

I laid my left hand in his, my right still gripping the tiny crystal tear. "You can call him Philipp, you know," I said, lacing my fingers through his.

"Right. Call the wealthiest tycoon in Erlangen by his first name."

Henning rolled his eyes, but I could tell he was teasing. Giggles welled within me, a welcome relief after such a heavy discussion. "Call my *Truhtein* Philipp, and call Herr Schneider Lorenzo. He's the reason I can make some Italian meals."

"I totally didn't realize Herr Schneider's Italian."

"His maternal grandfather did the blood-transfer. And you know who gave his blood for him?" I paused and wiggled my eyebrows, then blurted the answer before Henning could guess. "Philipp's grandfather!"

My Keyholder narrowed his eyes, our hands still linked. "Both survived the ritual?"

"Yep. Priests were better at Wuotan's rituals back in the 1800s than they are now." I stuck my tongue out at him, an unspoken challenge.

Henning smirked and tightened his fingers around mine. "Oh really? Guess I'll have to brush up on my blood magic to be worthy of you. Did Philipp or Lenz ever bleed you?"

I recoiled. "What? Why?"

"Some wives or consorts of Teuton priests find it soothing to be bled. But I'd never force that on you. If I ever push you toward something you don't want to do, please tell me. I don't ever want you to fear your *Leitaeri*." He crossed his left arm over his waist to touch where Erlangen's keys lay in his right pocket.

Even with the khaki cloth between his fingers and the keys, I felt the magic tingling along my spirit, another assurance of my *Leitaeri's* support. So I decided to be honest, embarrassment warring with arousal inside me. "Philipp bled me one time. To see whether my blood memories held any info that could nail the porn ring. I gave him my permission. And I . . . it kind of . . . ."

My cheeks flamed, and Henning traced a gentle circle on the back of my hand. "There's no shame in how the body and spirit respond to bloodletting by a trusted partner. I've been told many find it erotic."

"My blood helped Philipp and Lenz identify the rapists." I steered the topic away from Henning's observation, which was far too true. I had pitched a fit when Philipp refused to have sex with me afterward. Immature. But the memory sent my muses in a direction I had not yet considered. "I wonder . . . ."

"You wonder?" Henning prompted as I stared into space, lost in thought.

"Just something I need to talk to my *Anne* about," I said, uncertain whether I ought to open the subject with her or not. I gasped a second later and jumped off the bed, scattering pebbles across the floor. "Oh no! We've been in here who knows how long, with all your friends out there waiting! They must think I'm crazy!"

Alarm registered on Henning's face. "It's fine, Zehra. I asked Dennis to send everyone home after your *Anne* finished handing out the baklava. I'll follow up with all of them once you're sure you'll be okay by yourself. The outside world can burn. My Lady comes first, always."

I blinked at him in a daze, trying to remember just what had happened after Murat proclaimed I could bear countless magical children. I still had not told my *Leitaeri* that my brother was utterly wrong about that. Had I said anything before my demons overwhelmed me? Oh no . . . .

"They heard me say *'Truhtein,'*" I groaned, rubbing my temple in anguish.

"And right after that I lifted you in my arms and carried you here to your bedroom. They probably thought you meant me. Not Philipp."

"This all went so wrong. It was supposed to be a happy gathering with your friends. Why do I always ruin everything?" Regret twisted my stomach, my gaze drifting toward the mirror over the dresser. My braid had started coming undone, my sable hair frizzy around my head. I looked like a madwoman, not a *Leitalra*.

Henning stepped cautiously toward where I stood in the center of the room, frantically patting my hair down. He held his palms out as he approached, as if I were a rabid animal. "You don't have to apologize for how your trauma influences your behavior. You've come a long way toward healing. I can tell from all the time we've spent together and how bravely you revealed your past today. You don't need to worry about what my friends think. I'll handle it."

"Don't tell them I was in porn. And don't tell them about my *Baba*. Please." I folded my hands before me, a habit from days of old.

My Keyholder reached out to take my hands in both of his, the warmth in his touch restoring my spirit. "We can keep those secrets between us, until you're ready to share them with others. I'll never break your trust. I promise."

Henning's gaze lowered from my eyes to my lips. My hormones resurged as I realized he wanted to kiss me. Erlanga's spirit compelled me to accept, but I broke contact with him and turned to stare at the pebbles dotting the floor. "I have to clean this up. I hope I didn't leak a bunch of rocks while you carried me here."

"There's actually a quick way of cleaning up, since you're a stone witch." My companion tilted his head at me, appearing unfazed by my rejection. "If you focus on the stone within your spirit and expand that sense out slowly, you should be able to find each pebble and guide them into a pile without using a broom. Then you can make them follow you outside to wherever you want to drop them."

My lips parted in wonder. "Of course I can do that. I threw a much bigger rock at you last month. I just didn't think of using my magic that way."

I closed my eyes to center myself on my element while Henning chuckled. "The possibilities are endless, my victorious stone witch."

Henning stayed with me for the rest of the afternoon and evening, sitting down with my mother and Murat for a heart-to-heart about what had happened. I let him speak for me most of the time, his respect and insight impressing me. When we sat around the dry bar to eat leftovers for dinner, I realized Henning reminded me of Philipp. An honorable man who wanted to support those in need.

Maybe Erlanga's soul had planned this all along.

Late that night, while I sat in bed reading a Cornelia Funke novel in hopes of winding down enough to sleep, I sensed my Keyholder's fiery spirit hovering somewhere nearby. I laid the book face down on the empty spot beside me—what used to be Philipp's spot—and looked at the digital clock. Twelve twenty-five. Early Sunday morning, June 13th.

I've got something for you, Zehra. Henning's mental voice wove its way into my mind, making me smile. *Can I come into your room?*

"Of course!" I called out loudly, setting my bare feet onto the floor and lifting my arms for a stretch. My stone sensed his blue fire lurking just outside the front-facing windows, their deep violet drapes drawn for the night. I invited my stone to enhance my vision, showing me the spiritual realm alongside the physical.

Henning appeared before the drapes, azure flames enveloping his spirit in luster. In his left hand, he held a violet-black urn. Philipp's remains.

Chapter Fourteen

An Empowering Fate

Gratitude flourished inside my chest as I stepped forward to accept the urn from Henning. It felt warm to the touch thanks to his fire, swirls of black mingling with violet in a marble pattern. The base of the urn displayed a name and years in silver etching—my element identified it as pure silver. *Philipp Alexander Liebig. 1934-2004.*

I had mentioned my *Truhtein's* urn to Henning only once during my confession yesterday. Hours after he departed my home, he returned with Philipp's remains. I must have done something right to be blessed with a *Leitaeri* as perceptive as Henning.

"Thank you so much for remembering Philipp," I murmured, resting the urn against my cheek and imagining my *Truhtein's* spirit hovering beside Henning's, resplendent with flashes of dark energy. "I'll make a place for him here with me, where he belongs. So few people care that he's gone."

More people remember him than you realize, Henning remarked as I carried the urn to the bedside table, setting it beside Philipp's clock. I would prepare a proper shrine for it later. Tonight his ghost would guard me while I slept.

Your Truhtein *had a lot of contacts among our people, including most of the rich Teutons in Bavaria and Austria,* Henning told me while I stood back to admire how the urn looked beside the digital clock. The blue numbers cast an intriguing glow upon its surface.

"Is that so?" I asked my companion, tearing my focus away from the most meaningful gift I had ever received, apart from my freedom and Teutonic magic. Turning to regard Henning's spirit, I raised my eyebrows and combed my fingers through my hair, which was let down for the night. Affection wafted from his aura as he watched me, his flaming eyes taking note of my breasts for once.

Maybe I should wear a tank top in his presence more often.

Philipp was close with my Omi, like you said, and he also knew one of my Omi's dearest friends. A forest witch of air from the Austrian Alps. She and her priest have taken a stand against domestic violence for decades.

Interesting. "So Teuton males don't always respect their wives and children, despite the fact that witches are equal to them in magical strength," I translated, sitting on the edge of my bed. "Thanks to Remmi, that's not exactly news to me."

Remmi? Curiosity glimmered on my Keyholder's face.

"The Teuton who works for my *Baba*. He's dark energy like Philipp, and he cast a shield over the vault where they keep all the documents. That's why my *Anne* and Murat have to stay here until we can crack it open. They don't have passports or any other IDs. And *Baba's* got his minions hunting for them."

I know Herr Schnei—Lenz—is a retired investigator, so I assume he's doing most of the reconnaissance? Henning's thoughts were loaded with implications. *Do you think he'd like help? Some of my friends would love to take a crack at an energy shield. Kora and Oliver for sure.*

Oliver claimed the basic form of energy, the invisible kind that acted most like electricity. "Would it really be a good idea to involve him, with Bianca wanting to try to get pregnant soon?" I queried, swallowing the bile that threatened to rise in my throat at the subject. "He doesn't need to get hurt or killed.

Considering what happened to Leyla, my *Baba* is *not* above killing his opponents."

Henning grimaced, which looked odd on a spirit. His teeth reflected light blue sparkles. *You have a point. What about Kora? She was really kind to Murat after he talked about your sister.*

My little brother had mentioned Kora three times in conversation last night, seeming fascinated by her lightning magic and her as a person. But she had given off strange vibes when I let her in the house, my wariness barking warnings at me. "Maybe we should let Lenz handle it himself. None of us are trained to break into criminal bunkers. And my *Baba* might work with more Teutons than just Remmi. I don't want any of Erlanga's kin to get injured or killed."

Spoken like a true Leitalra. Henning beamed at me, his respect prompting me to blush. I meant what I said. My heart wanted all of the Teutons in my city to be successful and content, not putting themselves in harm's way.

"Lenz plans on getting a couple priests on the council involved, once he's worked out how to uncover enough evidence to arrest my *Baba* and free his slaves," I remembered. Had he found any fresh leads yet? I needed to call him on Monday and ask for an update.

He's probably thinking about Volli Ehrlich, the youngest member of the council aside from me. He's a cop who wields the element of metal. Not sure if metal could bring down an energy shield, though. He might need Herr Burkhardt for that, but I don't think he does that kind of stuff anymore. Henning rubbed his chin, gazing toward the door to the hall.

"What does Herr Burkhardt do?" Lenz had mentioned that name.

District attorney. The lead prosecutor in the case against your handler, as I recall.

"Oh." So the serious-faced attorney who had ripped my handler to shreds claimed Teuton blood just like me.

He's lightning like my cousin. If he and Volli worked together, they could probably crack that vault, both the shield and any solid reinforcements.

"But would law enforcement get involved without probable cause?" Philipp had explained that standard to me years ago, and it still perturbed me. If the potent magic I wielded as *Leitalra* had not destroyed my mother's anklet, we would have more than mere testimony to go on. Henning and I tossed ideas back and forth for a little longer; but by the time he wished me goodnight and sent his spirit back to his body, we remained stymied. At this point we would have to wait for Lenz to get it done right, focusing on our relationship instead.

~*~

Henning and I did just that during the second half of June, visiting each other almost every day either as spirits or in person. The Saturday after I hosted his friends, I summoned the courage to visit his house for a meal with his parents. Henning had told them the basics at my request—that I had been trafficked as a child and rescued by Philipp Liebig, who granted me Teuton blood. His father and mother treated me very graciously, offering their assistance with anything I might need as I integrated into the Teuton community. His mother, Christel, gave me a container of peanut butter cookies to take home to my family, informing me with a wink that her son had helped her make them.

Their acceptance heartened me, as did the compassion of Henning's friends. Kora tagged along to keep Murat entertained whenever my Keyholder visited the Liebig property in person, proving herself a lively chaperone as she and Murat tried to teach themselves bocce. My brother proved much better at it than she was, but she may have held back to boost his confidence.

While Henning and I gradually dismantled the barriers I had built around my heart as a result of my slavery, Murat faced struggles of a different sort. On the last Monday in June, he admitted he missed school. He had finished reading all of his textbooks and completed every homework assignment, sadness evident in his demeanor at the fact that he could not take the exams.

"I'm worried I'll be behind once Lenz finishes with Befreiung," Murat said as we lounged in the grass beside the pool. "I don't want to be behind. What will the principal say when she finds out I studied at home for a month and a half? That's illegal."

"We'll try to get it figured out before the next school year starts," I replied, the tragedy in my brother's tone wounding my heart. "If you and *Anne* stay here, you'll be going to a different high school, anyway. You can read all of Philipp's books this summer to keep your brain engaged."

Murat lay back and tucked his arms beneath his head, his dark eyes gazing into the elm leaves rustling in the summer breeze. "Why didn't Philipp send you to foster care?"

His question startled me. I tensed where I rested in the grass, my right hand reaching out to stroke the nearest stone beside the pool. "Why *would* Philipp send me to foster care, when I wanted to stay here? He and Lenz brought my abusers to justice, so I knew I could trust them. I couldn't trust random adults. Some of my handler's other cuties came straight from foster care."

"But you were fifteen by then, right? You could have gone out on your own. Become an apprentice like Henning." Murat turned his head to look at me, his large eyes inquisitive.

I smiled at him, not wishing to sully his innocent view of things. "Maybe I just wasn't as brave as you. And I wanted to be a witch, you know."

"That makes sense." My brother averted his gaze to the branches again. "Do you think Lenz would let me become a Teuton when I turn eighteen?"

I chuckled to myself and dropped my fingers back into the grass. "You'd better read up on the blood-transfer before you decide to become a Teuton. I still have nightmares about it every week."

"But you did it, and now you have a fated mate. It'd be nice to have a fated mate."

I jostled his arm with my left elbow. "That doesn't happen to most Teutons, remember. Only to the weird ones like me."

"Kora says Philipp's energy shield is scratchy," Murat said through a yawn, dropping yet another abrupt change of subject. "I like her. I wonder if she'd like me back, if I became a Teuton."

I resisted the urge to roll my eyes. "Kora already likes you. But she's also a little old for you." Murat needed to concentrate on his studies, not on girls.

My mother prepared a savory meal of lamb shish kebabs over flatbread with tossed salad for our dinner with Lenz that evening. Murat loved barraging the elder Teuton with questions about magic and his former career, and Lenz obliged him with tales that sounded far-fetched to me. He noted that one of his IT contacts was trying to hack into Befreiung's accounts in his spare time. Thus far, Remmi's dark energy had thwarted him, but he suspected the basement vault concealed at least one server that hosted all of Befreiung's business transactions.

We really needed another energy Teuton on our team. I had not known how essential Philipp's expertise had been when we took down the porn ring. Neither Oliver nor Kora used their elements to muddle internet protocol. I was starting to think we would have to raid the compound and breach the vault by force.

My mother sent Murat off to the upstairs library after the meal. Luckily, my little brother did not protest, for he had started reading the modern version of *Der Weg* several hours earlier, after our chat beside the fish pool. The Teutonic tome would keep him occupied while we adults gathered in the lounge to discuss things not fit for his adolescent ears.

Lenz inquired after my relationship with Henning, checking that the young *Leitaeri* was treating me with gentleness and respect. I assured him he was, gazing into the gas flames flickering in the fireplace between our dark gray armchairs. "He actually reminds me of my *Truhtein*. He never uses my past against me or pushes me to do things that make me uncomfortable. I should have just told him the truth from the start. Then we wouldn't have wasted time arguing."

"It's not easy for anyone to find peace with the workings of fate, especially when there's a mate involved." Lenz blew on the herbal tea in his mug, a knowing glint in his hazel eyes. My mother occupied a plush couch in the shadows, content to listen while sipping her own tea. It was the wildflower blend again, laced with dandelion, chamomile, and lavender.

"I'm so lucky Henning's not an abusive priest. He's told me about those, how they enslave their wives' hearts and make them unable to speak out. He's going to introduce me to a forest witch sometime soon, a lady who can give me pointers on how to recognize and support women in our community. I also need to get brave enough to absorb the gifts my predecessor left for me."

Henning and I had talked about the *Herzestein* more than once in recent weeks. He had no idea what the process would be like for me, when I reached out with my *Leitalra* magic to drain the essence the turquoise crystal harbored. He did not think it would change anything about me or my magic; my stone would not merge with light after I absorbed his Omi's gifts. He had never thought to question her about it before she passed away. Since that sort of mysticism was not common knowledge among the Teutons, we were pretty much on our own.

The *Herzestein* held unlimited potential and mystery. It worried me.

Lenz made a thoughtful noise and shifted his gaze to the fireplace. "It may be too soon to ask this, considering what you've been through. But there's been talk among the priests. Most still don't know who Erlangen's new *Leitalra* is, because your Keyholder gives ambiguous answers whenever anyone asks about you. Do you think you might be ready to appear publicly at his side?"

I tightened my grip on my mug, wishing the tea's warmth would soothe my spirit like my Keyholder's fire did. "Henning told me I'll have to present myself to the council at some point. Will our people expect more than that?"

"Some believe you've rejected the bond between Lady and Keyholder."

My mother gave a soft gasp from the couch, and I set my mug onto the side table, not wanting to spill any tea if this discussion progressed into tougher topics. Then I lifted my chin and looked Lenz square in the eye. "I haven't rejected the city bond. My heart longs to unite with Henning in every way possible. My body, too. But I don't want to move too fast, like I did with . . . . I mean, I feel like I can trust Henning, like he's a good man. But he still doesn't know . . . about . . . ."

A lump formed in my throat and I could not say the words, even though my companions knew how my former handler had broken my body. Lenz sighed and bowed his head. "I can't say I understand, but I think your Keyholder would embrace you, even if you physically could not mate. He's defended you anytime a new rumor crops up, whether from the priests or from the married witches with too much time on their hands."

"He shouldn't be doing that. He's supposed to be preparing for his exams," I muttered, staring blankly into the flames. Henning was scheduled to take both assessments—written and practical—that would elevate him to journeyman plumber in early July. My anxiety had been staging a party on his behalf, lately.

"Zehra, if your heart tells you it's right for you to marry Henning and seal the bond between you, I stand with you all the way." My mother's soft voice broke into the conversation, peeling away the glum veil distorting my self-worth. Turning away from the fireplace, I invoked my stone into my eyes so I could make out her expression. She nodded at me, appearing resolute.

"The two of you can accomplish more together than alone. I've seen it when he's helped you with your magic. You and Henning both show a strong desire to use your powers for good, so I believe you should set aside your hesitation. Claim your young *Truhtein*. Teach him the wonders of devoted love. And share your light with those who need an example of a triumphant matriarch."

When my mother fell silent, Lenz raised his cup toward her. "Hear, hear." He took one sip while holding her gaze, then dumped the last of his tea down his throat. I took up my own mug again, astounded that my mother viewed me in such an empowering manner. Another layer of uncertainty loosened its grip.

"I've been thinking about what you told me, Zehra," my mother continued, her gaze drifting from my face to Lenz's. "That my blood might hold worthwhile information about your *Baba's* crimes. I've decided that I'm willing. Willing to be bled."

Chapter Fifteen:
Blood Revelations

Nervousness smoldered in the forefront of my brain the following Monday, when I stood in the sunroom watching Lenz and my mother prepare for the bloodletting. She chose her favorite recliner as the stage—the place where she lounged every morning while drinking coffee and observing the birds and squirrels foraging outside. She declared that the mauve recliner and the openness of the sunroom relaxed her, an appropriate venue for the unveiling of her heart.

I had cleaned the recliner with my earthen magic and a handheld vacuum that morning, and again an hour before Lenz arrived. My failure to talk my mother out of the ritual left me feeling useless, unable to spare her from pain. How could she trust a Teuton priest she hardly knew to jab her carotid artery with a needle? What if Lenz did not stop her bleeding in time? Did she really want him privy to her secrets?

My mother brushed off each of my concerns, stating that from what she had seen, Lenz was a much nobler man than Remmi, my father, or any others she had encountered in recent years. She started a big pot of lentil soup just before Lenz arrived, leaving Murat to tend it in her absence. We would all eat dinner together afterward, an event that had become our

Monday tradition. My mother hinted that if I could not handle watching the bleeding process, I could help my brother with the soup instead.

Though I longed to accept my mother's offering of escape, my instincts kept me rooted to the floor five steps away from where she lay upon the recliner, the low neckline of her flowered summer dress baring her arteries to the Teuton priest looming over her. Lenz was dressed for the part, his element augmenting the robe's blackness as he reached two fingers out to trace the channel on the left side of her neck. My mother's brown eyes remained focused on his face, and she gave a short nod when he murmured something to her.

"Zehra, step forward and take your mother's right hand." Lenz's voice broke through my anxious haze, his cloaked arm gesturing me to the opposite side of the recliner from where he stood. "Your presence will comfort her, and you can keep tabs on her pulse throughout the process."

I hastened to obey, taking my mother's right hand in both of mine. Her gaze shifted from Lenz's face to mine, her aura projecting determination. "Be brave," she whispered to me in Turkish. I wondered if she meant those words for herself as well as for me. I threaded the fingers of my right hand through hers, then sought her pulse.

"I'll be draining the standard amount medical professionals take from blood donors," Lenz said, pulling a small beaker from a pocket within his robe and setting it upon the floor. "Five hundred milliliters. The jar will fill quickly, since blood flows much faster through arteries than veins."

"You've done this how many times?" I cut in, my fear rocketing toward the clouds at the sight of the syringe he held. Its needle appeared horrifically thick and sharp, a thin tube sprouting from the syringe's far end.

"More times than I can count. This is common practice when questioning Teuton criminals, remember. And no, I never let any of them bleed to death. Might have been tempted a few times." Lenz inserted one end of the tube into the beaker, then winced when he straightened, his age showing itself. He caught my gaze and smirked, his irises a hellish black.

"Don't tease my daughter." My mother narrowed her eyes at the priest, her expression implying exasperation.

"Very well. I ask you to relax as far as you are able, Arzu. Keep your eyes open and enjoy nature's beauty." He cleansed her skin with an antiseptic wipe, then inserted the needle deep into my mother's neck. Her eyes widened, and a soft gasp escaped her. I tightened my grip on her hand.

"Please forgive the pain I must cause you," Lenz murmured, his tone heavy with regret. I looked from my mother's face, her eyebrows crimped in anguish, to the crimson stream rushing down the tube. Thank goodness Philipp had drunk my truths straight from my neck, when I agreed to be bled. This method was far more terrifying, even if it was cleaner and safer.

My mother's breaths grew shallow, her gaze fixed upon Lenz's face, despite his suggestion that she look out the window. He stemmed the tide racing down the tube just as her pulse started to flutter; and seconds later, he extracted the needle from her neck. No stray drops of blood appeared on her skin before he laid a cotton swab against the wound, Lenz's skills at blood magic clearly evident. I had not yet delved into that aspect of Teutonic sorcery—stemming the flow from an injury. I would have to ask Henning to teach me as soon as possible.

This afternoon, he was taking the written exam in his path to journeyman plumber. Henning would get his results on Wednesday. He had invited me to share dinner with his family that evening, whether he passed or not. Hopefully it would be a celebration, and then he could shift his focus to the practical exam. Along with three other apprentice plumbers, he would take that one on Friday.

The events of this week tested my stability, without question.

"I'm so sorry I had to hurt you, Arzu," Lenz said to my mother, cupping her cheek gently in his hand.

"It's worth it," my mother breathed in a weak voice. "To break Kemal's hold on all of those women." She squeezed my hand, bringing my muses back to the present. Lenz turned his attention to the blood collected, casting a spell over it to protect it from decay. I ought to find my mother something to drink.

I let go of her hand and scurried to the wet bar, retrieving a bottle of mineral water from the small fridge. My mother accepted the bottle, her dark eyes shining with what looked like accomplishment. "It wasn't traumatic at all," she said to me in Turkish. "I've experienced far worse."

"Me too." I knelt upon the floor and leaned my head against her side as she drank, silently thanking heaven for the mystic wonders of Teutonic magic.

~*~

Lenz drank my mother's blood bit by bit, because he said that was the best way to identify what sort of useful information it held. When Teutons wished to read someone's blood truths, they could search for the person's general thoughts or seek specific things. Philipp had honed in on the faces of my handler's clients as they assaulted me, memories he used to track each of them down and bring them to justice. On Wednesday afternoon, Lenz noted over the phone that he had found something that should prove valuable, but he refused to say what.

His vagueness irritated me, but I knew he wanted to keep everyone on the Liebig property as safe as possible while conducting his investigations. My part in the process was pretty much finished, Lenz reiterating that I ought to concentrate my efforts on nurturing my relationship with my Keyholder.

I still needed to tell him what haunted me the most, along with opening up about my feelings toward sex. On Tuesday afternoon, while we spent time together beside the pool, Henning mentioned that his mother had a therapist colleague at the university who counseled trauma survivors on the side. And apparently, this colleague had told Henning's mother that most trafficking survivors acquired a deep-seated aversion for the mere concept of sexual intimacy.

While one of my most prized possessions was my vibrator.

As usual, I did not fit into the "expected" mold. My childhood abuse had rendered me a nymphomaniac, not asexual. And my *Leitaeri* was a virgin. He had admitted to it several weeks ago.

Awkward.

My brain was obviously broken, despite Philipp's attempts to repair me.

Henning called me after I hung up with Lenz on Wednesday, his deep voice infused with enthusiasm as he told me he passed the written exam. "I could have waited till dinner to tell you, but I didn't want you worrying about it."

His compassion made me smile, as always. "Now I can worry about Friday's exam instead, especially since it's going to take all morning and afternoon."

"It doesn't *actually* take that long. We have to watch the other apprentices finish their tasks, too," Henning reminded me, sounding amused.

Joy floated freely in the atmosphere that evening at dinner, as Henning and his father discussed their plans once they could officially go into business together. I slipped several bites of roast chicken to Lumpi, who wove around everyone's legs under the table, in search of samples. Eventually the cat realized I was the most generous among the humans gathered around, so he sat patiently beside my chair, his golden eyes watching my face.

Whenever I looked down at him, he favored me with a slow-blink-smile. I offered the same to him, along with tender head scratches.

Henning and I watched a game show with his parents after dinner, and then he invited me to join him outside. We walked hand-in-hand to the trampoline, climbing atop its springy surface and stretching out to observe the sky's changing hues as the sun sank toward the horizon. "Whenever I lay here like this and focus on that cord deep within, I sense this oneness with every Teuton in Erlangen. Like we're all part of something bigger," Henning said in a pensive tone.

"I feel that way when I sit on the stones by the pool. And whenever I send my spirit into the sky over the city," I admitted, remembering how awesome it was to sense the elemental magic rising from Erlangen the first time I separated my spirit from my body. "I'm so glad Erlanga chose you to be my Keyholder."

It felt so perfect to lie here beside Henning, the warmth of his fire caressing my stone through our entwined hands. "I feel the exact same way about you. And I can't wait to see what good we can do for our people, as a team."

Henning squeezed my hand, his essence glowing with devotion to a maiden shattered by her past. I took a deep breath and exhaled, praying for the courage to say what needed to be said. Keeping my gaze on the sky's deepening blue, I opened the first topic, tension awakening my element from its sleep. "Remember when you told me about that therapist your Mama knows? The one who's counseled other trauma survivors?"

"I'm reading a book she recommended right now, actually. To get insight on how to support you. I'm really lost with stuff like this."

Henning sighed, his fingers flexing on mine. My gaze followed the path of a kestrel high above, and I rubbed the fabric of my shorts with my free hand. "You've done a lot better than most people, actually."

"Not that first time I showed up on your property."

"You didn't know. You spoke out of ignorance that day. You've been so kind since then, and I just . . . there's so much I still haven't told you. I hardly know where to start." My body shivered and I edged closer to him, chilled despite the summer's heat.

"We can stay out here all night and talk. Doesn't bother me."

I pushed another heavy batch of air through my nostrils, then squeezed my eyes shut. *Just say it.* "Okay. You're a virgin. I'm not. We need to talk about sex." My entire body froze as I waited for Henning's response.

"I know you're probably not interested in sex at all. And that's completely okay. We don't have to—"

"No," I interrupted, opening my eyes to blink against the foolish tears trying to break free. "No. It's not that. I'm not like that about sex. I threw my body at Philipp over and over again. He got me a vibrator so I could take care of it myself. Even if Erlanga's soul didn't urge me to claim you as my mate, I would want to. I want to bind my stone with your fire. I've been trying to suppress it because I don't want you thinking I'm a whore. I know I'm not 'supposed' to want sex. But I do. I need it. I'm so messed up."

I sat up and pulled away from Henning, the trampoline's springs squeaking as I retreated to the far side. I hid my face behind my knees and wrapped my arms around my legs, not wanting to witness whatever expression adorned my *Leit-aeri's* face. Now he knew his Lady was an impulsive sex addict. A siren seeking a high.

"So you . . . *want* to have sex with me?" Henning sounded stunned.

"So much," I mumbled, my cheeks damp with tears.

"Okay. Wow. I just . . . Zehra . . . you know I have no experience with this." My Keyholder's awkwardness touched my spirit across the distance between us.

"But you've beat off, haven't you?" The question burst from my lips before I could call it back. Discretion? What was that?

"Um. Yes? Sometimes. In the morning." Henning cleared his throat.

Humor struck me, my tears subsiding as a new query arose in my mind. I peeked at him from over my knees, nervousness warring with curiosity. "Have you dreamed about . . . us?"

Henning's cheeks flushed beet red. He was sitting up, too, his gaze cutting quickly away from mine. "More and more often."

Delight chased the remainder of my tears away, and I plopped my legs down upon the trampoline's surface. "So you've beat off while picturing me. How sexy."

"Zehra!" My Keyholder sounded mortally wounded. He laid a hand over his eyes, his cheeks flaming.

"Let's clear the air, shall we? Since I'm sure you've been wondering how many STDs I've got." I halted there, beaming while I waited for Henning to look at me. After an extended pause, he let his hand fall to his side, cerulean fire glinting in his irises as he observed my expression. I laughed and raised my right fist.

"I've had syphilis once, gonorrhea twice, and chlamydia twice." Lifting one finger to indicate each illness, I waved my hand at him like a flag. "Thank goodness for modern medicine. No HIV and no hepatitis. Philipp had his doctor run tests on my blood twice, right after he rescued me and again three years later. I'm clean."

Henning blinked at me, a tiny smile curving his lips. "Okay then."

"Whenever you want to take our relationship to the next step, please don't be shy," I urged him, the fact that he had not yet rejected me dismantling the walls my past had erected around my heart. "I'll guide you away from things I don't like, things that would trigger bad memories. I know what works for me and I'd be honored to teach you. And I know how to please a man, too."

I favored my Keyholder with a sultry smile and crawled toward where he sat at the opposite side of the trampoline, undulating my hips along the way. Henning laughed and held up a restraining hand, though I saw his eyes tracing my curves. "To be honest, I'd rather wait until we complete the bond in marriage. To have sex, that is. My heart tells me it'd be a lot more meaningful that way."

Taking my former place beside him, I stretched out and offered him my hand. "That's how Philipp felt, too. I can wait a little longer."

Henning grinned as he wound his fingers through mine. "Then you want to marry me? Really?"

I raised my eyebrows at him, not comprehending his surprise. "Henning, I don't know who *wouldn't* want to marry you. You're the kindest, most honorable young man I've ever met." I pressed a kiss against his cheek.

He released my hand and pulled me against him, wrapping his arm around my back as we lay down to watch the stars appear. "You are a truly elegant Lady. I couldn't ask for more," he murmured, the desire in his spirit reaching out to dance with mine in the ethereal realm.

I relaxed my muscles to relish the moment, though I would have to bring up another subject before my hormones cast me atop this man. The fingers of my left hand had begun to slide down his T-shirt, seeking the hem and the skin beneath. *Get it together, Zehra. He doesn't want sex this soon. Now you need to tell him the price he'll pay if he chooses to marry you.*

I parted my lips to admit the truth but chickened out, confessing another secret entirely. "The first time we met at Pritzl, you asked if I was an alcoholic. I said no. But actually . . . that's something I still struggle with. My handler used alcohol to keep me compliant. Philipp tried his best to break me of that, but . . . well, whenever something bad happens . . . I kind of . . . drink."

Chewing on my bottom lip, I twisted my neck around to meet Henning's gaze. His eyes were gentle, supportive, so I told him more. "I drank for almost a week after Philipp died. Lenz pulled me out of it, or I wouldn't have stopped. Then I drank the whole bottle of Schnapps when I went home after you mentioned the Kebap stand. And I drank two bottles the night after you first visited me as a spirit. I don't want to do it. But it's so easy to give in . . . to use it to cope."

Henning stretched his left hand out to touch my cheek, his element's heat taking the edge off my shame. "I can help you fight it, once we're married. We can conquer that demon together."

The conversation shifted to the *Herzestein* not long after, and I resolved that I would perform the spell to receive my predecessor's gifts the night before we got married. That way I could represent Erlangen properly, when we stood before our priest at the Teutonic altar to join our blood in ritual marriage. I noted that I would like Lenz to perform our wedding and Henning agreed, saying it would be an honor to have him preside over the ceremony.

~*~

On Friday, a nightmare tore me from slumber just after five a.m. This time I had watched Wuotan himself drag Philipp's spirit into the depths of hell before turning his attention to my devoted Keyholder. The demon had whispered lies into Henning's ear and led him into perdition, blocking my screams from reaching him. I woke panting with my heartbeat racing, my element strengthening my blood in unnecessary defense.

If Henning passed his exam today, we might need to discuss completing our bond in marriage as soon as possible. Once my heart rested securely in his hands, he would gain the authority to carry me into a tranquil dream world, a place no enemies could harm us. I need never fear nightmares again, after Henning and I became true mates.

I struggled with restlessness that entire morning, trying to stay active in a vain attempt to banish my worries about Henning's exam. He would not be able to contact me until he had finished, and the endlessness of this day loomed over me in a shroud. I did two loads of laundry before my mother and brother awoke, my legs constantly twitching as we shared breakfast at the dry bar. Noticing my agitation, my mother suggested I walk to the grocery store, for we were running low on a few key ingredients.

Grateful for the distraction, I struck out toward the now-familiar section of my city, taking the long way to avoid the Kebap stand. My mother had compiled a short list of what we needed, grape leaves at the top. I planned to roll some with rice, onions, and spiced meat for tomorrow's lunch. That was my favorite out of all the Turkish dishes my mother prepared. Henning liked stuffed grape leaves, too. That meant I could make them for our family after we married.

Did Henning want to move into the Liebig mansion, or would he rather we get a townhouse or apartment of our own? I had not thought to ask him. It seemed appropriate for a Lady and Keyholder to occupy a grand property, reminiscent of centuries long past. Hopefully Henning would agree to join me in the master suite, bringing his crystals, CDs, and drawings along to make the chambers his own. I wondered if his parents would let us have Lumpi.

At the grocery store, I found everything on the list without difficulty. I had mastered the task of grocery shopping. These days I even managed to exchange a few pleasantries with the cashier on my way out. I picked up a bag of gummy bears to share with Murat just before I left, imagining his excitement.

My muses shifted back to Henning and his exam while I headed home, anxiety forming a familiar knot in my chest. I reminded myself that my *Leitaeri* was skilled and inventive. He would ace the assessment and get certified as a journeyman plumber.

As I wound my way through the side streets in my detour around the Kebap stand, my element detected a tingling sensation in the air, prompting my eyebrows to arch downward. I had not felt anything of that nature since Philipp's death, the creeping energy quivering along my skin. Why was I sensing mysticism here in this place? No Teutons lived in this area aside from my Keyholder's family.

Zehra Yildiz. A sinister voice crept into my brain and I ground to a halt, my eyes widening in horror. *You're not an easy girl to catch alone.*

My breath caught in my throat, the fingers of my right hand tightening upon my grocery bag. Only one Teuton would call me by *that* name, the one I expunged from my record on my eighteenth birthday.

The Teuton who worked with my father.

The Teuton whose dark energy prickled around me in an invisible net.

Remmi.

"This isn't the time or the place," I hissed under my breath, forcing my feet to move forward. I cast my gaze all around me, checking for witnesses.

Your little brother Murat would disagree.

I froze, the skin of my arms hardening into stone. "*What?*"

He took a quick jaunt out from under your pitiful shield right after you left this morning. Fell right into our trap. He's back where he belongs, under his dear father's watchful eye. Imagine the stories he'll tell about his time away!

Fury surged into my veins along with my stone, casting my vision in a veil of silver. I turned in a slow circle, looking all around for Remmi's spirit. I could not find him. Was he hiding in the clouds overhead?

"Don't hurt my brother." I pushed the words through my teeth, failure wrapping me in its vise. Of course Murat would eventually slip into the outside world, no matter how much my mother and I warned him against it. He was young, curious, and bored.

And now he was captured.

I'm afraid your father has little patience for a runaway boy like Murat. He wants the rest of his family back. His wife. His lovely daughter. And that powerful priest you call your mate. A Keyholder and Lady to bow before him.

I curled my lip into a snarl and set out at a brisk pace. "Never."

Pity. I'll tell your father to begin torturing the boy. Can't wait to try out my personal methods on his virgin body. Oh, I'd better warn you, it wouldn't be wise to charge into your father's territory in spirit form. If you do, he's agreed to let me cut the boy's throat.

Chapter Sixteen:
Rash Action

I hurried back home as fast as I could go without running, Remmi's wicked laughter ringing in my mind long after he finished foretelling my doom. My grocery bag and purse thudded against my leg and hip in an insolent manner, every aspect of the world around me amplifying my desperation, constricting my reason. Even the sun hid behind a thick gray cloud, and the driver of a bright blue sports car honked at me as he flew past along the main road.

Maybe Remmi had lied. Maybe Murat was still safe on the Liebig property. Maybe this was all an elaborate ruse to imprison Erlangen's Keyholder and Lady, to force Henning and me to expand my father's influence.

Did my father actually know anything about the bonds of a Teuton city? Or was this Remmi's attempt to seize more power for himself?

I could not figure this out on my own. Not with my brain awash in chaos. I concentrated on breathing steadily when I approached the iron gate, reaching out with my stone magic to open it. Philipp's shield passed over my body as I stepped onto the Liebig grounds, his dark energy welcoming its master's shining star. But Philipp's magic could not help me if my brother had fled its protection.

After closing the gate behind me and securing its latch, I stretched my spirit forth, expanding my element's sense to search the entire property. Within seconds, I pinpointed my mother's mundane spirit in the pantry. I detected no other spirits, mundane or magical. My mother and I were alone.

Murat was gone.

I fought a strong urge to sink down and collapse on the driveway before the fountain, its trickling rivulets not granting me any hint of comfort. I had brought my family here to protect them, and I had failed. Now my father wanted my mother back under his control. And his evil Teuton partner wanted my Keyholder and me to submit to his authority.

Henning would be away all day finishing his practical exam. I could not ask him for help, for fear of ruining his prospects as a plumber. Aside from that, I could not let Remmi capture both of us, especially if he meant to bend us to his will.

I suddenly realized I had wandered around the mansion to a side door, the one that led to the laundry room, pantry, and garage. Within moments, I would have to confront my mother. How much should I tell her? Did she know her son had disappeared? Had Remmi spoken to her, too?

He probably can't, because of Philipp's shield, I realized as I let myself in, trying to organize my thoughts enough to ask for my mother's advice. *Remmi said I'm hard to find alone, and that's because I've grocery shopped with Henning for the past month or so. He obviously can't get onto my property, and his outsider minions can't either, or else they would have snatched Murat a long time ago. To use him as bait. For* Anne? *For Henning and me?*

Who *was* Remmi? What did he want with Erlangen's Keyholder and Lady?

My mother awaited me in the doorway to the pantry, her eyebrows crimping as she took in my expression. "What happened?" She reached out to take the bag from me, guiding me into the pantry.

"Murat left the property," I said in a dead voice, propping my hip against the deep freezer. I laid my left hand upon its lid, images of my brother screaming provoking me to stiffen. I needed to do something about this. Now.

"You used your magic to check?" I nodded, and my mother's face paled. "He said he was going to visit the fish. That was right after you left. He couldn't be far. You were gone less than an hour."

I shook my head slowly, tiny pebbles working their way free from my eyes. "Remmi has him. He's going to torture him until I give myself up. He said if I try to rescue Murat in spirit form, he'll cut his throat."

The story spilled from me in jagged pieces, like the pebbles plinking against the tile floor. This was worse, far worse than anything I experienced as a child. All of my handler's cuties did our best to behave no matter what our abusers did to us, for we all faced punishment if anyone stuck a toe out of line. We shielded each other as best as we could. But I had failed to protect Murat. Now my father and his cruel minions would torture him until they had me. The audacious *Leitalra*.

"I have to go to the motel. To the compound," I whispered as my mother held me in her arms, the deep freezer keeping us upright. Sliding back into the old ways, I gritted my teeth and forced myself to dissociate from the terror seeking to throttle me. My brother needed the strong, brave Zehra that Philipp had believed me to be. Only that Zehra could free him from our father's trap.

"I should go, not you," my mother murmured, her spirit radiating distress. "Kemal wants me to revere him, like an obedient wife. If I go, maybe he'll let you and Henning live in peace."

"You can't go. You have to stay here." I pulled back from my mother and gripped her arms gently, meeting her gaze as I tried to explain. "It's not just *Baba* calling the shots right now. I think Remmi wants to use Henning and me to seize authority over the Teutons in this city. I don't know what he thinks he can do to a Keyholder and Lady, but my *Leitalra* magic is what destroyed the anklet."

"But that's why you *can't* go, not by yourself," my mother interrupted, tears dampening her eyes. "If Remmi gets access to your power—"

"No one can wield a Teuton Lady's magic but the Lady herself. And there's no Teuton sorcerer more powerful than a Lady and Keyholder, except for a Cursed One. I know Remmi's not dead. If he was, he could kill with his anger."

My mother grimaced, and I let go of her arms. "I can never keep up with all the types of Teutonic magic. You mean some Teutons can *kill* people just by getting angry?"

"Black Priests or Cursed Ones. Yes. They serve Wuotan himself, so it's not smart to ask them for help. But the point is, Remmi's just an everyday Teuton with everyday dark energy. Like Philipp. And earthen magic can absorb or disperse energy magic. I have to go so they'll stop hurting Murat, and then—"

The phone on the wall above the freezer abruptly rang, prompting me to jerk to attention. My mother reached for it before I could, her gaze remaining on me as she listened for a moment, blotting her eyes on her sleeve. Then she covered the mouthpiece with her free hand and said, "It's Kora. I forgot to tell you she called when you were at the store. She's bringing an apricot cake Henning's mother made. She's at the gate."

Perfect timing. "In her car?"

My mother frowned and turned back to the phone. In her heavily-accented German, she asked Kora whether she had come in her car. She nodded.

"Okay. Tell her I'll be out to get it in a second. Then I'll ask her to drive me to the compound." I snatched my purse off the floor and turned to leave.

"Wait!" My mother spat the word in Turkish before relaying my message to Kora and hanging up. Then she rounded on me, setting her hands on her hips. "You can't drag Kora into something like this!"

"I'm not dragging her into it. I'll tell her I need a ride to an appointment in the village and walk to the compound after she leaves. It's better than taking the bus and train, especially since *Baba* has people watching this property. If I ride public transportation, they might corner me and knock me out. Take me to some other bunker so I can't save Murat."

My mother heaved a sigh. "They could follow you in Kora's car, too."

"Her element's lightning. *Baba* doesn't have *that* many Teutons working for him. She can use her magic to protect herself if his minions try to hurt her."

Pursing her lips, my mother followed me as I threaded my way through the hallways to the vestibule. I would take the cake from Kora and ask her for a ride. If she agreed, I would bring my mother the cake and then be on my way. I could warn Kora to keep her element on guard, without telling her the entire story. She cared about Murat, too. She would want me to bring him home safe.

"I'm calling Lenz as soon as you've gone," my mother said when we entered the vestibule, my stone magic stretching out to unlock the front door. "I know we can't interrupt Henning's exam, but—"

I ground to a halt with my right hand reaching for the knob. "What if *Baba* knows Lenz has been poking around? On Wednesday, he said he found something useful in your blood. What if they captured him, too?"

I met my mother's gaze, but she shooed me out the door with a determined expression. "Either way, I'm calling him for backup. I can't let my daughter walk alone into a place like that, no matter how powerful she thinks she is."

Had I come across like a powerful matriarch, when I announced I must save Murat? Doubt churned in my veins along with my element as I marched down the driveway toward the gate. Kora's gray hatchback idled on the far side of its iron bars. I did not feel powerful, not at all. Was there anything in my purse I could use as a weapon? They would likely take my phone from me as soon as I reached the motel. Should I text Henning to let him know what was going on? Or would he check his phone at lunchtime and get too distracted to complete his exam?

I pushed my stone magic into my fingers, hardening my nails and extending them into short claws. Weapons that should make outsiders look twice . . . but did I want to display my magic before normal humans? Were all of my father's minions aware of Remmi's gifts? Maybe I should reach out to the stone walls like I had on my first visit to the compound. Maybe I could enchant the building to collapse on the felons inside while leaving the working women intact.

Maybe.

If nothing else, I had a switchblade in my purse.

Kora blinked at me as if I were a strange creature when I asked her for a ride to the optometrist in the village north of Erlangen. I had noticed that office on my walk from the bus stop to the motel, the day I rescued my mother and brother. "Can't you just use the one downtown?" she asked, handing me a covered dish with the apricot cake inside.

"Didn't have to wait as long for an appointment up there," I lied, accepting the cake and holding her gaze.

Her mouth twitched, and then she shrugged. "Okay then. I might expect a meal from McDonald's in return."

I could leave her a ten from my wallet after she dropped me off. No problem. When I slipped into the passenger seat soon afterward, snapping the seatbelt into place, I noticed her car smelled like cigarettes. The seat and floor looked like they had not been vacuumed in at least five years. Kora blabbered something about the latest Chanel perfume while she threw her car into gear and pulled onto the road, heading for A73. I worked hard to stifle my distaste. Philipp's cars were much nicer than this one. Cleaner, too. No perfume could mask the reality here.

"Does it freak you out to go to the eye doctor?" Kora asked as she merged onto the highway. "Tension's rolling off your spirit in waves."

Her muted blue eyes shifted toward me for a second, and I sensed her magic shimmering beneath her skin. "I've been meaning to get glasses for years." I lied again; my vision was perfect even without my element enhancing it. "Now seemed like the right time."

"Hmm. How's your little brother doing?"

I caught my breath, unsure why Kora thought to ask about him. "He's good. He's been reading Teutonic tomes lately. Pretty sure he has a crush on you." Murat might not appreciate that being out in the open, but his witchy muse ought to be aware of his interest.

Kora cackled. "I don't think my father would let me mate with an outsider."

"Then you're just leading him on? That's not very nice." Something about Kora's aura had bothered me from day one. She should know how a thirteen-year-old would interpret her persistent attentions.

"I'm just doing what my father told me to do."

An odd note in her tone prompted me to look at her, my thoughts drifting back to what little I knew about her. Kora lived with her mother, who worked with Henning's mother at the university. She had no siblings . . . and until today, I had never heard anyone mention her father.

Suspicion coiled in my stomach. "Who's your father, anyway?" My fingers flexed in my lap and my left foot nudged my purse, where it sat on the floor between my legs. Had I made a grave mistake?

Kora's next statement confirmed my fears. "The man who's using your little brother as bait." She spoke without any trace of sentiment or remorse.

My brain raced into overdrive, and I bent forward to reach for my purse. "I wouldn't do that if I were you. If your hand goes anywhere near your phone right now, you'll get a shock strong enough to stop your heart. For good."

Grinding my teeth, I straightened again, catching sight of the first sign for the exit where Befreiung's compound loomed in the trees. "I thought it'd be a lot harder to get you in the car with me," Kora went on, eyeing the highway ahead as though she had no care in the world. "Figured I might have to tie you up and dump you in the trunk."

"You're the one who lured Murat away from my home," I realized, my skin harder than usual thanks to my element's agitation. "You pretended you were his friend. Your father's torturing him right this second, and you don't give a shit."

"I didn't have a choice, okay?" Kora barked at me, defensive. She braked hard as her car carried us off the Autobahn toward the seedy motel. "I just wanted to reconnect with my father. To actually have a Papa like all the other kids. I didn't know what he did for a living. If I don't do what he says, he'll make my Mama into one of his whores. I can't let that happen to her."

Kora gave a loud sniff, her car slowing further as we neared the motel. While her excuse struck a chord within me, it hardly explained what her father planned to do with Henning and me. Why did Remmi need a Keyholder and Lady? Did he really think none of the Teutons under our jurisdiction would come to our rescue? Lenz might already be on his way, and he had connections with law enforcement—two priests on the city council.

Kidnapping the *Leitalra* should be enough cause for them to stage a raid.

I just hoped Murat and the working women would not end up caught in the crossfire.

Taking a quivering breath, I ordered myself to keep my head on straight, no matter what happened once they took me inside the compound. We had reached the motel, and Kora turned her car toward the back lot, around the motel's lobby. Another thought struck me out of nowhere.

Did Henning know that Remmi was his uncle? Did the blue-fired priest I had grown to intimately trust have anything to do with this? Had I misjudged his devotion to me? Was it all a sham?

"What does your father want with me?"

I voiced the question just as Kora parked her car in front of the compound, yanking the parking brake upward. Her eyes locked with mine for a second, a look of pity on her face. Then my vision blurred like an old TV with interference, a weird crackling noise scratching the edges of my brain. I tried to breathe but could not. And the world went black.

Chapter Seventeen:
Abject Cruelty

Realizations came over me in an indistinct haze, while my brain wrestled its way back to consciousness. I should never have trusted Kora, not at all. I should have followed my gut instinct, recognized what it meant when my brother said Philipp's shield "scratched" her. His shield repelled those with sinister intent. If Kora had been doing jobs for her criminal father this whole time, that evil would lurk within her soul, even when she wished to project an innocent aura.

Remmi's threats to Kora's mother did not matter. She could have shared her intel with the police, or urged her mother to take a long vacation. But no. She would rather help her father capture vulnerable people and force them into slavery.

She must have used her lightning to knock me out. Philipp had told me once what it felt like to be shocked by an energy element. The crackling, the distorted vision, the sense of detachment from one's body. He had also said aftereffects were common, especially for outsiders. Burns, neurological issues, hearing damage, loss of memory. Like being electrocuted by a live wire.

156

Since Kora's lightning was magic, just like my stone, my body ought to fully recover. Right? Awareness faded in and out, my eyelids not yet remembering how to open. I heard voices murmuring in German, the words not distinctly clear. Pain gouged my chest with each heartbeat, and I felt something cool touching the skin over my left breast. A dull ache pounded the left side of my throat, something worse stabbing into my wrists and ankles.

Wait. *Skin?*

What had happened to my T-shirt? My shorts? Was that really air traveling along the length of my body from head to toe?

They had stripped me naked, and I could not move.

Oh shit.

"She's coming around. Her heart rate is back to normal."

"Go. Bring the items Remmi requested."

That second voice belonged to my father. The first I did not recognize, but I felt the cool touch vanish from my chest as the man replied, "Yes, Mohammed."

Mohammed. What a joke. My father did not follow the prophet's teachings at all. Was he the only one in the room with me now? The gambling addict who sold out his family and prayed a hypocrite's prayer for forgiveness?

My eyes had not yet opened, so I reached for my element, wanting to count how many spirits occupied this place, how many ogled my naked body. A shooting pain seized my muscles the second I summoned my magic, a cry bursting from my lips as my stone did not respond. My Teutonic gifts were beyond my reach.

I was utterly defenseless.

Finally, I managed to pry my eyelids open, the bare bulb overhead casting insufficient light upon my location. Gray stone walls matching those of the hallway in Befreiung's compound. No door to be seen, which meant it stood behind me. To unhinge me further, of course. I blinked several times and squinted toward what looked like hooks screwed into the far wall.

Could I move the rest of my body yet? I tried, but my muscles still refused to respond to my brain's commands. Likely an aftereffect of the lightning. Right?

"My eldest daughter has thoroughly destroyed herself."

My father's voice, laden with repulsion, crept into my right ear. He marched around to stand before me an instant later, his dark eyes evaluating every aspect of my body. I did my own assessment at the same time. He wore a name brand gray suit and matching tie, the collar of his light blue dress shirt sharply creased, a pair of pricey black loafers on his feet. Dressed to impress—for his weekly trip to the mosque, quite likely.

Obviously, he would rather kidnap his children than worship God.

By tonight, he would be rolling the dice at one of the local casinos. Unless I figured out my role in bringing this operation down. Was Lenz rounding up a band of commandos right now? How long had I been here?

My father stepped close, reaching thick fingers out to trace the scars from my blood-transfer. He stood barely a handbreadth taller than me, his bearded jaw shifting in aversion. How exactly was I standing up when I could not control my muscles? Why did I not think of that earlier? My heartbeat quickened and I tried to look down. No luck there. Something held my legs apart and suspended my arms above my head. Probably the same "something" shooting pains into my wrists and ankles.

My father's minions were going to torture me. He may not take part himself, considering his attire, but . . . .

Having noticed my elevated heartrate and shortened breaths, my father dropped his hand back to his side and gave a low chuckle. "Yusuf transformed you into a rabid whore, thirsting for pleasure at a man's careless touch. And yet you ruined your chances for a lucrative career by taking part in a devil's ritual. There's nothing attractive about your body now, daughter. Nothing."

Hearing the name of my former handler prompted my insides to clench, my breath going out of me as horrors from years ago reared into the forefront of my memories. My father knew *exactly* what that bastard planned to do with me when he sold me. He knew. Not a hint of regret shone in his eyes.

"I never thanked you for paying off one of my largest debts." He folded his arms behind his back and met my gaze. "Yusuf gave me fifty thousand Marks for you. In cash. He made a lot more than that from your videos. A wise investment."

My own father had watched videos of his firstborn being ravaged by males. "You . . . are . . . dis . . . gust . . . ." I had trouble shaping the Turkish words, for my mouth felt filled with sand, my tongue parched by the desert sun.

"Your sister pulled a much higher price than you, though," my father went on, a pearly smile breaking across his face. "If I'd known what mafia bosses are willing to pay for their sweet prizes, I could have set myself up for life!"

What a lie. Even if my father earned millions from his trafficking, he would waste every cent at the casinos. "So your children mean nothing to you." I forced myself to speak in spite of my mouth's dryness. "You came to this country to give your family better opportunities. I remember you saying that when I was a child. Why did you let go of that for money? Empty, pointless—"

He stepped forward and backhanded me across the jaw, twisting my neck to the left. "You're the same as every female. Worthless, senseless bleeding heart. Yusuf should have taught you the *only* things that matter in this world are wealth and power. You can't get either of those things by playing fair or doing good. The darkness is too strong in this world. It always wins. You're better off shaking hands with it than tossing cute little sentiments toward it."

I tasted blood in my mouth, the ache in my neck punishing me further as my muscles and nerves began to awaken. I identified the surface supporting my back as some type of wood, likely that of an adjustable table. My instincts told me that once my father finished belittling me with words, the torture would begin. I needed to keep him in the room as long as possible.

"What about Murat?" I asked him with a sneer, running my gaze over his visage, seeking any signs of weakness. The corner of his right eye twitched, so I pressed forward. "Are you really letting Remmi torture him with his sorcery? Is he just another pawn in your game, even though he's your son?"

My father looked toward the door beyond where I stood shackled, his proud stance shifting just a bit, though he refused to give ground verbally. "He allowed himself to be poisoned by female tenderness. The fault is on your mother and you. My eldest son is a man. He understands the ways of this world." He took a step forward, this time easing himself between the right wall and my current cage.

"What do you want from me?" I demanded as he passed beyond my sight, my heart sinking into my toes. *More pain is coming. Prepare to detach yourself from this, Zehra. If you don't, the light in your spirit may dim into darkness.*

My father's chuckle reached me from some distance behind. "Oh, daughter. All I wanted was for you to leave me and my private business alone. But no, you had to embrace the devil's debauchery and become a witch, then attack my partner and confine my dear ones in a realm of foul enchantments. I have no use for you. My partner, however, has extensive plans."

The sound of a door swinging on its hinges sent tingles down my spine, and then two men shuffled around my cage to position spotlights in each corner of the wall across from me. My eyes widened as another man appeared to set up a camera, panic seizing me in its grip. Remmi was going to take photos of my torture. Maybe even a video.

He would put all of it on the internet. Maybe even tag my stage name.

The anonymity I had valued since my body blossomed into adulthood would crumble to dust. Erlangen's *Leitalra*, the starlet of hardcore porn.

Remmi had bled me before I regained consciousness. That had to be why one side of my throat retained a raw ache. He bled me without healing the wound, then bound my magic beyond my reach with the shackles constricting my wrists and ankles. Aside from poison, the only method an outsider could use to render a Teuton helpless. Something I had read in one of Philipp's tomes, never expecting to face it in real life.

What else had Remmi seen in my blood? Had he sought only for the best ways to break me? Or had he looked for the source of my wealth? All of Philipp's investments and accounts . . . had he read the passwords in my blood? Had he seen my mother's plan to call Lenz, the priest who might rouse his forces to save me?

What did he want with Henning?

The three minions setting the stage departed, leaving me exposed before the harsh glare of the spotlights and the camera's teasing eye. It was an expensive camera, a large one that reminded me of the ones zooming in on my anguish so many years ago. It was turned off, but its mere presence ruined me, my body quivering in terror. This was the end of those beautiful dreams I cherished, of guiding my people toward the light at my Keyholder's side. Remmi would distribute his videos of my humiliation far and wide, revealing Erlangen's *Leitalra* as a weak toy.

Two fingers touched the pulse at my throat and I gasped, shifting my gaze away from the camera to the man who stood at my left side, his features obscured in darkness. He wore the robe of a Teuton priest, whether he had earned it properly or not. I swallowed as he continued to track my pulse, panic rendering me mute.

Remmi breathed out a sigh, his fingers sliding downward to my collarbone, then to the tip of the scar closest to my sternum. "I am truly honored that you came to me willingly," he crooned in Teutonic dialect, his deep voice igniting a peculiar yearning in my core.

His fingers continued their exploration, tracing their way between my breasts before cupping each one in turn, a murmur of amazement passing through his invisible lips. "Your *Leitaeri* has not given you what you need, has he? I drank the craving in your blood, how desperately you long to twine your element with his in ardent passion. But he has withheld himself from you, and you suffer."

His fingers had made their way below my navel, slipping down to rub my clit once, as if in curiosity. My body shuddered, heat building within me against my will. "No. I want my *Leitaeri*, not you. Never you."

"Is that so?" Remmi slid one finger between my folds, and a pitiful cry spilled from my lips. "Your heart may not want me yet, but your body certainly does. It longs for a master who can grant its darkest desires, the ones you have yet to share with that youth who holds the keys. But they will be mine soon, and then you'll learn the wonders of deep servitude, lovely Zehra."

He gestured with his free hand, and one of the minions came forward to reposition the camera and switch it on. So I closed my eyes and ordered myself to dissociate, to set my soul apart from this place where a cruel tormentor forced my body to betray me.

Chapter Eighteen:
Soulless Villain

Cool water soothed my lips sometime after Remmi deemed himself satisfied, his minion switching the camera off as his boss showed me a gentle façade. A game I knew well, since my handler often added "aftercare" scenes to his porn. A hollow attempt to persuade viewers that it was okay to exploit little children. Not so evil, not when the abusers cuddled their victims afterward.

My parched throat welcomed the water, while my mind continued to seethe with hatred. I had closed my senses off to what Remmi did to me and how my body reacted to him. He recited the same lies again and again, but I desperately clung to what Philipp had ingrained into my ravaged soul. *You are not what they say. You are worthy just as you are.*

But the doubt that still polluted my healing resurfaced, telling me I should have known better. If I had not handed myself over to my father's vile partner, I could have spared myself this humiliation. Maybe some part of me yearned for the rush of release, no matter who provoked it. Consensual or not.

I had come here to save my little brother. I could not do that while shackled to an adjustable table with my element leashed. I had tried to reach out to the stone walls around me while Remmi ravaged my body, but my attempt sent harsh pains into my bound wrists and ankles, the stone silent to my call.

How long would it be before Lenz came to rescue me? Or did these criminals already have him locked away? Should I reach out to Henning through our incomplete bond, a feeble cry for aid? Had he finished his exam yet?

"You have been trained well to accept a master's care, Zehra." Remmi's voice tore me from my thoughts, and I cracked my eyes open to glare at him. He slurped a giant gulp from the same water bottle he had offered to me, the veil of dark energy lifted from his features. A firm jawline, colorless lips, midnight blue eyes absent of sympathy, yellowed canines disturbingly sharp, brown eyebrows flecked with gray sprouting on either side of his arched nose. His fingertips screwed the cap back onto the water bottle before setting it beside one of the spotlights. Their brilliance still hurt my eyes, baring each of my flaws.

Remmi ordered the cameraman to depart, to edit the video "as we discussed earlier." The man muttered his compliance and lugged the camera out of the room, his glance meeting mine for a half second as he passed around my right side. There might have been a hint of pity on his face. A chill seeped into my blood at the implications of Remmi's order.

He's going to upload the video to the dark web. Then send it to every online Teuton community. Email the link to the priests on Erlangen's council, to anyone with influence among our people. Erlangen's Leitalra, certified slut.

Henning would never want to complete our bond after this. Especially since we were expected to invite each priest on the council to our ritual wedding. What man would face public ostracism by marrying a whore? I had not been able to stifle all of my cries throughout the ordeal. My body had betrayed me, like always.

Another one of Remmi's minions arrived to clean the mess on the floor between my spread legs. To my surprise, the man also rinsed my thighs with soap and warm water. I longed to relax and cherish these fleeting moments of peace, no matter what would come later. But that horrid Teuton of dark energy stared at me in silence, his eyes binding me in dread. Once the floor—and my legs—were clean, Remmi ordered the man to depart. Then he stalked toward me and extended his right hand to massage my chest, right over my throbbing heartbeat.

"Erlangen's previous *Leitaeri* should have given the keys to me, not to that doe-eyed apprentice. I've brought lovely ladies to their knees for decades, a strong Keyholder who can protect our people from modern idiocy. Did you know that the number of full-blooded Teutons has decreased for over sixty years? Too many of us wish to embrace outsiders as equals, and young people no longer care about raising the next generation to honor their heritage."

He held my gaze throughout that entire spiel, concern seeming to soften his features. But then he looked down at my pussy, something he had neglected during his rampage. "Once I hold the keys myself, I'll claim you as a *Leitaeri* should. I will mold your heart until you worship me like you worshiped that elder you once called master. When we are wed, I'll grant you the privilege you've longed for since you were fifteen. To bind your body and element with potent dark energy, the height of Teutonic supremacy."

Traces of his element seeped into my muscles through his touch, agitating my heart, which belonged to another man entirely. "Do you really think Henning would give Erlangen's keys to someone like you?"

That was the longest sentence I had spoken to Remmi yet. Nothing I could say would sway him from his objectives, but I needed to understand just how he expected to seize a Keyholder's power over me. Teuton priests who accepted the keys of a city retained that authority for life. That was why Keyholders summoned prospective successors while they lay on their deathbeds.

And there was no way possible to break my connection to Erlanga's soul. Remmi could never create a standard heartbond with me. The city's essence and her departed legions shielded my heart against rape.

Remmi smirked, his laughter sending ice down my spine. "Oh, you poor, sheltered child. You ought to know that men like me couldn't care less about *how* they get what they want. Once your *Leitaeri* comes to rescue his captured princess, he'll have to defeat me to claim you."

Remmi's hand traveled upward to cup my cheek, and he leaned close to murmur in my ear, "My daughter's lightning didn't stop your heart permanently. But believe me when I say, my dark energy knows no limits."

"You're going to kill him," I gasped, terror racing along my nerves. I should have expected this. Dark energy was more than capable of such devastation. Philipp had called his element the great consumer.

"And take Erlangen's keys myself when the deed is done, since I am her child, just like you. Then I'll bend your heart to my will using sorcery your boyish crush has never thought to wield."

Remmi pressed his face into my neck and bit down on my artery before I could think of a response. His teeth tore into the right side of my throat, opposite the wound he had given me earlier. The pain was brutal, the palm of his right hand still stroking my chest as if to alter my heart's yearnings through touch alone.

Weakly, I tugged at my restraints, ignoring the agony such gestures sent into my nerves. The shackles that sealed my stone beyond my reach were imbued with dark energy, like the working women's anklets. Without my magic, I had no hope of breaking free, of clawing my way to where my brother was trapped.

By the time Remmi stopped drinking, blood loss had weakened me further, my lucidity ebbing. The bastard had bled me twice in one day without access to the heart of my soul—which meant he could not direct the blood of Wuotan's river to replace what he took. If he did it again, I might go into shock. Teuton priests knew better than to treat anyone like this, prisoner or not.

Remmi must not be a priest, even though he dresses like one, I realized, the edges of my vision blurred as I watched him wipe my blood from his lips. His dark blue eyes glittered with possibility, and he strode past me to call for someone in the hallway behind. *He probably just saw all the passwords and codes that'll give him access to Philipp's wealth. My wealth. There's got to be some way out of this.*

An atrocious howl pierced my ears from further down the hallway. It was my brother's voice, and he sounded agonized. "Murat!" I screamed out his name until my voice gave out, sobs shaking my body as I faced a strong urge to just give up. Give Remmi whatever he wanted, if he would set my brother free.

As I stood there shackled, tortured by my brother's cries, the real choice hit me square between the eyes. My father said he wanted nothing to do with me or Murat. We were here only because Remmi wanted to be the Keyholder of Erlangen. In order to do that, he must murder my blue-fired priest. Remmi would hurt my brother until I used the city bond to summon Henning to this compound.

I sensed the ethereal coverings of the bond encircling my heart, my instincts telling me if I called for Henning, he would come. The manacles barring my magic affected my element alone, not the power vested in me as Lady Erlanga. Could I figure out how to use *that* strength to break my chains? I had freed my mother in similar fashion just two months ago.

But how? With effort, I worked to ignore Murat's painful cries and focus on my epiphany that might save us both. Since my blood-transfer, I had used *Leitalra* magic only once, when I broke my mother's energy-infused anklet. Or was it twice? That may have been how I blessed the Teuton community that first time I hovered over my city as a spirit.

How could I take hold of that dominant force? I shut my eyes and sought for it deep inside, the incomplete bonds around my heart flaring in response. My eyelids sprang open as I caught my breath, a new quandary looming before me. Henning had sensed it both times I wove an enchantment as his Lady. That meant if I used that magic now, he might run to assist me.

Where he would fall right into Remmi's trap.

Tears gathered behind my eyes and I groaned. This was impossible.

"Thank heaven above you stopped screaming that name." Remmi stalked back into the chamber, and I heard objects clattering behind me when he shut the door, smothering my brother's anguish to some extent. Fury coiled in my chest as I awaited my tormentor once more, this time resolved to spit in his face. I cleared my throat, hocking up some saliva at the same time.

"You know why your little wimp of a brother was screeching like a tortured cat?" A dull-faced man rolled a TV screen in front of my cage, prompting my focus to waver. Then Remmi ran his fingers up the right side of my neck and I jerked, the shackles cutting into my wrists and ankles in the process. I turned my head to meet his gaze, wishing I could shoot stone darts from my eyes.

"He was just given the privilege of watching your unedited porn video," the man told me in a saucy voice. "You and your mother have poisoned his manhood, just like your father said. He sobs for the sister he can't save, not for himself. He barely made a sound when I worked on his body—the video you're about to watch."

I loosed a projectile of spit onto Remmi's nose and mouth as he grinned at me, inciting him to back up and scowl. "You impertinent slut! You'll pay for that." He wiped my slobber onto the sleeve of his robe, gesturing for his minion to switch on the TV.

Then Remmi forced me to watch the most abhorrent video I had ever seen. Whenever I tried to look away or shut my eyes to it, he sent a sharp jolt of dark energy into my most sensitive places, the pain searing me from the inside out. I shrieked the first time he punished me, then gritted my teeth and chewed on my tongue each time afterward. Remmi got off on others' pain. He had parted his black robe to display his snug trousers, and I saw him getting hard.

He would rape me again after Murat's disgrace played out on the screen.

I gained several seconds of relief when someone called to Remmi from the hallway and he left me alone before the TV, his robe flapping behind him. As soon as he disappeared from my line of sight, I shut my eyes, mentally reeling from what I had watched that criminal do to my little brother. Had he tortured each person who came through Befreiung's channels, too?

I could not submit to this man, if he triumphed over my *Leitaeri* and seized authority over me as Lady Erlanga. I had read that a Lady and Keyholder could not kill each other, once their bond was finalized in marriage. But maybe I could kill him before that. I could not let Remmi take control of my city, or he would lead the Teutons to ruin. He might even revoke the secrecy protecting us from outsiders in a mad grab for magical supremacy. That had happened a few times in centuries past, the devastation apocalyptic.

While I mulled over my options in the confines of my mind, a snap of energy brought me back into my bleak reality. Remmi had turned off the TV, beckoning his minion forward to cart it away. Why he did not have the spotlights removed or switched off was anyone's guess. He had likely seen how those spotlights unearthed awful memories from the depths, that last time he drank my blood.

"So tell me, lovely Zehra," Remmi began in a conversational tone, his arms clasped casually behind his back. "Are you prepared at last to call your *Leitaeri* to meet me here and face his destiny?"

The man was as hard as a rock. If I refused, I knew what he would do next. Could my body withstand his brutality again? I sent a silent prayer to Philipp's ghost, to his God, and to Lenz, a final entreaty for otherworldly courage. Then I lowered my chin to glare at my tormentor.

"Not until you send Murat back home to his mother."

Remmi threw back his head and laughed, his Adam's apple bobbing. "Oh, sweet child, don't you realize this world holds no place for him after I altered his body? Besides, we don't need him squealing to the authorities, do we?"

For the first time since I awoke in this chamber, I grinned. "He already has." Remmi's eyes widened, his proud stance faltering. I pressed on. "Your trafficking operation ends today. You'll never see the Keyholder's face until you stand before the council to be judged and imprisoned."

The door swished open behind me, and an anxious voice broke the silence. "Herr Remmi, we have a problem. The internet's down in the entire compound and the motel."

Remmi snarled and brushed the man off. "Lock the video in the vault. I'll take care of it when I've finished here." His minion mumbled an agreement and left; and then Remmi advanced, taking hold of my face. "I don't believe you. If your pals were ready to invade this place, I'd have seen it in your blood."

Pals? I curled my lip at my tormentor and said, "Get ready to watch all of your power slip through your fingers."

Remmi growled and backhanded my face again, his blow making my vision darken and my ears ring. "Lie all you want, but it's time you obey your master. See what my daughter just stole from your precious *Leitaeri's* bedroom?"

He drew his right hand forward, showing me a turquoise crystal. Alarm shot through me from head to toe as I recognized it. The *Herzestein*. He must have seen it in my blood, for Henning and I had never discussed it in public. The mysticism simmering within the crystal whispered to me as Erlangen's Lady, the successor to Frieda Dahlhausen's magic and experience.

The truth dawned on me in an instant. If I had already done what I ought to do as Erlangen's Lady—absorb my predecessor's gifts—I would already know how to summon my *Leitalra* magic. How to bring this arrogant son of Erlangen to heel. But now Remmi held the crystal and raised it high overhead, away from me.

"If you don't summon your Keyholder here right now, I'll smash this stone so you'll never reach your full potential as Lady. Weakened and forlorn, you'll be a much easier conquest for your rightful Keyholder. Me."

Dark energy sparked in his irises as he smiled a wicked smile and raised the *Herzestein* higher. All of my hesitation evaporated when he brought his hand down hard, the crystal slipping through his fingers. "*No!*" I shouted.

As the *Herzestein* shattered, Erlanga's sorcery burned within my heart, the whispers of my fallen children invigorating me. Blue flames ignited the chamber's walls and Henning appeared as a blazing spirit, grabbing Remmi by the throat.

Chapter Nineteen

The Bonded Pair

Undulating currents of magic churned in the air around me as my heart opened itself to the power of the whole. My awareness expanded, inviting Erlanga's ethereal entity to join me, to strengthen her *Leitalra* beyond mortal capacity. The fetters around my wrists and ankles splintered like the *Herzestein,* stone arising within me after a long slumber. I stretched my senses out to touch the chamber's walls, questioning whether my Keyholder's flames damaged their integrity. Finding that his element acted like Philipp's energy shield at present—protective, not destructive—I turned my attention to where my Keyholder held Remmi pinned between the spotlights.

My *Leitalra* magic had erupted like a volcano when that wicked man broke the *Herzestein,* protesting his disrespect. It had brought Henning to me instantly as a powerful spirit, the heat of his light blue flames restoring me, body and soul. I had seen him arrive despite my element's suppression, my senses enriched to taste the fear surging from Remmi's aura, as the evil Teuton lashed out at Henning's ethereal arms. Violet-black dark energy charged along Remmi's fingers in a mad attempt to loosen Henning's grip on his throat, but my *Leitaeri* did not waver, his glowing visage severe.

What has this monster done to you, my Lady? Henning's mental voice vibrated with inherent authority, the Keyholder's sway.

"*What he did does not matter.*" I responded to his query in kind, Erlanga's essence infusing my words with certain doom. Stepping forward, I halted beside my Keyholder to glower at Remmi with the eyes of the Lady he had betrayed, robes of luminous marble cloaking my naked body from his sight. "*He wishes to assassinate his* Leitaeri *and claim your sovereignty for himself, to force our sons and daughters down the dark path.*"

Henning tightened his grip on Remmi's throat and the man squeaked, his energy still clawing at his captor's vivid flames. *A slave of Wuotan, just as his past implies. This fraud has no right to clothe himself in priestly attire.*

Henning relaxed his grip enough for Remmi to cry out as the flames sizzling along the wall burnt his black robe to ash. My element had unified with that of my Keyholder, Erlanga's soul relishing our oneness even in a situation as grim as this one. Remmi croaked out some nonsense implying I had lured him into this, that I longed to pervert the city bond into tyranny over our people.

"*How dare you speak such untruths about your* Leitalra?" Erlanga directed me to rouse the stones of the wall. My lips formed a spell to shift the wall's earthen particles, which took hold of Remmi's sparking wrists, trapping his arms. "*We shall bring this man before the council to be judged publicly.*"

So be it. My *Leitaeri* leaned into Remmi's face, breathing smoke up his nostrils as he appended, *You ought to realize no* Leitalra *can lie while speaking with her city's voice. You will pay dearly for your crimes, your sins broadcast far and wide among our people.*

Remmi's arrogant expression cracked at last. He wailed, "*Mutti!*" before Henning squeezed his throat again, cutting off his breath until he passed out. His heart continued to beat beneath his shirt, stone confining his arms against the wall.

My nerves released a spoonful of their tension as I recognized that the worst threat in this compound had been neutralized. For the moment. Henning's spirit rotated around to face me, his cobalt eyes dropping from mine to the translucent layer of marble clothing my body. *Zehra . . . .*

"My little brother is here," I whispered, shivers of belated shock quivering along my skin as Erlanga's soul eased away from mine. My senses still enhanced, I knew I would find Murat in a cell further down the hallway, along with two other mundane spirits. Conflict seethed from that chamber like a pulsing beacon.

Henning reached a hand out cautiously, the warmth of his fire caressing my face. *Can you hang onto Erlanga's magic long enough to find him? No one, Teuton or outsider, can hurt you with her essence as your guard.*

The blue flames licking along the walls shrank into nothingness, as though they had not existed in the first place. They had not given off a puff of smoke, but they dimmed both spotlights in their departure. Erlanga's presence slipped further away from me, gradually relinquishing her hold upon her human avatar. Henning's concern bled off of his spirit, his right hand cupping my cheek in fiery solace. I had no time to relish his comfort or to question my fizzling vitality.

"I have to save my brother." I pushed my way past the table that had served as my torture site, preparing to shove the door open and breach the hallway. Henning remained at my side, his element reinforcing my strength.

Go. I need to give Volli an update on what's going on here. If anyone tries to harm you, I'll be with you instantly.

I stopped with my hand on the metal doorknob, my gaze locking with that of my loyal Keyholder. My staunch supporter and partner, come what may. My jaw trembled, but I nodded, acknowledging that he needed to go. Apparently, I had not been wrong when I told Remmi law enforcement would raid this compound soon. My element identified Lenz's spirit of darkness not far away, along with two other Teutons I did not immediately recognize. This was Befreiung's final day.

When Henning's spirit vanished, I gathered all of my nerve and entered the hallway, my elemental senses on alert as I headed for where Murat was being held prisoner. The spiritual cloak Erlanga's soul had granted me whispered against my skin, her essence empowering me to continue on, even though exhaustion waited in the wings. If my Keyholder returned by the time I freed Murat, I would likely collapse in his arms. The adrenaline rush was fading fast.

My nightmares would have loads of new material with which to torment me now. I needed to come clean to Henning about everything this very night, find out whether he still wanted to claim me as his Lady and complete the city bond. If he rejected me, it would drive me to despair. The cruelty I had faced today revived all of my demons, even the ones Philipp's care helped me vanquish years ago. Slut. Worthless. Broken. Masochistic. Ugly. Sex addict. Passive. Failure.

"You are not what they say. You are *not* what they say," I repeated to myself in a quiet voice as I reached a closed gray door exactly like the one belonging to my torture chamber. With an errant brush of magic, I asked the stones comprising the walls to seal that chamber's door—to ensure Remmi could not escape, even after he regained consciousness. I did not know how long it would take law enforcement to arrive, but dark energy could consume bullets. Teutons needed to take control of that wretch, anyway.

Just as I wrapped my fingers around the door handle to pull it open, another scream pierced the walls before fading into a gurgle. I yanked the door open, terror driving me forward, then stopped short as I cast my gaze over the chamber before me. An adjustable table stood in the center, its leather straps lying empty. The stench of blood inundated my nose, along with what smelled like Kebap breath. My father leaned in the far corner with his arms crossed.

And there beside the table stood my brother Faruk, his teenage face set in a stern grimace, his right hand gripping a bloody dagger. Murat's bruised body lay face down upon the cement floor, dark blood spreading from his neck. His own brother had murdered him, his father looking on without sorrow.

Faruk had stolen Murat's chance at a bright future.

"Why did you kill him?" I forced the question through my lips in German, unwilling to address either person before me in our family's preferred language. I swallowed a sob, the fingers of my left hand still wrapped around the doorknob.

Faruk met my gaze, his thick eyebrows coming together in confusion. "I defended our family's honor by purging the abomination." He gestured toward Murat's body with his dagger, sprinkling his back with extra droplets of blood.

"My son did his younger sibling a service, or else he would have stumbled through life unable to reproduce." My father ran his gaze over my ethereal clothing, a sneer contorting his upper lip.

I tugged a neutral mask over my face and stepped back into the hall, closing the door and directing the stones to seal my father and Faruk inside. So that was how both of them viewed people who could not have children through no fault of their own. Unworthy of life. I backed away from the door until I hit the far wall, sinking to the ground as the last of Erlanga's essence departed from me. Now I was nothing but a drained stone witch, broken in all possible ways.

Faruk had slit my little brother's throat, imagining he did him a service.

I had failed to save Murat. And failed to absorb my predecessor's gifts from the *Herzestein* before Remmi eliminated that possibility forever. My element contracted into my spirit, leaving me bare and cold. Erlanga's soul should have chosen some other Teuton female, not me. I tucked my head between my knees and shivered, grief turning my insides into ice.

Henning's spirit reappeared while I sat unseeing in that bland hallway, the rest of the world receding from my awareness in my *Leitaeri's* presence. *Zehra, I've found your clothes. Please let me help you get dressed.*

He lifted me to my feet, his vibrant element granting me stability as he slid my underwear back into place, followed by my jean shorts. Tears welled in my eyes when my Keyholder straightened to meet my gaze with a helpless expression, his hands proffering my black bra. I tried to force my lips to smile at him, but could not.

"My brother cut . . . Murat's throat because . . . Remmi used his . . . energy to make . . . him infertile." My voice broke in strange places, my arms hanging dead at my sides, unable to take my bra from Henning's hands. "My *Baba* said . . . there's no point . . . in living if . . . you can't . . . have kids."

Angst darkened my Keyholder's visage, and he glanced toward the closed door. *They're in there?*

"I can't have kids!" The truth burst from my lips without warning and I sank to my knees again, choking on my tears. "I can't . . . I can't!"

Henning crouched beside me and tucked me against him, his spirit holding me in security as I lamented the entirety of my life all at once. I could not fathom that the Keyholder of Erlangen would agree to bind himself with a Lady who could not become a true matriarch—a mother of magical children. My handler had taken that privilege away from me right after I had my first period, something he did to each of his cuties to prolong their "shelf life," as he called it.

He took me to a surgeon in the dead of night who cut my Fallopian tubes and burnt their edges, detaching my womb from its creative sources. I could not carry on Henning's lineage or bear Teuton children. The worst possible role model for the witches in our community.

While I wallowed in a miasma of emotional turmoil, my *Leitaeri* helped me put on my bra and my T-shirt, holding me to his chest while his free hand smoothed my tangled hair. *I'm not leaving you again,* Henning promised, his mental voice soothing all of my unmet needs. *Do you think you can pull yourself together long enough to speak with Lenz? He and his contacts are collecting a bunch of evidence from the vault right now.*

I sniffed and blotted my tears on the front of my shirt, surprised that they remained damp the entire time I mourned. My stone permeated my spirit like a faithful companion without intruding on my grief. Trying to concentrate on what my

Keyholder had said, I took a deep breath, working to sort my thoughts. Here I stood in Befreiung's compound, clasped against a spirit's chest. The cops—most of them outsiders—were on their way.

We needed to get out of here. I was in no state to speak on record about my experience this day, nor did I want to get sent to the hospital. I could learn what repercussions Remmi's brutality left on my body later.

"Lenz," I managed to whisper, leaning into Henning's embrace. How a spirit could support a mortal human, I could not even begin to explain. But I sensed no repulsion in his aura, only a gentle acceptance that fortified me, and a respectful silence that might have been reverence.

I'll carry you, Henning responded, his fiery arms lifting me off the floor. *Hide your face against my chest and close your eyes. I'm not going to travel at human speed.*

"Just don't pass through any walls," I murmured as I shut my eyes, a frail hint of humor peeking through a stony crevice in the midst of destruction. Maybe my Keyholder wanted me even though I was barren. Maybe he loved me.

As incredible speed enveloped us both for a split second, I realized for the first time that I might love him back. A deep, abiding love that stemmed from more than just Erlanga's influence. Henning was an honorable man, one who used his authority as Keyholder to stand against evil.

I longed to meet the future at his side.

Herr Schneider, my Lady is safe with me. The administrators of this place are in sealed chambers by her command.

Henning projected his mental voice to the other Teuton spirits I sensed not far from where he had come to a halt. He did not set me onto my feet, but I opened my eyes and rolled them at how he referred to Lenz. "It's *Lorenzo,*" I said far too loudly.

The next thing I knew, Lenz answered in Italian, his darkness casting a shadow over where my Keyholder cradled me against him. I blinked in confusion when I looked up at him. My stone confirmed Lenz was here in spirit form, but somehow he wore standard attire for a private investigator. Khaki trench coat and trousers, matching cap pulled low over his face, leather gloves, and what looked like a scarf concealing his features.

Your Anne *is so worried about you, Zehra,* Lenz said, reaching a hand out to touch my right cheek. *She called me in tears several hours ago. I would have come much sooner, but the bastard cast a shield over the entire property. A poor one, since my contacts and I breached it a half hour ago, but—*

"Is my *Anne* okay? She's still on Liebig property?" I interrupted him as fear raced into my blood on my mother's behalf.

Safe and sound beneath Philipp's protection. Don't you worry. But unless you're planning on giving testimony to law enforcement, you and your Leitaeri might want to disappear. Volli and two other Teutons just pulled into the parking lot. They'll hold the regular cops back until we've cleared all evidence of sorcery. There's not much, thankfully, since Remmi's shields have failed.

I cast my gaze over Lenz's outfit again, weariness muddling my thoughts. *I noticed several young women moving around the parking lot when I came to collect my Lady.* Shifting my attention back to Henning, I saw admiration reflected in his eyes. *No dark energy bound them. That means you shattered their anklets with your Leitalra magic when you summoned it down upon this compound. All of those women are free now because of you.*

My lips parted in shock as I looked from Lenz's disguised face to Henning's. "You're saying . . . when Erlanga's power called you here . . . it dissolved everyone's anklets . . . not just the shackles that were stifling my stone?"

Henning nodded, approval brightening his countenance, while Lenz gave a mental hiss. *That bastard used shackles to chain your element?*

My Lady has decreed that Remmi be judged before the council. You shall pass that directive to Volli and the others. The outsiders here shall face standard judgment. A trace of the Keyholder's influence wove through Henning's thoughts as he met Lenz's gaze. Then he glanced down at me, checking to see if I agreed.

As satisfying as it would be to toss my father and Faruk into a dungeon from the Middle Ages, I knew those two must be tried as regular humans. So I nodded, and Lenz bowed his head. *I'll see it done, Leitaeri. You two had best get going. Our comrades will be here soon.*

"Wait!" I cried out as Henning turned to go, likely expanding his senses to pinpoint the best exit strategy. "Lenz . . . did you use what you saw in my *Anne's* blood . . . to breach the vault?"

My stone assured me that the potent energy shield around Befreiung's vault was long gone. Henning and I had met Lenz before its reinforced entrance, which stood open, the door's breadth as thick as my forearm was long. Too exhausted to bother with the vault's contents, I trusted Lenz and his two contacts to collect every piece of damning evidence. His companions were also in spirit form, one of them popping in and out of existence every minute or so. My elemental sense identified them as a Teuton of air and another of earth.

Your Anne *has been inside this vault on multiple occasions,* Lenz answered, having left Henning and me in the hall to return to his work. *Her memories of its interior are quite detailed. While she doesn't know the lock's combination or how to lower the shield, a Teuton spirit like me doesn't need such things to change reality around him. Remmi's spells attempted to stop me, but my intent was much stronger, with you and your brother in danger.*

"You took out the internet?" I got the question out before visions of Murat's motionless body invaded my brain, causing me to quail against my Keyholder. His spirit offered me another breath of support, but I detected his impatience. The rest of my questions must wait until later.

No? Lenz's reply came softly, for Henning had already sent his spirit away in a blaze of blue fire. I heard nothing more as we blew by the three Teuton cops, Henning dropping a quick note in their minds of where to find Remmi, my father, and my brothers. Then the fresh atmosphere of evening brushed my skin, my lungs seizing as much of that glorious relief as they could. My body started shaking again when my *Leitaeri* paused beneath the grove of trees behind the compound, worry evident in his glittering eyes.

Do you want me to take you straight home, Zehra? The journey will likely be somewhat uncomfortable for you, since you're in your mortal body and I'll have to dart into the clouds to avoid attracting attention. Hopefully. It's still light out, so this won't be the simplest thing to do. Haven't carried a mortal human this far as a spirit since the initiation.

Henning pressed his lips together, his eyes shifting from my face to the sky. It was more complicated for a spirit to carry a living being, human or animal, from one place to another. Physical bodies could not withstand the pressure of altering location through magic and intent alone—how Lenz had penetrated the vault and how I had first sneaked into Henning's bedroom. But wait . . . .

"Did you finish the exam? Where did you leave your body all this time?"

My fiery priest grinned down at me, his essence surging with satisfaction. *I passed my exam this morning. Just had to watch my three buddies complete their assignments after that. As for my body, well . . . I kind of stuffed myself into an empty dumpster. Didn't have another option. My Leitalra summoned me when I was on my way home, so I had to jump off the bus in the middle of downtown. Threw myself into a dumpster next to a building owned by a Teuton. Pretty sure I scared him to death when I roared for him to safeguard his Leitaeri.*

The amusement replete in Henning's thoughts prompted me to giggle as his fire flared and hurtled us into the ether, my devoted priest carrying me home.

<h1 style="text-align:center">Chapter Twenty:
Commitment</h1>

"You are truly a wonder, Zehra," Henning told me while we shared dinner late in the evening, seated at the dry bar with my mother and Lenz. Upon our return, my mother met us in the back garden as my Keyholder carried me to the mansion, wrapping me in maternal comfort once we reached the sunroom. She had guarded Lenz's blackened mortal body for a long while, unable to focus on any household tasks while awaiting news of her children.

At that point, I had been unable to communicate verbally, grief overflowing in a fresh round of sobs when Henning quietly informed my mother of what little he knew. The two of us clutched each other while we mourned my brother's loss, depression tearing my soul to pieces. It seemed impossible that I would never hear Murat's voice again, never catch him sneaking up on me when I fed the fish, never bounce crazy ideas about Teutonic magic off of him. My little brother was gone forever. I had failed him.

My mother clung to me as she whispered a prayer, her tone conveying her brokenness at the knowledge that she had only one child left. The witch child. The one who renounced her heritage at the cost of her brother's life.

I would not be able to handle this without alcohol. Unless my *Leitaeri* agreed to stay with me this night. My reason had crumbled into desperation, a need for something, anything, to assuage the pain.

My mother pulled herself together long before I did, whipping up a dinner of scrambled eggs, spicy sausages, tomatoes, and peppers. She informed my Keyholder that he must attend the meal in his physical body, so she could feed him. She trusted Lenz would return in time to join us.

My mother was the wonder, a resilient matriarch. Not me.

I felt as if I hovered on a plane somewhere apart from the earth, detached in a sea of sorrow. Henning brought me into the kitchen so my mother could look after me while he retrieved his body, noting in a strained attempt at humor that he would have to speak with the Teuton who owned the dumpster before he returned to us. My mother rattled off some platitudes she had learned from religious texts, her phrases fading in and out of my brain. I tracked her movements from where Henning had placed me at the bar, my fingers digging into the stool beneath me.

My mother was my sole connection to Turkish traditions now, her maroon dress swishing around her as she moved from stove to countertop and back again. She had her hair down today, its length something I aspired to match in the future. She no longer covered it, and I suspected that had a lot to do with how Lenz's eyes admired it whenever he visited. Somewhere along the line, I would have to probe into my mother's affairs, ask whether she thought it wise to pursue a romance with a Teuton priest, when she claimed no magical blood herself.

At least Lenz's darkness was not destructive. He could let his element run free if they got intimate. A privilege Philipp— or Henning—could not claim.

Now I sat in stoic silence, stuffing food into my mouth without tasting it, while Henning retold the tale of how my *Leitalra* magic freed the working women from their anklets. I shut my ears to his praise and concentrated on my food, not wanting to see the amazement on my mother's face or the reverence on Lenz's. So what if Erlanga's power had destroyed Remmi's mystic bondage? Maybe if I had figured out how to channel it earlier, Murat would still be alive.

I did pay attention when Henning and Lenz discussed the information they had collected about Remmi. Like we had guessed, his legal name was far different—Albert Florian Morich. The man was not related to Henning at all. He had studied for the Teuton priesthood and attempted the initiation while dating Kora's mother, who ended their relationship after he failed to earn his priestly robe. She became pregnant with Kora around that time, but her ex remained unaware of his daughter's existence, having left Erlangen to seek his fortunes elsewhere.

Apparently, Remmi tried to pass the initiation again in another city, failing a second time. After that, he went to the Black Castle in the Alps to cut a deal with a Cursed One, pledging to use his gifts to serve the demon, Wuotan. He vanished into the edges of Teutonic life afterward, resurfacing only once—when Henning's great-grandfather lay on his deathbed. Remmi had tried to compel the Keyholder to give him Erlangen's keys, but the dying man refused. Henning's Omi chased the power-hungry mage out of the house using her elemental magic, and the keys were granted to Henning not long after.

So Remmi had crept back into the shadows, waiting for an opportunity to seize Erlangen's keys by force. He reconnected with his daughter, then collaborated with her to set Henning up for death, to make it look like an accident rather than a murder. But then the *Leitalra* barged into his compound and freed his partner's wife and son. Priorities changed, and my family faced the fallout.

Despite my mental turmoil, I recognized what that meant. If Philipp and I had not started investigating Befreiung's affairs before his death—and if I had not insisted upon rescuing my mother and Murat as soon as possible—Henning would have been murdered. Then the city bond would have swept me beneath Remmi's authority, Erlangen's children doomed to suffer.

Maybe I was not entirely a failure, after all. Lenz said that my father and Faruk had been carted off to the local jail to await trial, along with the minions who had not left the property before the raid. Some of them had the sense to scram when my *Leitalra* magic exploded into a seething entity; but Lenz assured us they would be caught, along with other criminals along the trafficking route. All of the servers had been confiscated, legal names of suppliers and buyers revealed.

The working women had been offered trauma support, the community opening its arms to help them integrate back into the world.

That might be something I could venture into, once Henning and I decided how to move forward as Keyholder and Lady. Maybe I could volunteer at the local shelter, donate funds to expand services to survivors. Both Henning and Lenz had mentioned the issue of domestic violence in Teuton circles, something my instincts compelled me to challenge. If I introduced myself to every witch in my jurisdiction, I could tutor the ones with feeble magical skills.

Every Teuton witch was worthy and powerful, whether her culture taught her that or not. That was a cause I could get behind, as Erlangen's *Leitalra*.

~*~

When Henning walked me to my suite after dinner, he lingered in the doorway, his fingers sliding away from mine. I turned back to look at him, and he said in a quiet voice, "If you want me to stay with you tonight, I will. But if you'd rather be alone, I can respect that, too. I'll have to meet with the council tomorrow, to figure out when and where to conduct Remmi's trial. I promise I won't let them schedule it until you're ready."

His azure eyes gazed into mine, no hint of flames enhancing their color. My *Leitaeri* embodied the perfect mixture of austerity and kindness; he wielded his authority well. I ran my gaze over the chestnut locks of hair draping his shoulders, then looked at his hands, his fingers casually tapping his belt, the keys of Erlangen hanging at his right hip.

"Stay," I whispered, returning my gaze to his face. I needed my Keyholder to sleep beside me tonight, though we could not yet bind our elements. I would have to call Philipp's physician tomorrow, ask if he could run the standard infection tests on my blood for the third time.

Henning pledged to return after packing a backpack with toiletries and extra clothing, and in his absence I retreated to the shower. The steaming water relaxed me at long last, rinsing away all traces of Remmi's brutality. I soaped my skin until the scent of wildflowers purified my muses, my spirit yearning to rest in my *Leitaeri's* care that night. After sealing my emotions off for most of the day, my heart burned to open itself to the one man it trusted, the man Erlanga chose for me.

I allowed myself to drift into a light snooze while Henning showered, my body comfortable in a tank top and gym shorts. No horrors disturbed my slumber, and when my Keyholder stepped into the bedroom, I cracked my eyes open to gaze at him in adoration. He wore naught but a pair of cobalt blue boxers, his damp hair tied back in a rumpled knot, the leanness of his torso belying the strength I knew his muscles harbored. He quirked a grin at me as he approached.

"Enjoying the show?" He stopped at the edge of the bed, glancing at the empty spot beside me as if uncertain whether he should occupy it or not.

Grinning back, I held my left hand out toward him. "You belong beside your Lady. Don't ever doubt that."

Henning beamed and climbed into bed, slipping beneath the covers before taking my hand in both of his. "I'm honored that you find me worthy."

I chuckled, closing my eyes to concentrate on our elements weaving together invisibly along our fingers. "You really want me as your partner, even though I can't have children? Even though I'm emotionally stunted, a sex addict and a recovering alcoholic? Even though I can't ever absorb your Omi's gifts, since I was too scared to do it sooner? Even though—"

Henning cut off my self-hatred with a gentle smooch, my eyes opening in surprise while he gathered me to his chest.

"Zehra, I love you for who you *are*, not the impossible standards you set for yourself," he said when he broke the kiss, holding my gaze with his. "We can walk this road together. You'll be strong when I'm weak, and I'll be strong when you're weak. I don't care how society expects us to act or to look. If I did, I wouldn't have hair like this, anyway."

He snagged a stray lock of his hair and stuck it in his mouth, prompting me to giggle at his silliness. "You got me there. But I really should have absorbed your Omi's gifts when you first told me about the *Herzestein*."

Henning blew the lock of hair out of his mouth, and it landed in my face. I snorted and brushed it away, my *Leit-aeri's* lightheartedness refusing to permit me to wallow in my failures. "Not every Teuton Lady absorbs her predecessor's magic from the stone. I know of three right now who haven't done it, not including you. That's just one of many ways to learn what it means to be a *Leitalra*. We can explore those ways together, if you'd like."

Leaning my head back on his right shoulder, I gazed into my priest's eyes, astonished at the dedication shining within them. My thoughts drifted back to what he had said earlier, warmth blooming in my chest like a vibrant rose. "You love me?"

"With every beat of my flaming heart and all the little deaths in between." He pressed a soft kiss to my forehead and my eyelids fluttered shut, happiness sweeping my uncertainties away. This was where I belonged. With Henning, my fiery Keyholder, the Teuton priest who loved me for who I was.

"Could you do something for me?" I asked as he ran his fingers through my hair, his touch relaxing me further.

"Anything."

Opening my eyes, I tilted my head up to meet Henning's gaze. "Would you bleed me?"

His eyebrows came together, hesitation creasing his face. "I'm not sure that would be good for you right now. I saw the bruises Remmi left on your throat before your *Leitalra* magic healed them. He bled you twice today. With our bond incomplete, I can't channel blood from Wuotan's river into your heart."

"You can give me some of yours first." I eyed his left hand, entwined with mine in my lap. "But . . . maybe not. I don't know if Remmi gave me any infections."

I winced, the impracticality of my yearnings crushing my bliss. The two of us needed to confront what Remmi had inflicted upon me today, but I was not ready to talk about it yet. If Henning could bleed the truth from my heart, he would understand how that wicked Teuton had modified his tortures specifically to break me. But we could not safely share blood, not even in medieval fashion.

Remmi might have given me an STD, even though he used a condom and kept his dark energy contained. Disappointment clouded my hopes, my shoulders sagging as I hid my face against Henning's chest.

He stroked my back, his chest expanding in a sigh. "Maybe I could bleed you for just a couple seconds. You want me to look for what that fiend did to you, right?"

"Yes." My body shuddered, and I clutched his left hand more tightly. "I don't have . . . the words . . . to explain . . . it was so bad. I need . . . you to know. I need you. Please."

"Okay. I'll try. But you're going to have to drink an entire bottle of water after I'm done."

"Then I'll have to pee a lot." I snickered and pulled back. My Keyholder was looking toward the minibar on the other side of the bed, likely wondering just how much water he could find inside. Its contents had changed in recent weeks thanks to him. Now it held no hard liquor—only juices, waters, and champagne. If Henning had not agreed to stay with me, I would have drowned myself in wine from the bar downstairs.

"As long as you don't climb over me on the way to the bathroom, that won't be a problem." Henning smirked at me, adjusting my position on his lap to tilt my head back against his shoulder, his hand releasing mine to gently touch the pulse below my jaw. Tingles ran along my nerves, desire escalating.

"I'll use your gut as a springboard every time I have to pee," I promised him, sticking my tongue out. His fingers pressed more firmly against my pulse, and a groan built within me, my eyes closing of their own accord. "Hurry up, or I'm going to want way more than a little vampire bite."

Henning snorted. "You silly witch. I'm directing your blood flow to fill this artery, so I don't have to drink for long. You're not permitted to pass out on me."

"Yes, *Truhtein*." The response fell automatically from my lips, the heat of his fingers departing from my flesh. Moments later, his teeth sank into my skin and my body released its tension, a moan of pleasure breezing from my soul. *Safe and protected. Let this priest see all of my fears, share in all of my struggles.*

Henning drank my blood for too short a time, his magic knitting my artery together before a stray drop escaped. The experience was incredibly erotic, the steady beat of my heart pleading silently for the hands of a priestly master to shield and preserve it, to instill it with the love it craved. We needed to finish this bond between us soon, for Erlanga's desires amplified mine.

If it always felt like this to be bled by a priestly master, it made perfect sense that most consorts begged for such things. The tomes described this, and now I understood. This was how my *Leitaeri* could truly know my heart.

"Drink, Zehra." Henning's deep voice eased into my brain, summoning me back to cognizance. I opened my eyes to find myself resting in his lap, a bottle of mineral water held to my lips. My gaze traveled to my Keyholder's face and I opened my mouth, inviting the water to refresh my spirit.

I drank, and relief lightened Henning's grim expression. "Finally. I was starting to think you had disobeyed your *Truhtein*."

He supported the back of my head with his right hand while I drank, my forehead crinkling at his declaration. The amusement in his eyes assured me he meant it in good fun. But my spirit sensed his despair, his reaction to what he had seen in my blood. When he pulled the lip of the bottle from my mouth, giving me a short reprieve, I swallowed and leveled him with a glare.

"I would *never* disobey my *Truhtein*." I folded my arms across my chest and narrowed my eyes at the priest who held me in his lap. The inexperienced youth who now knew how damaged his *Leitalra* truly was.

"You play a dangerous game, my precious Lady." Henning uttered the sentence in Teutonica, his gaze dropping from my eyes to the place where my heart beat defiantly against my ribcage.

His meaning abruptly became clear. "Lucky for me, Erlanga's soul chose an honorable man to claim the keys to my heart," I responded in Teutonica, letting my hands fall into my lap and shifting my attention to the half-full bottle.

Henning brought it back to my lips and I drank, focusing on his countenance as the darkness crept along his features. "No words . . . in any language . . . would be enough to describe . . . how angry I am at that man . . . at every man who hurt you. Zehra, you'll never carry any of this alone again. I promise you that. We will bring that wretch to justice, and he'll wish he never shook hands with our demon lord. If anyone taunts you for being unable to have kids—*not* your fault—they'll answer to me. And we'll be married as soon as you want. I saw how deeply you've suffered, and I'm so sorry. I never imagined . . . but I'll make it right. We'll heal together in our dreams. I promise."

His sincerity clasped my spirit in reassurance, and I shut my eyes to revel in the wonders of devoted love, my own spirit brimming with gratitude. I swallowed the last of the water, and Henning released me to set the bottle atop the shelf over the minibar. I dropped my head back onto my pillow and stretched, grateful for the privilege of sleeping at my Keyholder's side. Whether my demons came for me in my dreams or not, I would wake beside my fiery priest, my vital defender.

"I think we should get married at dusk on the same day we judge that fiend before the council," I said when Henning eased his body toward mine beneath the covers, inviting me to rest in his arms. "It just seems fitting, to conquer Remmi and seize our greatest triumph that same night."

"Hmm. When you put it that way, I have to agree." Henning tucked me against his chest and kissed my hair. "How soon do you think you'll be ready for such a big day?"

I considered for a moment, his gentle caresses luring me into a trance. "One week from Saturday. The seventeenth of July. All I need is a dress that emphasizes my element, so I'll have to see what I can find in the designer catalogues."

"I'm thinking marble. Or better yet, some type of gemstone."

"I like how you think." I nuzzled Henning's chest, planting soft kisses upon his muscles. He smelled like a campfire crackling in the forest, alluring and warm. Erlanga's soul hummed with pleasure in my heart, augmenting my commitment to this fiery Keyholder.

"I can't believe you called me *Truhtein*," Henning murmured in a gravelly voice, sounding half asleep.

"You earned it," I told him, reaching up to mold my lips with his. He kissed me back, his arms tightening around me, our elements blending into one as we memorized each other's tastes. A low groan rumbled in Henning's chest, and then we ended the kiss, his eyes not reopening.

"My master," I whispered to him in Franconian dialect, the word feeling wholly right to me. Then I snuggled against him and allowed my exhaustion to win the fight, confident in my *Leitaeri's* closeness.

My bladder awoke me only once that night, and I remembered to exit the bed on the far side, not wishing to disturb my Keyholder's slumber. Afterward, I cuddled close against him again, his left arm draping itself subconsciously around my waist. Reassured of his devotion, I sank into another repose, thankful that my demons had left me in peace thus far.

This time, my dreams led me into a woodland reminding me of the Liebig grounds, a natural waterfall trickling into a tiny brook that chattered over pebbles in its personal quest for the sea. I walked beneath aged oak trees amid patches of wildflowers, sultry aromas on the breeze rendering me carefree and content. Until I caught sight of a young man leaning against an oak at the brook's edge, his black hair slicked back from his face, his blue-gray eyes oddly familiar.

"You've surpassed my wildest expectations. I'm so proud of you."

My eyes widened and I stopped about a meter away from my unexpected companion, my brain working to rationalize what I saw and heard. The man spoke with Philipp's voice, but he looked much younger. *Of course.* I grinned, more to myself than to him. "This is a nice dream."

The man raised an eyebrow. "Have I ever looked like *this* in your dreams?"

Chapter Twenty-one:
A Peek at Eternity

Philipp's remark gave me pause. I looked him over again, this time noticing his clothing and carriage, along with his features. He wore a crisp pair of dark blue jeans, a collared short-sleeved shirt of black brushed with shimmering violet, and a pair of upscale black sneakers—the exact pair he always wore when we played bocce with Lenz. He reclined against the tree trunk casually, his right thumb settled in a pocket of his jeans, his left palm resting against the bark. His haircut was the same one he sported in my memories, the obsidian grandeur of his locks reflecting the ambient sunlight.

He appeared to be in his early thirties, at most, but I had seen photos of him from those days. The 1960s. He had worn his hair differently then and sported a mustache. This manifestation of Philipp resembled the clean-shaven magnate who rescued me from a perverted handler . . . but much younger.

Would my subconscious conjure up such a vision? In my dreams, Philipp usually appeared elderly, like I remembered him. Or like a flickering spirit of dark energy that had already chosen defeat, dying in Wuotan's river.

Dread tainted the tranquility of this glade. "Am I dead?" I looked down at myself, patting my body to ensure it felt mortal rather than spiritual. I wore a sinuous gown I had never seen before, satin veils cloaking me in sparkling sapphire. A row of crystal buttons rose from its waistline to the décolletage, which plunged between my breasts, baring the upper scars from my blood-transfer.

I looked from the scars to Philipp's youthful face, my reason not yet having caught up with where we stood and how we were together. "I assure you, you're certainly alive. Check that essence abiding in your heart. Erlanga's soul would have freed you if you'd left the earthly realm permanently."

I tilted my head at my companion, my braid tickling my back as I did. One normal thing in all of this weirdness—my hair was pulled back in a braid. "Left the earthly realm permanently. Does that mean we're not on earth right now?" I did sense Erlanga's soul inside my heart, along with those silvery threads that bound me to her Keyholder.

"We are not. You'll be going back once we're done here. But I have a divine court to return to, of course." Philipp smiled, his spirit exuding pure peace.

"Tell me about your heaven," I requested, curiosity superseding my dread. Philipp implied it was safe for us to be here, that I would have no trouble returning to earth later. That meant I needed to learn all I could now, in the brief time we were given.

"'My' heaven. It's everyone's heaven, Zehra." The sound of my name on his lips sent a rush of awe through me. I took two steps forward, wondering if we were permitted to touch in this place . . . or whether he would permit us to touch. A deep urge to embrace him coiled within my spirit; but I curbed my desires, my fingers plucking at the veils of my dress.

"Come. Let's sit by the brook, and we can talk." Philipp straightened and held out his right hand, an invitation.

His dark energy tingled along my skin when I took his hand, his aura radiant with fondness. I stared at his face as he led me forward, amazed at the familiarity there in contrast to his youth. His hand firm against mine, I sensed no danger, his spirit welcoming mine in the atmosphere around us. Whether this was a dream or something else entirely, I would cling to it as long as possible.

When we reached the base of the waterfall, Philipp sat in the grass without hesitation, no hint of discomfort in his bearing as he situated himself. "I think these are becoming rather unnecessary, wouldn't you agree?"

With an impish grin, he gestured at his shoes as I sat beside him, leaving a proper gap of space between us. "I can take them off for you," I offered, recalling how his feet used to swell after a long day, how I would free them from the confines of his shoes and swath them with slippers.

"Ah, no need to baby me in this place. I'll take care of them myself. You've got your own pair to deal with, it seems."

His response took me off guard, but I turned my attention to my own feet, currently hidden beneath my airy dress. I had not bothered to notice my footwear. Poking them out from beneath the sapphire veils, I discovered I wore a pair of slippers that looked as crystalline as the buttons on my dress. They fit me perfectly, not having rubbed my ankles at all while I navigated this enchanted forest.

I took one of the slippers off and weighed it in my hand. "If I'm Cinderella, are you the handsome prince or the guardian about to die on a journey?"

Grinning at Philipp, I set my slippers upon a smooth boulder beside where I sat. He laughed, the sound dancing along my eardrums in a sweet melody. "I think we both know the answer to that. You have a new *Truhtein* now. A young man who carries his responsibility with honor and grace."

Philipp tossed his shoes and socks across the brook, and they vanished into nothingness on the far side, confirming the wizardry of this place. I wrinkled my eyebrows as my brain came to terms with that, my companion dipping his bare feet into the brook with a delighted sigh. Whatever this was we had right now was not meant to last. Devotion stirred within me when Philipp mentioned Henning, the fiery priest who had seen my heart and accepted me anyway.

"Did you decide to die in Wuotan's river . . . so I'd have the opportunity to become the Lady of Erlangen?" The puzzle pieces had begun to fall into place, but my inquisitiveness remained.

Philipp leaned back in the grass, propping himself up on his hands as his feet swayed in the waters. He turned his head toward me, where I sat at his right side, my feet tucked beneath my dress again. His blue-gray eyes studied my face for a long moment, our elements swirling together in the glade, celebrating our reunion. A hint of regret darkened his brow.

"I was dying already by the time I gave my blood for you," he admitted. "I should have been forthright with you about it, but I didn't want you to bear that burden along with your own. Frieda told me about Henning, of the goodness of his heart and his desire to combat the darkness Wuotan casts over our community. A notion grew within me that I couldn't ignore, the notion that Erlanga might choose you as our city's next matriarch. In my mind's eye, none of the other Teuton witches could match you for splendor and grace. The last time I spoke with Frieda while we still walked the earth, I knew I'd have to free you in Wuotan's river, or you would have tied yourself to an aging man with no future."

The tragedy in his eyes wrecked me, his remorse rousing the emotions I had long hidden. I pulled my knees up and wrapped my bare arms around the veils of my skirt, the truth spilling in a deluge from my heart. "It shattered me completely . . . when I saw your spirit dissolve . . . in Wuotan's flaming blood. I *felt* your energy . . . felt it when our fingers touched. I tried to drink the pain away . . . but it's still there . . . it's still there. *Why* did you leave me? *Why?*"

"Oh, Zehra, I couldn't stay with you. I couldn't!" Philipp's arms bound me in a tight embrace as my grief clawed to the surface, mingling with betrayal in loud sobs. He rocked me against him while I cried, his hands gently massaging my back. "Our relationship was never healthy. You clung to me like a god, something I could never be. You're destined to be strong and triumphant, not a subservient damsel who worships her *Truhtein*."

With effort, I forced myself to stop crying, for I ought not to waste time while we were here together. The frankness of Philipp's words sliced through me like a knife, and I buried my face in his smooth shirt. "I've already failed," I mumbled, my desperation during last night's bloodletting saddling me with embarrassment. "I'm not strong, not like I should be. I told my *Truhtein* . . . Henning . . . I told him I'd never disobey him. I begged him to bleed me like a needy masochist."

"Hmm. You can reserve that part of your heart for Henning alone. There's no shame in such yearnings. No matter what you pledge in the heat of passion, I don't think you'd allow him to drag you onto the dark path. Consider your reaction to that fraud of a priest. There's nothing wrong with being vulnerable before the man who guards your heart in honor."

What he said made sense, but the worthlessness drilled into me during my childhood barred me from fully accepting it. "I never wanted to be Lady Erlanga," I confessed, lifting my face just enough to gaze at the rivulets splashing over the waterfall. "I wanted to be Zehra Liebig. Your wife."

Philipp released me from his embrace, giving my shoulder a solid pat, an indication for me to return to my previous spot in the grass. "I'll admit I nearly faltered, when I saw you rushing through those currents toward me, fire sizzling along the edges of your spirit. You glowed like a perfect diamond, the essence of earth's most powerful element. The reflection of the light in your heart, my shining star. I almost stayed with you, though it would have damaged us both."

He took my left hand in his right, his face repentant as he looked at where our fingers twined. I blinked the last of the tears from my eyes and squeezed his hand, his apology lifting part of the shroud that mired me in mourning. "Tell me about heaven. Please," I asked, bringing the subject back around. I wanted to be sure he was happy in the celestial realm, that he had found a place for himself among the angels and the human souls already in residence.

Radiance returned to his countenance, and he smoothed his thumb across my wrist. "It is beyond anything I could have imagined, while I lived with you on the earth. The lands are so vast and exquisite, the mansions grown from living stones and plants, flowers and fruit abundant. The perfect place to explore and craft the wonders sin polluted for people on earth."

I pulled my knees up again and laid my head upon them, gazing at Philipp in fascination. "Is your mansion bigger than the Liebig property on earth?"

He smiled, lifting his gaze to admire the sky. "Size doesn't matter in eternity. There are no limits to the glories you can explore. My home is the perfect size for me. And Lenz has a cozy place springing up just a short walk from mine." Philipp turned his face to look at me, possibilities glittering in his eyes.

"Do you think . . . my home . . . won't be all that far away from yours?" Part of me was nervous to ask that question, especially after what Lenz had said about his friendship with Philipp. The two of them might not want me bothering them in eternity.

"You and Henning own lovely places that beautify themselves each moment. We share the lush grounds in between, and Lenz's recent muse has taken root not far away. I'm afraid you're going to have to share."

Philipp grinned at me, dark energy glinting in his eyes for the first time since we rendezvoused in this place. "I can share," I assured him, joy smoldering within me at the prospect of sharing eternity with my dearest friends. Philipp and Lenz, Henning and my mother. But what about . . . .

"Have you . . . happened to run into . . . Murat?" My body quivered a little as I stifled memories of his brutal end.

"Last I knew, he was celebrating with your sister, Leyla. Their homes aren't as close to mine, but distance means nothing in eternity. You can travel like a spirit there, transforming reality around you." Philipp winked at me, his feet playing in the brook once more.

"Wow," I whispered, entranced by this wondrous peek at the celestial realm. "I can't wait until we're all together there."

"Don't hurry along. The earth needs my shining star a while longer," Philipp advised, releasing my hand and leaning back into the grass.

"Yes, *Truhtein*."

"Ah, Henning hasn't cured you of that yet?" My companion chuckled, his gaze on the waters before us. "No man can serve two masters, Zehra."

"Good thing I'm a woman," I shot back, straightening and dipping my own feet into the brook. Its waters invigorated my spirit.

Philipp burst out laughing and I joined him, delighted to poke fun at my odd tendencies with one of the two males I thoroughly trusted. He chided me for my defiance but assured me I would grow into my relationship with Henning as the years went by. He noted that he had watched over me from time to time since his passing, keeping his distance in an effort to let me find my own way, rather than simply trailing along his coattails. He would be in attendance at Remmi's trial and at my wedding, although mortal eyes—physical or spiritual— could not see celestial beings.

"I really appreciate you watching over me," I said, burrowing my toes into the sand of the brook's bed. "And I understand why you've let me work through everything by myself. You've been teaching me to do that ever since you rescued me. Your energy shield is still active, even though I don't know how it connects with that generator in the root cellar. It makes me feel safe at home. Thank you for that."

Philipp smiled, trailing the fingers of his right hand along one of the veils comprising my skirt. "That's actually not my doing. You're the one who powers the dark energy that shields Liebig property."

"Me?" I squeaked, astounded.

"Yes, you. I wove a spell upon you in our last months together, then sealed it when you clasped my hand in Wuotan's river. The dark energy protecting your property answers to you alone, without draining your natural vitality. As a witch of stone, you draw power from the earth itself, so no enemy of yours will ever be able to breach that shield." Philipp favored me with a look of respect.

I stared at him, bewildered. "Can I summon dark energy myself, then? Or just to power the shield?"

"Few Teutons train themselves to invoke or manipulate elements far afield from their own. But if you'd like some instruction on that, I'd advise you to meet with the forest witch Henning knows. Her name is Lady Ilsa, one of the cleverest witches I've ever had the privilege of befriending. She could share some of Frieda's endeavors with you, help ease your mind about your destiny as *Leitalra*."

"Really?" That sounded like a fairytale come true.

"Really." Philipp nodded firmly, his expression austere.

"Wow. Lady Ilsa. I'll have to ask Henning about her in the morning."

Philipp hummed in agreement, and then the two of us sat in silence for a while, enjoying each other's company. Our elements still drifted in a joyous dance around the glade, the brook's waters invigorating me for my journey ahead. While Philipp might not be there to guide me, I had my devoted Keyholder, the priest I would name my husband in just one week. Then I could finally discover the glories of mating as *Leitaeri* and *Leitalra*, the victory of intimacy mingled with love.

My gaze shifted back to where Philipp lounged at my side, traveling along the planes of his face to his shoulders and torso. Despite Erlanga's bond pulling me toward Henning, my desire to truly know Philipp had not faded. Especially in this peaceful glade with both of us dressed in finery, our mortal faults polished away as our elements whirled in unity. He would refuse me if I asked. I should keep my hormonal longings to myself.

"So you still crave the elderly freak who hid you away from the world like a pirate's treasure." Philipp dropped that bomb in an amused tone, his attention on the waterfall.

"I'm . . . sorry?" My cheeks flamed hot and I dropped my gaze to my toes in the brook. "I know you don't want my body. I'm not going to—"

"You'd be surprised." His eyes slid toward me, taking note of my dress' tight bodice, the veils draping my curves.

My lips parted in shock and I glared at him, hurt blazing through my chest. "If you've wanted my body all this time, *why* didn't you let me meet your needs? You know I'm fully capable. We've talked about it!"

"Zehra, you were a *child!*" Philipp's black eyebrows slanted downward as he turned to face me. "Your body didn't interest me at all when we first met. It got more and more difficult to say no every time you offered to please me as you grew into a woman, an utterly gorgeous maiden. If I hadn't hoped for a grander destiny for you, I would have pushed through the blood-transfer and taken you that night, binding your stone in my dark energy and forcing you to cry out my name. I would have done it. But you deserve so much more than I can give."

Disappointment cooled the heat raging in my blood along with my element. I stared down at the sapphire veils of my dress, their color muddled by my tears. *Are you a glutton for punishment, Zehra? Don't ask him. Don't ask.* "If I could have you here, in this place . . . it would be enough. I know we'll probably . . . never meet again until I die . . . but I wish . . . I wish."

I shut my eyes against my tears. A moment later, Philipp's thumb lifted my jaw, his touch as tender as always. "Look at me, Zehra." One of my tears escaped before I could squelch it but I did as he asked, violet-black enhancing his irises. My desire intensified, my heart rate increasing in desperate hope.

"Would it really be enough for you, to bind ourselves fully in this place?" His thumb glided upward from my chin to trace my bottom lip—the most intimate gesture he had ever offered me. My heartbeat escalated further.

"If we don't . . . I'll be wondering about it for the rest of my life," I whispered, my breaths shortening as he stared into my eyes. My hands had crept up to clutch his shirt, yearning to touch the muscles underneath.

Philipp chuckled, his lips spreading into a wicked grin. "We don't want that, do we? Would you have the master, or the equal?"

Hunger simmered in his eyes, and I fell apart before him. If his hands had not taken hold of my upper arms, I would have sunk to the ground to grovel. Instead, I managed to gasp, "Command me, Philipp. Please."

His lips met mine seconds later, and I shut my eyes to concentrate on the torrent of sensations consuming me. His fingers worked on undoing my bodice as we kissed, our tongues relishing the love and craving we had leashed for years. He lifted me bodily out of my dress at the same moment his sleek shirt hit the ground, his mouth releasing mine as he pillowed my back against our clothing. His fingers had already found my nub and I whimpered, my body shuddering.

"So deliciously wanting," he purred, his fingers leaving me behind to free himself from his jeans. I would have done that myself—in fact, I *should* have—but my body had turned into a quivering heap, tingling all over at the prospect of true union. "You're going to have to control yourself, my shining star. Don't need you shattering far ahead of your master."

"Yes, *Truhtein*." I opened my eyes to look at him through a veil of elemental silver and black lashes. A growl rumbled in his chest as he set himself between my legs, dark energy charging along his skin. The size of his length made me tremble all over again. How long had it been since I had last taken something like that? Five years? Longer?

Never. I had never taken a man who loved me into myself.

When we lay in each other's arms beneath the sunlight afterward, needs wholly sated and spirits fully joined, I played out the experience in my mind over and over again. In grim determination, I demanded these new memories supplant my previous wounds, the thousands of times beastly males had assaulted my body. Philipp's love swept me away in a cloud of satisfaction, dark energy empowering my stone with the grandeurs of magic and adoration. He had ordered me to come, just like I asked . . . and I had complied, our cries cementing the truth I had always known.

I loved Philipp Liebig. Even if my loyalty to him was unhealthy, tainted by my past, he had elevated me from victim to victor, a witch who might be willing to accept everything about herself after all. While Erlanga's soul assured me, even as we rested together, that Henning Glossner embodied my destiny, I could not have granted my heart to him freely without knowing this man first.

"Is it enough for you, my shining star?" Philipp asked me after a time, his right hand tracing my spine as I lay atop him.

Lifting my face from his chest, I met his gaze, marveling at the love shining in those familiar blue-gray eyes. "It is enough. Thank you *so* much for sharing your love with me, Philipp. For showing me how wonderful it can be."

"Your *Leitaeri* will show you far more than this." Philipp smiled fondly at me, then caressed my lips in a gentle kiss. I shut my eyes as I drank his goodness one last time, a final memory to carry with me until we met in eternity.

We rose to our feet shortly thereafter, leaving our clothing behind upon the grass, since Philipp assured me it would vanish once we went our separate ways. I looked around at the oaks and multicolored flowers sprinkling our glade with life, then ran my gaze upstream along the brook's bed to the waterfall. It stood just a bit taller than the two of us, mosses growing along the boulders that formed it. An idyllic place to come together with the man who shaped me into a strong witch.

I breathed out a sigh and squeezed Philipp's hands, raising my head to meet his gaze, while we stood facing each other before the chattering brook. "Thank you for bringing me here. Whether this was just a dream or something more, it helped me more than you can imagine. Now I'm not afraid to give myself to my Keyholder, thanks to you."

Philipp bowed his head, appearing humbled. "Don't forget to have Henning introduce you to Lady Ilsa. She'll guide you along your way."

"I won't forget. But I have one more question." My intuition told me I must return to Liebig property soon, to awaken beside my Keyholder and greet the new day. But something else had occurred to me, my eyes narrowing in thought as I studied Philipp's face.

"The internet went out at Befreiung yesterday, before Remmi's minions got a chance to put my torture video online. And the energy shield around the vault failed, too. Lenz wasn't sure how either of those things happened. Was it you?"

An accomplished smirk brightened Philipp's countenance. "You caught me. Even though I try not to interfere with earthly events, I refuse to permit anyone to dishonor you that way. Some of heaven's residents send their loved ones cardinals or pennies. But I prefer actions that make a real difference."

"I love you, Philipp," I whispered, folding my arms around him.

Chapter Twenty-two:
Ancient Justice

The subsequent week passed in a whirl of activity. Aside from choosing a wedding dress for myself and getting it sized, my mother took charge of arrangements for the ritual, from the stage to be set beside the fish pool, to the refreshments offered in the dining room. Lenz would conduct the ceremony for Henning and me, and he brought some of the necessary items onto Liebig property throughout the week. A hewn post of oak to be raised beside the pool. A flask of water from the Regnitz River. A branch from our city's only silver oak, to allow our marriage to be blessed by the tree fairies.

I unearthed Philipp's old version of *Der Weg Teutonisch*, the one containing every Teutonic spell written out in dialect. Lenz could read the wedding vows from there, along with the traditional statements describing the duties of husband and wife. Henning and I decided to use the Liebig family dagger to unite our blood, for he expressed an interest in taking my surname along with his. That gesture touched me so profoundly that I agreed to do the same. Herr and Frau Liebig-Glossner, the Keyholder and Lady of Erlangen.

Henning and I planned to take a long honeymoon in the Tyrolean Alps next spring, so we could get to know Lady Ilsa and her husband, Horst. Along the way, we would visit four other Teuton cities—Regensburg, Passau, Salzburg, and Innsbruck—to forge relationships with our fellow Keyholders and Ladies. While Henning already had a good friendship with Nürnberg's Keyholder, I hesitated to explore that further, thanks to my murky history in that city. I also wavered about visiting München, the place where my father prayed to a deity he did not serve. Maybe in the future I could conquer those fears, but I had no wish to stain our first journey as a couple with dark memories.

When she spoke with me on the phone Friday that week, Lady Ilsa gave me some tips to help me delve deeper into my connection with Erlanga's soul. I related some of the damning evidence the priests had pulled from Remmi's blood and from the documents in the vault, admitting that the notion of that fiend languishing in the dungeon did not sit well with me.

"He studied sorcery with a Cursed One," I told her, uneasiness churning in my blood at the prospect of Remmi gaining the trust of other Teuton prisoners—potential accomplices. "Erlangen's priests haven't had any problems with him yet, because they've stifled his element with dusky spurge. But not all sorcery stems from the elements. My *Leitalra* magic is something else entirely. My instincts have been warning me he might be able to invoke dark spells, even trapped in the dungeon."

Lady Ilsa sighed on the other end of the line. "You're not wrong about that. Black Priests walk the dark path and use unseemly methods to weave enchantments. All Teuton prisoners have their elements suppressed, rendering them unable to reach the spiritual realm. But a prisoner who knows blood magic could gain the opportunity to charm a guard into compliance through regular bleeding."

"Or find out how to escape, if they look for that in a guard's blood," I added, my disquiet forming a brick in my stomach. "Remmi has to be put away for life, the priests have agreed to that. But if he ever manages to escape, he would go after Henning and me again. The shield around my property can stop him, but the two of us can't just hide away from our people."

"If the man does get out, the guards should inform you and your *Leitaeri* immediately. But you might have another option, if you're willing to channel your city's essence in front of the council."

Erlanga's soul seemed to hum softly in agreement, as I held the phone to my ear. "The trial is set to happen tomorrow morning at the Teuton meeting place of Erlangen. It's open to the public, so it won't be just the council there. One of the priests is going to cast a shield so outsiders don't stumble into it. But you think if I ask Erlanga's soul for aid, she'll cut Remmi off from any magic?"

"All Teutonic magic stems from the blood, first and foremost," Lady Ilsa reminded me. "Since Remmi is Erlanga's son, you have the authority to take that from him. You'll need to present yourself carefully, if you choose to do such a thing. It's said to be frightful to witness. Anyone in attendance will likely be terrified of crossing you afterward."

"That might not be a bad thing," I said, though I knew that would make it harder for me to connect with the witches in my community. As long as Henning's friends did not shun me, they could help me smooth things over. They would all attend our wedding tomorrow night—Gabi and Lukas, Bianca and Oliver, and Dennis and Till.

The council had already sentenced Kora to two years in the dungeon and four years of community service after that. She had been found guilty of luring and kidnapping a minor—my brother—along with a handful of others Befreiung had bound into prostitution. She had pleaded hollowly for mercy, declaring that it was all her father's fault; but her mother approved of her punishment, stating that Kora had sought her father out against her advice. New priorities would be instilled in her during her confinement, guiding her back to the proper path.

The road to justice would be much longer for my father and Faruk, of course, since their cases must be processed and sentenced in the German courts. My mother and I hoped to find the courage to attend their trials when the time came. Henning and Lenz both pledged to support us, whether we chose to observe their punishments or not.

~*~

I woke shortly before five on Saturday morning, my nightmares having torn me from sleep four times that week. My Keyholder's presence in the bed soothed me to some degree, but I knew my trauma would not release me in slumber until we finalized our bond that evening. This was the last morning I would ever have to stand before the bathroom mirror, counting my breaths and begging my heart rate to slow. I would never see my little brother's prone form in my dreams again, hear Faruk's dead voice declaring he had salvaged his family's honor.

This night, I would grant my heart to Henning, and I would be free.

But first, I must ensure Remmi could never harm anyone again, Teuton or outsider. Once I got my panic under control, I slipped outside to the pool, situating myself upon my favorite stone and inviting Erlanga's essence to awaken within me. As my spiritual senses expanded outward, identifying and blessing every Teuton under my jurisdiction but one, the city's soul assured me we would handle Remmi together. She advised me to wear my wedding dress to the trial, since its design signified the blending of blue fire and solid earth.

After Henning awoke, we scarfed a quick breakfast of buttered bread and coffee, my mother having promised to cook a hearty meal for us to enjoy when we returned from Remmi's trial. As an outsider, she was not permitted to attend. Lenz, however, had vowed to describe the entire event to her sometime this afternoon, while they made final preparations for the wedding.

While we dressed ourselves for the trial, I shared Erlanga's intentions with my Keyholder, hoping he would not order me to restrain our city's vengeance. "So you're going to take his Teuton blood," Henning said in a stoic tone as he adjusted the belt of his priestly robe, the keys of Erlangen clipped to his right hip. "Good."

"You know about that practice?" I shot a glance in Henning's direction, then turned back to the full-length mirror in our bedroom, ensuring my dress garnished my body appropriately. It was of dark blue satin splashed with a marble pattern of lighter blue, the flared sleeves and cinched bodice sprinkled with turquoise crystals in homage of the *Herzestein*. The blue represented Henning's fire, while the marble represented my stone. Not exactly the norm for Teutonic weddings, since a female usually wore clothing indicative of her element alone. But I wished my gown to reflect the equal partnership I cherished with my Keyholder.

"I've read about it, but I'm pretty sure no Lady has done it in centuries," my *Leitaeri* responded, coming to stand behind me, the hood of his robe lowered to reveal his hair pulled back from his face. "After everything we've learned about Remmi's crimes, I'd say it's warranted. I'm actually of the mind to toss him into Wuotan's realm, so he can burn to death at his demon lord's feet. Erlanga's idea sounds even better than that."

Henning laid his arms around my waist and set his chin upon my shoulder, his eyes admiring my reflection. I had turned my attention to my makeup, giving him a gentle swat as I applied foundation. "You might want to give me some space unless you want your face painted, too."

He heeded my wish, dropping back but remaining in a spot where he could watch me do my makeup. He looked amazed by the process, reminding me again of his overall inexperience. Tonight would be very interesting, once we chased our guests off the property and retreated to the cozy dell where we would sleep beneath the stars. I could hardly wait to admire his body in the starlight.

"I just hope our people don't think I'm a wicked witch after today," I said before concentrating on my clear lip gloss. Navy blue eyeshadow and waterproof eyeliner completed the look, my hair pulled back in a simple blue clip. My mother intended to style it later for the wedding.

"They won't. Once I read the list of Remmi's crimes and two of the council members relate the sins in his blood, every Teuton in that clearing will be longing for justice. The *Leitalra* embodies justice. After Remmi has been allowed to speak his defense—an ancient custom that doesn't help the accused at all—that will be your moment to step forward and summon Erlanga to discipline her son."

The trial proceeded exactly as Henning predicted. The traditional meeting place south of Erlangen proper was a larger forest clearing than I expected, though I recognized it needed to provide space for all of the Teutons who called Erlangen their home. Most of the time, the clearing was used for smaller events like ritual weddings, priestly initiations, or today's trial. But twice per year, all the Teutons in the city were invited to celebrate two customary holidays as a group—the May dances and the New Year's festival.

The New Year's festival of 2004-2005 would be my first public appearance as *Leitalra*. Today's trial did not count, at least not to me. When my Keyholder and I took our places beneath the branches of an aged linden before the fire pit on the north side of the glade, my element detected only twenty-six Teutons present. Eighteen spectators, the five priests on the council, the Keyholder and Lady, and our prey.

Herr Burkhardt, the district attorney, had cast a sizzling shield of invisible lightning to hide the clearing from outsiders. He and Volli Ehrlich, the policeman, led Remmi from the trailhead to where his judges gathered, all of them dressed in black robes except for me. The witnesses assembled along the woodland stream in respectful silence, most of them in casual attire except for the other three priests in attendance. I recognized only the priest of darkness, Lenz. His presence boosted my courage.

I had invited my element to enhance my senses and my blood while Henning and I walked to the clearing, Erlanga's soul observing the proceedings through my eyes. Remmi wore dull khakis and a matching shirt, the typical outfit for a Teuton prisoner. My stone sensed no element suffusing his aura, but mystic potential still flowed in his blood, bound but existent.

Not for long, Erlanga's soul whispered in my heart, a sentiment I shared. Especially when Remmi's captors shoved him to his knees before his judges, and he raised his chin to stare directly at me. The Lady of Erlangen, the prize he yearned to claim. He bared his teeth at me, and suddenly I feared what he might say when offered the chance to defend himself. He might tell everyone in the clearing that he had raped me . . . and forced my body to climax.

He might reveal that Lady Erlanga was a child porn star. A whore.

I barely listened as Henning stepped forward with a clipboard to read the complete list of Remmi's crimes. He described them all thoroughly and declared at the end that the official report would be mailed to each Teuton household in this city. Henning also mentioned that Remmi's mother resided in a retirement complex in Bamberg. We had agreed to ensure she was well cared for in her son's absence, his depravity no reason to abandon his sole dependent. Henning and I intended to keep an eye on Kora once she was released from prison, too.

Remmi's soulless eyes continued to bore into me as his captors secured him for the second step in the trial—the revelation of blood truths. The Old One of the council, Herr Thiel, bled Remmi first, the fiend's eyes continuing to stare at me even then. Henning sensed my edginess around that time and moved to stand in front of me, blocking me from Remmi's view. As Herr Thiel wiped the blood from his lips, a middle-aged priest on the council, Herr Amacker, bent down to drink from Remmi's neck.

It surprised me to realize I knew Herr Amacker. He owned the landscaping company Philipp hired to maintain the Liebig grounds. I had seen him only once this year, the first time I scheduled his people to tidy the property; that was before I honed the ability to detect whether a person was a Teuton or not. He glanced at me briefly after finishing with Remmi and gave a slight nod. I nodded back, reassured by his presence.

Herr Thiel and Herr Amacker listed the horrors they saw in Remmi's blood in unison, their voices taking on a rote quality as if under a spell. Murmurs arose from the spectators, and my spirit sensed disgust hanging heavy in the atmosphere. Turning my attention to those eighteen—my people—I noticed

Henning's friend Lukas poised beside an elegant matron I judged to be his mother. Astrid Felder, the woman who took over Philipp's position when he retired.

I wondered what she would think of me, after she saw me wield Erlanga's sorcery to drain the magic from Remmi's blood.

"Let the accused now speak his defense, if he can formulate any justifications that would prove valid against the truth in his blood." My Keyholder's deep voice resounded through the clearing, his black-clad body still blocking me from Remmi's sight. My muscles tensed, despite Erlanga's confidence.

"Let it be known that the *Leitalra* of this city is a harlot who pleads for a master's discipline." Remmi projected his dark voice even further than Henning's, shifting his position to speak directly to the onlookers gathered beside the stream. "See how she hides behind her *Leitaeri*, weak and ashamed? She behaves this way because she knows this trial is a sham. Her heart begs for my authority, for all her pitiful *Leitaeri* refuses to give her. I could bring this city—"

"*Enough!*" Henning marched forward to tower over Remmi, the fingers of his right hand winding dangerously around Erlangen's keys. Power surged in his aura and Remmi stared up at him, no words escaping his open mouth. "No matter how you wish to twist reality to conform to your vision, your blood —as well as the blood of my precious *Leitalra*—has revealed you a liar, a fraud, and an abuser. The sins you committed against your city's matriarch one week ago are unforgivable, for they did not merely shame an honest witch. They shamed Erlanga herself. That is why she shall determine your fate."

Henning's fingers fell away from the keys as he stretched his right arm out toward where I stood, my emotions reeling from Remmi's accusations and my Keyholder's defense. *We do not stand alone,* Erlanga assured me, her soul nudging me forward. *Now is the time.*

Hardly knowing what I did, I advanced until I stood a half meter from Remmi, my Keyholder moving to stand at my back, ever supportive. My skin began to tingle with otherworldly sorcery and I elevated Erlanga's soul to the fore, my body her instrument. Stretching one hand forth, she spoke in a terrible voice.

"*You believe you have shamed me, the ethereal mother who granted you the magic in your blood. All Teutons have the choice of which path they shall take, and you chose to align yourself with the demon lord who blinds this world with evil and darkness. It is I who am ashamed of you, Albert Florian Morich.*"

Remmi flinched when the city's essence spoke his legal name. The air grew tight as glistening blades shaped themselves from Erlanga's sorcery, forming a ring around where Remmi quailed upon the ground. "*Your deeds have dishonored your* Leitalra, *Erlangen's beacon of justice and light. What was given shall be taken from you this day, never to be reclaimed.*"

What happened afterward is difficult to describe—frightful, as Lady Ilsa had warned me. The spiritual blades hovering around that wretched criminal seemed to crack the ether itself, a howling current descending to siphon the magic from his blood and spirit. Erlanga's essence continued to speak through my lips, reciting each aspect of magic Remmi could never wield again.

The blood sorcery of healing, rending, directing its flow, drinking its truths. The ability to separate his spirit from his body. The absolute power over another that the heart-bond granted. The gift of drawing vitality from the elements to direct spells and enchantments. The keen senses that elemental magic offered, and the elemental sense itself.

The final power Erlanga took from him was the dark energy sparking in his blood and spirit. A *clap* echoed in the clearing when she siphoned away his last vestiges of Teuton blood, leaving him sobbing on the ground. The ghostly blades vanished and the atmosphere settled, my right arm descending to my side. My city's soul whispered a promise to my heart as she released her grip upon my body. *He can never hurt any of our children again.*

Volli and Herr Burkhardt carted Remmi away in the aftermath, intending to hand him over to the Teuton authorities in charge of the dungeon. He would be locked in solitary confinement, never permitted to enjoy the light of day. His name and fate would be spread throughout the community as one whom the Lady had cursed, one who lost his Teuton blood by deviating too soundly to the dark.

A sense of accomplishment came over me, as the three council members who remained took a moment to assure me of their enduring support. Each of them—even the Old One—lowered his gaze in deference. Henning came to stand at my left side, entwining the fingers of his right hand with mine. The city's keys hung at his belt between us, their influence shimmering along our skin, beckoning us to seal our bond forever that night.

"My precious, triumphant *Leitalra*," he murmured to me in Teutonica, pressing a kiss to my temple. The heat of his fire warmed the inherent coolness of my stone, a contented smile curving my lips.

Several of the spectators paid their respects to us before departing, wishing us well on our upcoming matrimony. Lenz favored me with a meaningful wink and advised us not to linger too long, for fear of missing out on my mother's brunch. Lukas confirmed that he and Gabi would be there for our wedding, that they could hardly wait to celebrate the Keyholder and Lady's formal union.

But his mother's accolade struck me the most, the matron who claimed an executive role in Philipp's former corporation. She met my gaze and held it before saying, "A significant action for the witches in Erlangen. Thank you, *Leitalra*."

Chapter Twenty-three:
Destiny Affirmed

My *Leitaeri* and I walked side by side toward the fish pool on Liebig grounds right before ten p.m., the late summer night just beginning to descend upon Erlangen. The night of the new moon, true darkness would last only three hours, the stars and the fiery glow in Henning's eyes sufficient to guide us into elemental oneness. We had spread blankets and pillows in a dell of conifers not far from the pool, the crisp scent of needles mingling with the atmosphere to caress our bodies, after we bound our blood in ritual marriage. Philipp's doctor pronounced my blood clean of infection a few days earlier, and my anticipation to seize the carnal privileges of *Leitaeri* and *Leitalra* eclipsed all of my latent uncertainties.

Even a maiden traumatized in childhood could represent a Teuton city with dignity and grace. The events at the trial had proved that to me, my spirit certain of Philipp's glorified presence looking on as a pale blue glimmer lightened our path through the woodland. Our guests spoke quietly amongst themselves, falling water freshening the pool and providing oxygen for its fish. Enchantment infused the air around us, Erlanga's soul welcoming us into her protection.

Henning slowed before the trail curved to the right, where it would open into the glade where our friends and families gathered for the ceremony. He gave my left hand a reassuring squeeze, his cerulean eyes revealing his features despite his hood's attempt to shade them from me. "You're sure about this? When a Lady and Keyholder marry, they're bound for life. No possibility of divorce, even though everyday Teutons have that option."

His smile never faltered. He was as confident of my loyalty as I was of his. I flashed him a saucy grin. "As if some 'everyday Teuton' could take your place in my heart. Let's get married."

Several of the ladies breathed out quiet sighs when we appeared in the light of Henning's fires, whether from the elegance of my gown or from my Keyholder's assertive posture, I could not guess. I cast my gaze over our guests in the seconds it took us to reach the table before the waterfall, where Lenz awaited us, his darkness concealing his face, his hands holding Philipp's old version of *Der Weg*. The five priests from the city council stood nearest to the trail, black specters here to witness their leaders' joining. I recognized Henning's parents to the right of the priests, then our small group of friends—Gabi and Lukas, Bianca and Oliver, and Dennis with Till. My mother stood at the far edge of the group, closest to the oaken post . . . and closest to Lenz. She wore a striking violet dress that flattered her shape, her sable locks pulled back from her face and curled.

This was where I was meant to be.

Henning had lit the traditional fire using the magic of his spirit alone, while we were in our suite preparing for the ritual. A blatant display of his elemental skill, for it flickered skyward from a stone ring with no wood fueling it. His gentle nature notwithstanding, Henning was neither weak nor uneducated as a priest. He would rise to claim me in conquest, once I showed him how. Of that I was certain.

"Tonight, we come together to bind two Teutons by blood, oath, and love, representing the incomparable union of the Keyholder of Erlangen and his Lady." Henning and I had taken our places before the table, our hands still joined as we regarded Lenz, our priest. Apparently, he wished to shade his features in darkness throughout the ceremony. Even my elemental vision could not make out his face.

"If either party wishes to renounce this binding, may he or she speak now, before these leaves meet the fire." Lenz laid the book down and took up the braid of silver oak leaves he had fashioned from the branch earlier this week. Neither my Keyholder nor I would back out, no question about it. We stood in respectful silence as our priest cast the braid into the fire, a breath of silvery magic rising to signify the tree fairies' blessing. Erlanga's soul hummed within me, pleased to offer her grace to all magical beings in her city, not just the Teutons.

As Lenz paced around us toward our group of friends, to inquire whether two agreed to perform the duties of ritual witnesses, I suddenly realized Henning and I had not discussed which of our guests should sign our marriage document. Two must sign in ink—the ritual witnesses—and a pensive frown creased my brow as I considered who deserved that right the most. His parents? Two of the council members? My mother could not sign, as an outsider.

Lenz returned to his place behind the table to prepare for the first wedding rite while I thought about it. Lifting the tome from the table again, he explained that he must cut each of our wrists with the dagger we had chosen—Philipp's family blade —to collect a small portion of our blood for the cup of sorrows, and to create the scars of marriage. Light pink marks would remain on our wrists permanently, despite the healing properties of Teutonic magic. Until death parted us, those scars would serve as a visual reminder of our commitment.

I presented my left wrist to Lenz first, as was proper, maintaining a solemn appearance even at the slice of pain. I watched as he turned my wrist downward, my blood trickling into the wooden goblet I found among Philipp's heirlooms. The cup of sorrows was supposed to be of unadorned wood, in reference to the simple seasons of life we would experience as a married couple. Lenz pressed a silver oak leaf to my wrist for a moment, allowing its magic to heal the cut; then he turned to my Keyholder and repeated the process.

The healing power of the oak leaf eliminated any possible scab, the skin of my wrist already smoothing into a pale scar that would grow more distinct after the fourth and final rite of Teutonic matrimony. I smiled as I studied the mark in the firelight, grateful for the strong *Leitaeri* who stood at my side, taking my hand again as Lenz added items into the cup of sorrows. Next, both of us would have to drink from it. Henning had promised it would taste awful.

I could not keep the grimace from my face when I swallowed the necessary sip. Water from the Regnitz, dust from the earth, bitter herbs from the gardens of Erlangen, vinegar from a nearby vineyard, and Teuton blood tasted disgusting when combined in such a way. Henning smirked at me as I handed him the cup, likely a reaction to my revolted expression. Then he took a sip and chucked the cup over his left shoulder, an act symbolizing the triumph of love and loyalty over trials. Somehow, he managed not to display any hint of nausea on his face.

My *Leitaeri* had me beat on impassiveness, even though I did not flinch when Lenz cut my wrist. I needed to work on that.

Our priest lifted the tome again to read the customary lines on the duties of husband and wife, then invited us to face each other for the exchange of vows. My Keyholder spoke them first, his deep voice awakening an ardent yearning inside my core, his flaming eyes not straying from my face. My element strengthened my grip on his hands, devotion pervading my voice as I repeated the vows to him.

"On this night I pledge my body and heart to you, Henning Robert Glossner, before these witnesses of earth, fire, air, water, and soul. I give you myself as your wife, with my faults and my strengths, and I take you to myself as my husband, with your faults and your strengths. May we live from this night forward as Teuton partners, of one mind and blood, in all matters of life. I pledge to stay with you and you alone, as your wife, until we are parted by death."

I caught sight of fiery tears shining in Henning's eyes when I finished the vows, his love for me surging from his essence in alluring warmth. His response to my commitment amplified my craving, and I pressed my thighs together beneath my skirt. I wore naught but a black-laced thong down there, which meant I had to keep my urges under control until we finished feasting with our guests.

Henning and I had agreed to evict everyone at midnight, whether they liked it or not. The sky continued to darken, but I could not impale myself upon my *Leitaeri's* body for over an hour. And when the time came, I would have to guide his hands to my sensitive places, explain that I yearned for him to take control once he felt comfortable doing so.

The anticipation fashioned its own form of torture, one that would end in ecstasy. *But you have to eat first, Zehra. Enjoy some peach Schnapps. Share some conversations with Henning's parents, our friends, and the council members. And maybe whisper to Lenz that he ought to spend the night with* Anne.

Our priest had finished describing the final rite of Teutonic marriage while I bundled my desires into a corner, taking a deep breath of summer's sultry air. Now we must unite our blood in the most absolute way possible, placing our hands atop the oaken post so Lenz could stab them with Philipp's dagger. Henning had assured me neither of us would feel pain in that moment, mysticism energizing us as we kissed. Lenz would drain our blended blood into a silver bowl, and we would use the blood to sign our marriage document.

I positioned myself with the pool to my left, once I neared the post, placing my right hand upon its smooth surface while gazing into my mate's flaming eyes. He drew close to me, his right hand covering mine while I reached for his cloak with my left, clinging to the fabric. One rush of nervousness breezed through me as Lenz pronounced the concluding words: "May the couple seal their marriage with a kiss, and may the union be complete!"

Henning leaned forward to kiss me before Lenz finished speaking, magic binding our bodies and spirits together while our priest united our blood. Warm hands closed over my beating heart somewhere in the realm of the spirit, my *Leitaeri* shielding my deepest self within his fiery spirit. It was not exactly like what I had read about the Teutonic heart-bond—with a priest removing my spiritual heart from my chest to cradle it in his hands. My heart simply seemed to manifest itself under my Keyholder's guidance and protection, his joy flowing straight into my soul while my heart infused his soul with devotion and trust.

My husband broke the kiss long before I finished marveling at the profound sense of belonging pulsing within my heart. I felt connected with every Teuton who called Erlangen their home, wisps of excess magic vibrating along my skin. Shaking my head in wonder, I lifted my gaze to Henning's, the adoration gleaming in his eyes prompting me to sink against his chest. His steady heartbeat soothed me, his arms granting me stability.

"We need to sign our marriage certificate," Henning reminded me, as I shut my eyes to listen to his heartbeat. "I can carry you to the table, if you want."

"That probably wouldn't be wise." I sighed, opening my eyes and ordering myself to return to reality after savoring that spiritual euphoria. "The Keyholder and Lady should appear strong and resilient, even if the Lady just discovered she's lived as a half-self all this time."

I chuckled through my nose, and Henning laid his arm around my waist as we paced back to the table. Lenz had the certificate prepared, the iron pen holding the paper down with our bowl of blood sitting off to the side. I took the pen to sign first, since Henning had said our blood would thicken over time, so the second person to sign would have more difficulty. The pen itself seemed spelled, for the crimson ink clung to its tip the instant I dipped it into the bowl.

"Did it really feel like that for you?" my *Leitaeri* whispered in my ear, while I inscribed my full name onto the document. *Zehra Saliha Liebig-Glossner*. "Like you've been incomplete until now?"

Delighted to learn that my husband and I shared the same amazement about our union, I handed him the pen and said,

"Thank goodness the other half of me is you, not some freakish Keyholder who wants to enslave me."

"You enslaved me the first time we met, Zehra," Henning responded while signing his own name using the same hyphenation as mine. "Soon enough, I'll be calling you *Truhtein*."

Lenz cackled quietly, having overheard our exchange since he stood so near. "Do that in the heat of passion and she'll melt in your hands, *Leitaeri*."

Henning's cheeks flushed, and he muttered something under his breath as he stepped back from the table. I trailed him and glanced at our guests, none of whom had come forward to sign as witnesses. Henning beckoned his father to the table, where Lenz handed him a regular pen. "Who would you like to sign for you?" my Keyholder asked me, looking curious.

I eyed his father's back as he bent over the table, and then a buzz of dark energy wafted through the hair draping my neck, sending an unspoken message. He had promised to be here—my guardian—and that meant he must sign. Pivoting to face Lenz, I declared, "Philipp will sign for me."

Lenz had released his grip on his darkness to some degree, for I saw his lips part in astonishment. Before he or anyone else could question my intent, the pen Henning's father had laid down rose to stand on its point, an invisible hand moving it across the paper to create a signature I knew well. Lenz's eyes bulged, and he crossed himself and mouthed a Hail Mary. I skipped away from my Keyholder's side, returning to the table to beam at the new signature adorning our marriage certificate. *Philipp Alexander Liebig*.

True peace bloomed in my heart as we celebrated with our guests afterward, for I knew I had taken a major step toward an encouraging destiny. With Henning at my side, we could explore the wonders of Teutonic possibility, our love increasing each day. While the ache of Murat's absence remained a festering wound in my heart, my mother had begun to experience honest affection for the first time in many years. Together, we would rebuild our personal spheres into something beautiful, as long as we remained on this earth.

~*~

As agreed, Henning and I excused ourselves from the celebration right at midnight, my husband advising our guests to clear out unless they wished to help my mother with the cleanup. Bianca instantly volunteered, along with Henning's mother, Lenz taking charge of separating the trash and recycling. My Keyholder guided me outside before I could join them, uttering a suggestive phrase in my ear that rekindled my earlier desires.

"I think it's time you teach me your techniques, graceful stone witch."

By the time we wended our way into the dell of conifers, I was sopping wet, Henning's seductive remarks igniting flames in my blood. "At the rate you're going, I'll come the second you touch me, even if you go in the wrong hole," I chided him good-naturedly, kicking my sandals off before stepping onto the thick blanket we had spread over the needle-covered ground.

"I would never do anything that cruel to you." Henning crouched to untie his black sneakers, his chin raised as he watched me remove every clip, tie, and pin from my hairdo. I dropped each into a small pile at the edge of our blanket, along with my discarded sandals.

My need escalated further at my husband's heartfelt promise. Two nights earlier, we had discussed what sorts of sexual exploits would trigger memories of my abuse, so Henning would know to avoid them. He admitted to curiosity about many things, but anal was not one of them. We would concentrate on discovering how to satisfy each other tonight, beneath a myriad of stars.

The junipers ringing our dell opened our blanket to the sky, the stars offering enough light for us to admire each other's nakedness. My hair let down at last, I shook its tresses out around my shoulders and straightened to look at my Keyholder. He had taken off his shoes and socks, his hands thrust into the pockets of the robe cloaking him in mystery.

"So . . . uh . . . are we going to strip tease now or something? Or do you want me to take your dress off, while you . . . ." Henning's voice trailed off, and he cleared his throat. Despite our marriage, doubt had not yet released its grip on him.

Accepting that I must take the lead, I swayed my hips and placed my hands upon them, my eyes not deviating from his face. "Strip tease sounds perfect. You start. You have more layers than I do. This dress just has a zipper in the back, and then . . . well . . . use your imagination." I slid my tongue across my bottom lip.

Henning groaned out a plea for heaven's mercy, his fingers working to undo his belt. "You're not the only one who's going to come too soon, you mischievous witch." He laid his belt atop his shoes and socks, setting Erlangen's keys aside with an air of reverence.

I beamed and continued undulating my body for his pleasure, watching through silvery-hued vision as Henning cast his priestly robe into a pile, revealing the plain T-shirt and black jeans underneath. He blazing eyes riveted upon me, he tugged his shirt overhead first, his pale skin standing out in the darkness. I ran my gaze along the muscles of his torso, a soft whistle passing through my lips. Even though I had seen his bare chest more than once already, the experience seemed more meaningful tonight.

At long last, every barrier between us had dissolved into irrelevance.

My husband paused before removing his jeans, chewing on his bottom lip as he looked from my face to my breasts, my fingers toying with their edges to tease him. He expelled a heavy pant that turned into a low growl, then granted me a split second to gawk at the tent in his boxers before he spun around, displaying his ass.

"I am *not* interested in your butt, silly priest!" I complained as he bared it, bending to place his jeans and boxers in the pile with his shirt. He straightened and flexed his hands at his sides, the muscles of his back rippling when he rolled his shoulders. "You're not going to be able to appreciate *my* strip tease if you keep your back turned."

I reached behind myself to snag the zipper, pulling it down slowly, the noise piercing the atmosphere and loading it with tension. Henning's shoulders sagged, and he ran a hand through his hair, which plunged halfway down his back, even when tied in a low ponytail. "I'm sorry, Zehra. I don't know. Part of me is kind of scared you'll think I'm not good enough. Especially after you had Philipp."

His deep voice sounded both embarrassed and nervous, his honesty fueling my respect for him, along with my need. Shrugging my way out of my dress, I left it on the edges of the blanket and stalked toward my husband, reaching my hands out to stroke the silken locks of his hair. Henning gasped at my touch, then relaxed as I loosened the band confining his hair, dropping it beside his shoes.

Winding my arms around his neck, I stood on my tiptoes to croon directly into his left ear. "Philipp Liebig could never give me what you can give, Henning. Because you're the mate destiny chose for me . . . and the *Truhtein* I choose for myself." I touched my lips to his neck and he groaned, his hands reaching up to clasp my wrists. "I need you to turn around now. Turn around and look at your wife. That's it."

He circled slowly to face me, his hands sliding to my forearms while I kept his neck in a loose embrace. Azure flames flickered in his irises as they stared into mine, so I took one step back, letting him admire my body in the starlight. His eyes opened wider at the sight of my breasts, his lips parting to speak, though no words came out.

I slipped my arms out of his grip to take hold of his hands, directing them downward. "Free your wife from her thong, *Leitaeri*," I murmured.

He bent just a little to obey, his gaze following the path of his hands as he tugged the thong over the curve of my ass so it could fall to the blanket. His warm fingers settled onto my waist, and I laid a hand over his heartbeat, its powerful throb entrancing me. The hands of his spirit closed around my heart at the same time, devotion and longing spilling into the mortal world as I moaned, my hands creeping down to grasp his firm cock.

Henning hissed, one of his hands taking hold of the back of my head while the other remained on my waist. "Not yet, lovely *Leitalra*. Don't force me to come before I can give you all you deserve." His lips drew forward to caress mine, his gaze boring deep into my eyes. "Direct me, Zehra. Show me how to please you."

I chewed on my lip for a second, then released my grip on his length, the heat of his element luring me to continue my explorations there. But my *Leitaeri* wanted to please me first, and I must obey. So I guided his right hand from my waist to my core, teaching his fingers the motions that would lead me to the brink and beyond. Wrapping my arms around his back, I shut my eyes and moved my hips along with his rhythm, short pants escaping my lips.

"Just like that. Don't stop. Please," I begged as elation built within me.

Since I had my eyes closed to relish the sensations, it shocked me when my *Leitaeri* bit down on my artery, the sting sending me over the edge. I cried out and dug my nails into his back as he drank, his spiritual hands drawing infinite blood into my heart from the infernal source that had granted me this glorious destiny. I was lost forever now, a hopeless slave to my Keyholder's will.

Absurdly, I had never felt so empowered in my life.

I reopened my eyes when Henning backed away from my neck, his fingers tenderly tracing the wound his skills at blood control had already healed. He shook his head slowly, his fiery eyes meeting mine in wonder. "That was spectacular," he told me, his arms binding me in a strong embrace.

I raised my eyebrows at my husband, the truth growing clear as I studied his expression. "Did you seriously bleed me just to find out how I climax?"

His cheeks darkened in the starlight, and he lowered his gaze. "I've always wondered what it's like for a female."

Extracting myself from his embrace, I laid a palm on his chest, then looked down at his cock, somewhat surprised it had not yet spilled. Time to change that. "Lay down, *Truhtein*. It's time I repay you," I ordered, a trace of steel in my tone.

Henning followed my instruction without delay, anticipation smoldering in his eyes as he watched me straddle him, his hands kneading my breasts at long last. This time, when I brought him to climax, I found my second one simultaneously, stone and blue fire entwining into an invincible entity, casting its blessing over our city as a whole.

And I knew, when Henning used his priestly sway to lull me into our private dream world, that every soul in Erlangen passed a wondrous night.

Chapter Twenty-four:
Mingling of Cultures

Four months later, my family and I prepared to celebrate *Ramazan Bayram*, or the Festival of Sweets, as non-religious Turks referenced the holiday. We decorated the sunroom with colored ribbons and hanging lights, my husband contributing a light blue flame to each candle. On November 13th, my mother and I spent most of the afternoon readying the grand feast we would enjoy at sundown, the scents of Turkish delicacies tantalizing my nose.

We had invited Henning's parents and our friends to join us for the feast, along with Lenz, who spent as much time on Liebig property these days as he did at his townhouse. My mother was in the process of divorcing my imprisoned father. Once she was free, she and Lenz planned to marry at the city courthouse. She had no desire to become a witch herself; but Lenz adored her without prejudice, fully intending to move in with us after he could lay his claim upon my mother.

While my mother would celebrate the religious aspects of the holiday, my German friends and I would give thanks for our friendship and the multitude of blessings we experienced throughout the year. In honor of Philipp's traditions, we would eat the meal in the formal dining room, then gather in the sunroom to enjoy the sweets and each other's company. Baklava, rose pudding, dates, and pastries drizzled with syrup were on the menu—foods that awakened memories of joyful moments in my childhood.

Murat's absence had weighed heavily on me as autumn progressed. I missed his fresh insight and his thoughtful questions about Teutonic magic and culture. His remains had been interred in the same cemetery as the Liebig family crypt. Tomorrow morning, my mother, Henning, and I would pay our respects to our departed loved ones—a custom that would mean much more to me this year than ever before. Then we would visit Henning's parents for the midday meal, a thorough mingling of Teutonic culture with Turkish.

As evening descended, my mother sent me off to the vestibule to greet our guests, enlisting my husband to cart each finished dish to the table. The main dish was a traditional lamb stew served over eggplant and topped with melted cheese and butter. I had prepared the stuffed grape leaves, including spiced beef along with the onions and rice, since I knew Henning's mother did not like lamb. Lentil soup, fried bread, and zucchini fritters rounded out the meal. Our guests had been asked to supply the drinks. We would distribute leftovers in covered dishes after everyone ate their fill.

Bianca and Oliver arrived first, bearing two six packs of Apfelschorle, since she had sworn off alcohol during her pregnancy. Lady Ilsa had requested aid from the elemental spirits to awaken Bianca's womb; and she was three months along now, just beginning to show. I gestured Oliver to take the sparkling apple juice to the dining room, then embraced his wife excitedly, smiling as she described how their baby looked at her most recent ultrasound.

"I can hardly wait to meet our miracle baby," Bianca gushed, her dark curls bouncing as she touched one palm to her abdomen. "I know you and Henning are off to the Alps at the end of April, but I hope you'll be back home in time to celebrate with us."

"We should be here, unless your little one comes early," I assured her, delighted that my friend had finally seized her long-awaited dream. "I'm going to ask Lady Ilsa for some tips on the witchy stuff, find out if there's any way I can use Erlanga's magic to invigorate the wombs of her daughters who want children."

Bianca squealed and clutched my right hand in both of hers. "Do you really think that's possible? That would be so amazing! I know Gabi and Lukas are trying for a baby right now!"

The aforementioned couple appeared at the door an instant later. Lukas had a small keg of Kellerbier under his right arm, his left touching Gabi's back. They greeted me with enthusiasm, and Oliver reappeared to help Lukas tote the keg to the dining room. I inquired after the silver oak fairy on Gabi's family's property, curious how long she intended to maintain the shield of spiritual fire around its tree. I had only just learned about the drama surrounding her family's tree, all a result of the ridiculous blood prejudice she had mentioned when we first met.

"I may actually be able to dissolve that shield soon, since Callen Heising got a job in Nürnberg last month," Gabi related, her upper lip curling into a sneer. "He was the source of all the rumors there. Apparently, he's finally decided to strike out on his own, because he told Lukas he's moving into an apartment close to his job."

"He's just jealous you found someone better," Bianca said, nudging Gabi's right arm in a playful manner. Then she waved at the next two guests approaching the portico. "Your little brother's here, along with Till!"

Lenz showed up right after I managed to herd my friends toward the dining room, the number of people crowding the vestibule grating on my anxiety. Healing was a continuous process, one I must work at for the rest of my life. Henning had helped me find peace with that prospect, his support instrumental in my growth since our marriage.

Lenz tipped his flat hat at me when he paused in the doorway, his hazel eyes alight with gratitude. "*Eid Mubarak,*" he said, offering me his right hand.

My mother had taught him Turkish holiday traditions. "*Khair Mubarak,*" I responded, planting a kiss on his hand and lifting it to my forehead. "You're the only person who's bothered to say that to me today."

"Might have to correct your *Leitaeri* when I see him." Lenz grinned.

"Ah, don't worry about it. We've spent most of the day cooking, too busy to bother with ritual greetings."

Lenz extracted his left hand from his trench coat, revealing a bottle of peach Schnapps and a small package wrapped in brown paper. "Bought this drink just for you, but if you're trying to cut back, I can take it home with me. Picked up this package for you from the post office yesterday."

He handed me the package, which was about the size of a Bible, but heavier. "Schnapps is fine, thank you. In honor of the festival, I'll enjoy one glass. Oh! This is from Lady Ilsa!" I squinted at the cursive on the return address, happiness stirring within me. Two weeks ago, she had promised to send me a gift for the holiday, and now it had come.

"I'm sure she'll be thrilled to learn what you think of it. Now if you'll excuse me, I believe there's a lovely lady in here whom I need to track down and greet." Lenz headed toward the hallway with a spring in his step.

"*Anne's* in the kitchen," I called after him, setting Lady Ilsa's package onto one of the steps leading to the second floor. Henning's parents were crossing the portico alongside Volli and his wife, our final guests for the feast.

The celebration passed in wonderful fashion, Henning and I seated beside each other while we dug into the tasty foods that marked the end of Ramadan. My mother had fasted during daylight hours for the entire month, her countenance gleaming with happiness at the opportunity to share the occasion with our friends. Everyone spoke of successes they had experienced in their work and personal lives throughout the year, the atmosphere brimming with joy.

~*~

After our guests took their leave much later, my mother, Lenz, Henning, and I loaded the dishwashers and sorted the garbage, our stomachs and hearts content. My mother, attired in an airy dress with flowing sleeves, sidled up to Lenz and laid her head on his shoulder, quietly asking him to stay the night. I smiled to myself when I heard him agree, catching Henning's eye and nodding in the direction of our suite. It was time we stage our private celebration.

I retrieved Lady Ilsa's package from the staircase before joining my husband in our bedroom, thankful for the festive evening we spent with friends and family. "I'll admit, it's nice that we have two cultures between us," Henning said through a yawn, his formal shirt unbuttoned as he stretched. "Three, if Teutonic traditions count. Extra holidays to go around."

"You're not wrong." I tossed the package onto our bed and slid my arms into my sleeves on my way out of the velvet dress I had worn for the occasion. "And I'm really looking forward to visiting the cemetery tomorrow. To tell Murat and Leyla all about this destiny I've found."

Though we did not know what had become of Leyla's body, discarded into the sea by a mafia boss, we had purchased a memorial stone for her and set it beside where Murat's ashes were interred. It seemed right to do that, since Philipp had told me my two youngest siblings remained close friends in eternity. I knew Murat would want me to live my life to the fullest, since he and our sister rejoiced in heaven's domain.

"I know they're proud of you," Henning murmured, casting off his shirt and coming around to my side of the bed. I stood with my bare feet buried in the rug, clad in naught but my underwear as I gazed at the package, lost in thought.

"I hope so," I whispered, breathing out a long sigh. "I still miss my brother. Just like I miss Philipp."

My gaze slid to the left, where Philipp's urn stood beside his digital clock. I had decided not to move it after all, preferring to keep his remains beside me when I slept. My *Leitaeri* guarded me in my dreams, while my first *Truhtein* guarded my sleeping body. It comforted me to know I had two powerful males protecting me, while I sought to honor Erlanga's presence within my heart.

"It's completely healthy to miss them," Henning reminded me, wrapping his arms around my waist and kissing me gently on the cheek. "Murat and Philipp will always be a part of our lives, and we'll meet again someday."

Twisting my neck around so I could meet my husband's gaze, where he had laid his chin atop my right shoulder, I offered him a fond smile. "Then you'll have to share."

"Hmm. I suppose. Now why don't you open that package? The suspense is killing me, even though it's your gift and not mine." Henning smirked and backed away, giving me space to sit on the bed and run my fingers along the brown paper.

"Lady Ilsa didn't have to get me anything, technically. I'm wondering if this is one of her witchcraft tomes or something." I weighed the package in my hands, then set it onto my lap and loosened the paper. Henning sat to my left, the warmth of his fire caressing my skin.

Inside the package, I found a sturdy pine box with an intricately carved sun adorning the lid, a metal clasp latching it shut. A folded note with my name on it awaited my attention, but I lifted the box to my nose first, inhaling its woodsy aroma. Visions of forested peaks filled my imagination, anticipation for my spring honeymoon with my Keyholder prompting me to smile.

"If that's what I think it is, you're about to embark on a journey few have taken," Henning said, eyeing the box with a look of satisfaction. "My Omi told me some of the stories from her past when I was growing up, and more when I became her Keyholder. But I always got the impression she kept a lot of secrets."

"You think this is her diary? Or her memoir?" I traced the sun pattern on the box's lid, a perfect representation of my predecessor's radiant element.

"She and her *Leitaeri* brought some Nazis to justice in their day," Henning told me, fire flickering in his irises as his gaze met mine. "Not that history would record the accomplishments of a witch."

"Wow. That's incredible! Now I really wish I could have known her."

"My Omi prayed for a successor with similar objectives as hers. A desire for justice and fairness, an open heart, and a deep love for her community, Teutons and outsiders alike." Henning reached out to stroke my hair, my eyelids sliding closed while his spiritual hands imparted his devotion into my heart. "You embody everything she wished for and more. My precious *Leitalra*."

The box could wait, for my Keyholder had distracted me. I pushed Lady Ilsa's gift aside and bound Henning in my arms, reveling in the magnificence of shared love and respect. And afterward, while he showered, I read the brief note the forest witch had written for me.

Zehra, may your predecessor's wisdom and faults ease your doubts as you continue forward. The path of light may not always be safe, but it is certainly worth walking. We will meet soon. Lady Ilsa Vorbach.

Epilogue:
Six Years Later....

In mid-August, 2010, Henning and I visited Lukas' family home along the Main-Donau Kanal to attend his daughter's fifth birthday party. Many of our friends had children of their own by that time, their youthful exuberance bringing life and light to every gathering. I lounged on the back deck with the other witches, keeping an eye on the children playing in the yard with their fathers and Winston, Lukas' silly pug. The pug seemed to have mastered the art of wiggling away whenever a kid tried to pounce on him, shrieks and playful barks punctuating the carefree mood of the summer afternoon.

"I can hardly believe Finn will be starting school just next year," Bianca observed, taking a sip of her mojito. "It feels like time is just flying."

"They grow up way too fast," Gabi agreed as her daughter—the birthday girl—scampered by in a princess dress and tiara, waving a plastic wand with a star on top. "But I'm excited to find out whether Rita takes after Lukas or me, when she discovers her element."

"Finn is going to be some kind of energy. No question about it," Bianca said, fanning her face with a look of tolerant exhaustion.

234

I straightened in my chair, about to launch into a diatribe of which elements Bianca's and Gabi's children could potentially summon. Teuton children tended to discover their elements somewhere between the ages of five and seven. Before that, even their parents' elemental senses could not pinpoint which type of magic their offspring might claim. My phone buzzed in my purse just as I opened my mouth to recite the list, so I tucked that thought away for the moment, digging my phone out and checking the name.

"It's Lady Ilsa. I have to take this," I apologized to Gabi, rising to my feet as I accepted the call. Gabi mouthed that it was fine, waving for me to go take care of business. So I wandered toward the far side of the deck where Oliver manned the grill, flipping burgers and sausages. Henning perched against a brick ledge not far away, a Paulaner beer can in his hand, sunglasses hiding his eyes from me.

But his hands caressed my heart as I drew near, a subtle brush of adoration.

"There's a young lady in my village I think you ought to meet," Lady Ilsa told me, after we exchanged pleasantries about the birthday party and the summer weather. "She's only a year younger than you, and you've got some rather pertinent things in common."

My forehead wrinkled as I wondered where the forest witch was going with this. Lady Ilsa was someone I respected very much; but when Henning and I went to the Tyrol to visit her, we did not usually socialize with the Teutons in her town. "What kind of things?" I prompted.

"She likes stuffed grape leaves."

My eyebrows ascended toward my hairline. "Is she Turkish?" My muses traveled in a new direction, interest brewing within me.

Lady Ilsa chuckled. "Not quite. But she's not a Teuton, either."

"Hmm."

"Yet."

My jaw dropped. "Is she thinking about doing the blood-transfer?" A skeletal hand clasped my throat. Were the Alpine

Teuton priests skilled at rituals like that one, or did my soon-to-be-peer totter on the brink of death?

"It's more than just a thought at this point, but she and her sister are trying to keep it quiet," Lady Ilsa said, a hint of disapproval pervading her tone. "I've given them all the advice I know, but since I've never done the blood-transfer myself, my wisdom only goes so far."

"I can tell them both how to survive. It should be easier for them, anyway, since they're the same gender. How soon do you need me to visit? Next weekend?" I headed toward where my Keyholder chatted with Oliver, ready to tell him we had another journey to plan.

"That would probably be best. I'm pretty sure they're going to do the ritual after school starts. Oh, and Zehra?"

"Yes?"

Lady Ilsa held her peace for a moment, her hesitation sprinkling my blood with anxiety. Then she spoke one cryptic phrase. "They're not just sisters."

~*~

Thank you for reading *Gift of Stone*. Zehra and Henning are deeply honored to have you along for the ride.

The *Elemental Bloodlines* series will continue with a tale of two sisters—one Teuton, one outsider—in *Gift of Darkness*.

If you'd like to read a bonus novella detailing how Ilsa fell in love with her priestly husband, Horst, sign up for C.L. Carhart's newsletter to get your eBook copy of *Gift of Air*.

Book III comes out in May 2023
Order now from your preferred retailer!

If you enjoyed reading *Gift of Stone,* please consider leaving your review where you purchased the book. Reviews help other readers find the stories they long to enjoy.

Gift of Stone is available on library platforms! Please ask your local library to order it in eBook or paperback so more readers can discover C.L. Carhart's works.

Want to stay informed about forthcoming stories in the Teutonic Fantasy Realm? Join C.L. Carhart's newsletter to get first dibs on where her writerly muse meanders.
https://bf.clcarhart.com/6w57qgfhc9

Want exclusive opportunities to read, discuss, and influence C.L. Carhart's works in progress? Check out her VIP reader program.
https://www.buymeacoffee.com/clcarhart

Follow C.L. Carhart on social media.
https://www.facebook.com/CLCarhartAuthor
https://www.instagram.com/c.l.carhart.author
https://www.pinterest.com/clcarhart
https://twitter.com/clcarhartauthor
https://www.bookbub.com/authors/c-l-carhart

Translations

Anne – mother (Turkish)

Apfelschorle – sparkling apple juice

Baba – father (Turkish)

Befreiung – liberation

Cin – djinn (Turkish)

Der Weg Teutonisch – The Teutonic Way

Döner Kebap – Turkish specialty, seasoned meat cooked over a rotisserie, often served in a wrap

Eid Mubarak – blessed festival (Turkish/Arabic)

Franconia – German region including the northern section of Bavaria

Frau – Miss/Mrs.

Herr – Mr.

Herzestein – heart stone

Jägerschnitzel – breaded veal with mushroom gravy

Kellerbier – cellar beer

Khair Mubarak – good wishes for the person who wished you a blessed festival (Turkish/Arabic)

Landjäger – spiced sausage of beef and pork, usually eaten as a snack

Leitaeri – Keyholder of a Teuton city

Leitalra – Lady of a Teuton city

Löwensenf – German brand of spicy mustard

Manti – seasoned dumplings with lamb or beef filling, served with garlic yogurt, spicy butter, spicy tomato sauce, mint, and chili flakes (Turkish)

Mutti – mom

Omi – grandma

Ramazan Bayram – Ramadan feast (Turkish)

Taubenball – Dove Ball

Teutonica – ancient Teutonic dialect

Truhtein – master

Vollkornbrot – brown rye loaf sprinkled with seeds

Wuotan – demon lord of the Teuton people

Pronunciation Guide
(for names and commonly used words)

Anne – AH-nay
Baba – BAH-bah
Befreiung – beh-FREYE-oong (eye is pronounced like eye-
    ball)
Cin – jin
Der Weg – Dare Veg
Erlangen – AIR-lahng-en
Frau – Frow (ow is pronounced like cow)
Gabi – GAH-bee
Herr – Hair
Herzestein – HARE-tseh-stein (stein is pronounced like a
    beer stein
Leitaeri – Leye-TARE-ee (eye is pronounced like eyeball)
Leitalra – Leye-TAHL-rah (eye is pronounced like eyeball)
Taubenball – TOW-ben-ball (ow is pronounced like cow)
Teutonica – Too-TAHN-ih-kuh
Truhtein – TROO-tine (tine is pronounced like a fork tine)
Wuotan – VOH-tahn
Zehra – Zeh-RAH

About the Author

C.L. Carhart has been writing since the age of 4, dabbling in everything from children's books, to fantasy, to historical fiction. Eventually, her lifelong interest in European history inspired her to create a mystical other-world based on the Teutonic people groups. Her Teutonic fantasy realm is chock full of heart-pounding adventure, dark magic, and swoon-worthy romance.

A book addict, stray cat rescuer, and unashamed metalhead, you can find her plotting out fresh stories deep in the night with a can of diet soda and a fun-sized panther infringing on her progress.